Ja... **his hand a**... **could feel his heart pumping. It gave her a peculiar but exciting thrill to know that she could affect him in such a way.**

This is a foolishness,' she said breathlessly, and yet you are so clever. No doubt you are practised in the art of persuading women to do what you will. But how can you talk of marriage when you have only just arrived ere, wounded and exhausted? Marriage is a rious matter and needs much consideration fore a decision can be made.'

cholas gave her a weary look, but there was o a hint of bewilderment in his hazel eyes he released her hand. 'If there is one thing ave learnt on my travels it is that one has seize the moment as it might never come in.'

AUTHOR NOTE

For those who enjoyed MAN BEHIND THE FAÇADE, and wanted to know what happened to Nicholas and Jane, who appeared in that book, this is their story.

It isn't ever easy writing a romance where love doesn't run smoothly when it is obvious from the beginning that the hero and heroine are so right for each other. And to weave in a historical background without it impinging too much on the love story is also a fine art. Films and television programmes have brought the Tudor years to the fore because they were interesting, exciting and scary times.

This book, just like the previous one, is set mainly in Oxfordshire. I owe thanks for a large part of my research to my eldest son, Iain, who was a student at Brasenose College, Oxford, a few years back. More recently we visited not only Oxford but the town of Witney whilst on Retreat. Witney was founded on sheep and the wool trade and was famous for its blankets. My husband and I were given one by my mother-in-law, Ellen Elizabeth Frizzell Francis, as part of our wedding present almost fifty years ago.

I'd like to dedicate this book to her memory, and also to my husband, John, and three sons, Iain, Tim and Daniel, for all their forbearance when I've been lost in a different world. At least this has ensured they can all whip up a good meal as well as change their beds and vacuum the carpet!

THE ADVENTURER'S BRIDE

June Francis

First published in Great Britain 2013
by Mills & Boon, an imprint of Harlequin (UK) Limited.
Harlequin (UK) Limited, Eton House, 18-24 Paradise Road,
Richmond, Surrey TW9 1SR

© June Francis 2013

June Francis's interest in old wives' tales and folk customs led her into a writing career. History has always fascinated her, and her first novels were set in Medieval times. She has also written sagas based in Liverpool and Chester. Married with three grown-up sons, she lives on Merseyside. On a clear day she can see the sea and the distant Welsh hills from her house. She enjoys swimming, fell-walking, music, lunching with friends and smoochy dancing with her husband.

More information about June can be found at her website: www.junefrancis.co.uk

Previous novels by this author:

ROWAN'S REVENGE
TAMED BY THE BARBARIAN
REBEL LADY, CONVENIENT WIFE
HIS RUNAWAY MAIDEN
PIRATE'S DAUGHTER, REBEL WIFE
THE UNCONVENTIONAL MAIDEN
THE MAN BEHIND THE FAÇADE

(*The Adventurer's Bride* features characters you will have met in *The Man Behind the Façade*)

Chapter One

Oxfordshire—March 1527

The blizzard took Nicholas Hurst by surprise and caused his spirits to plummet. He knew that if it continued snowing so heavily it would soon blanket out the unfamiliar Oxford–Witney road. Pray God, he would reach Witney before nightfall. He had made a promise to a certain lady and it was that, and the safety of his daughter, which were of the uppermost importance to him now. God only knew what Jane Caldwell would have to say when he arrived there with Matilda, although the vision of her that he had carried with him in the last few months had caused him to hope that she would welcome them both.

Nicholas still found it unbelievable at times

that he had assisted at Jane's second son Simon's birth—an event that he sometimes spent too much time thinking about. Even so he was flattered when she had asked him to be godfather to the child. But he was also confused by his feelings towards Jane; he certainly felt a responsibility towards her and her son that was almost as strong as that which he felt towards his new daughter, but there was something else... During the three months he had been away in Europe, he had visualised the widow impatiently awaiting his return and had prayed that she would not tire of doing so. Yet surely he could not be in love with her? His feelings towards her were so different to how he had felt towards Louise, the Flemish mistress he had parted from last summer. Besides, he had vowed never to love again and had even considered joining the church. Jane was certainly no beauty like Louise and yet there was something about her that drew him...and he wanted her in his life.

He remembered his first sighting of Jane in Oxford last year. He had travelled there in company with his brother, Philip, who was intent on visiting Rebecca Clifton, whom they had known since childhood and who lived with Jane. His younger brother had in mind that Nicholas should marry Rebecca, but he had

soon made it plain that was out of the question.
Soon after that meeting, though, Jane had come
towards him, shouting and waving a stick, hell-
bent on frightening off the cur trying to reach
the kitten cradled in the arms of her son, James,
standing at Nicholas's side. Naturally, he had
been doing his uttermost to defend the lad, despite suffering from a broken arm at the time
after an attack on him in London. Her appearance had come as something of a shock for she
was heavily pregnant.

That maternal aspect of her nature had been
very much to the fore then, but it was during the birth of Simon that her strength and
courage had hit Nicholas afresh. He had experienced emotions then that he had never felt
before and when he had seen his baby daughter for the first time, he had felt overwhelmed
by similar sensations. A baby was so frail, so
precious. He had determined to provide for
Matilda by whatever means lay in his power
and Jane had formed part of his plan. Widowed the same day she had given birth, he had
deemed that, given time, it was possible Jane
might agree to what he had to say. He suspected
that her first marriage had been one of convenience and although she might have grown fond
of the husband, who had been twenty years her
senior, he doubted she had loved him.

Whilst away from England, gathering information for King Henry's chancellor, Nicholas had imagined he had seen Jane's likeness in paintings and statues in every great house or church he had visited. Why he kept picturing her as the Madonna, a paragon of virtue, was curious, for she had cursed like a fishwife during Simon's birth. And yet from the little he had learnt of her from his brother, Philip, and Philip's wife, Rebecca, they believed her to be a woman of high moral standards.

Suddenly his conviction of Jane's warm welcome wavered. It was possible that he was mistaken. She might not approve of his actions in accepting responsibility for the daughter of his erstwhile Flemish mistress who had deceived him. He groaned inwardly. It would have been wiser if he had kept quiet about the passionate feelings he had felt towards Louise. He must have been crazed to speak of it to Jane, but he had thought to take her mind off the ordeal of childbirth at the time.

Dolt!

What must she have thought of him?

And then to have told her, too, of the pain and deep disappointment he had experienced after discovering Louise had deceived him! Jane had actually thought to ask what he would have done if Louise had informed him earlier that she was betrothed to a Spanish sea captain. Would he still have fallen in love with her or had she been irresistible?

Jane's question had taken him by surprise and he could only answer that he had no answer but that Louise's failing in doing so had resulted in a duel with the sea captain and several attempts on Nicholas's life after the Spaniard had died from the wounds inflicted during their duel, his younger kin having vowed vengeance. Nicholas sighed heavily. It would have been better for all concerned if he had refrained from visiting his own kin in Flanders after his travels to eastern Europe and the Far East.

A deeper sigh from the wet nurse behind him interrupted his thoughts. No doubt Berthe was wishing that she had never agreed to come to England with him due to the unseasonal spring weather. It was not that he had never experienced such a storm before, but his daughter's wet nurse had obviously not. She began to complain in high-pitched Flemish as the thick, white flakes whirled and swirled as if tossed by a giant hand. He managed to control his impatience. She had proved extremely satisfactory in caring for the child, but now he was concerned that Matilda might catch a chill.

'There is naught I can do about the weather, Berthe,' he said in Flemish, turning in the saddle to the wet nurse where she sat in a pillion seat, nursing the baby in a blanket. He saw the child blink rapidly as a snowflake landed on her pretty nose, and frowned. 'Pass Matilda to me and I will put her inside my doublet where she will be safe and warm,' he said abruptly.

Berthe's plump face fell and she shook her head and clutched the child more tightly and muttered something that he did not catch. 'Do what I say at once. We cannot afford to delay,' he ordered.

Still she clung to the child. He let out an oath and, gripping the horse's flanks with his thighs, let go of the reins and took hold of his daughter and forced Berthe to relinquish her. The woman let out a cry of anguish which took him by surprise, but he had Matilda safe now.

Opening his riding coat, he unfastened his doublet, kissing his daughter's cold face before easing her between his linen shirt and padded doublet. Then he drew his riding coat close about him and fastened it before reaching for the reins.

He urged the horse into a trot, aware that Berthe was cursing him in her own tongue, which was disconcerting. He had treated her well since hiring her in Bruges and she had seemed grateful, but since their arrival in Oxford, her behaviour had changed and she had grown sullen and more possessive towards the child, reluctant to allow him to handle her. He would be glad when he reached Witney and Jane.

He drew down the brim of his hat in a further attempt to shield his eyes from the falling snow and fixed his gaze on the road ahead, not wanting the horse to veer off into the ditch to his left. To his right the snow was swiftly concealing the grass verge, beyond which there were outcrops of rocks and budding trees.

As he rounded a bend in the road, the wind appeared to strengthen so that the flurry of snow that hit him in the face almost blinded him. For a moment he did not see the two figures on horseback that blocked his path. Then the two horsemen started towards him and instinctively he reached for his short sword. As he raised his sword arm and drew it back, there came a shriek from behind. He scarcely heeded it, too intent on defending himself from the attackers in front of him. Angry desperation enabled him to swiftly disarm one of them with a mighty thrust of his elbow and the force behind the blow dislodged the man from the saddle.

He wasted no time seeing what happened to him, but managed to jerk his horse around to face his other assailant. Aware of Berthe's screams as the beast's hooves slid in the snow, she must have accidently caught him a blow on the head with a flailing arm as she tumbled from the pillion seat. Then he was fighting for his life as the other man thrust his sword directly at his chest. Fearing for his daughter's life as well as his own, Nicholas succeeded in twisting his body in the saddle. A fist smashed into the side of his face and then he felt a blade go through coat, doublet and shirt into the hollow beneath his collar bone. The pain made him feel giddy and sick, but, summoning all his strength, he brought his weapon down on the man's forearm. The resulting agonising screech seemed to vibrate in Nicholas's head, but his attacker had fallen back, clutching his arm as his sword fell from his grasp.

Nicholas jerked himself upright in the saddle and dug his heels into the horse's flanks. At the same time he heard the babble of women's voices. As the beast started forwards, its hooves slithered in the snow and for a moment his heart was in his mouth; somehow the horse managed to get a grip with its hooves and the next moment they were off.

He heard the women cry out in Flemish, 'Stop him. He's got the child. Stop him!' One was Berthe's, but he did not recognise the other.

Aware of blood seeping through his clothing and his daughter grizzling close to his heart, he dismissed the women from his thoughts. Dizzy still from the blows he had received, he could scarcely believe what had taken place in such a short space of time. He could only pray that Witney was near and they would arrive before the light faded.

'He should have been here by now,' said young Elizabeth Caldwell. She was kneeling on the cushioned window seat and in the act of rubbing the condensation from the diamond-shaped pane with her black sleeve. She put her eye to the glass in an attempt to see out.

'Master Hurst has a long way to come,' said her stepmother, Jane, trying not to betray the misgivings she felt and which gave lie to the outer calm she presented to the children. She laid her four-month-old son in his cradle and added, 'We might have to give Master Hurst a few more days to get here.'

'But he promised he would arrive in time for the fourth Sunday in Lent,' said nine-year-old Margaret agitatedly. She was the older sister, fair-haired and blue-eyed and more slender than Elizabeth, so that the black gown she wore hung on her spare frame. 'We cannot have the ceremony on that day without him being here.'

'That is true,' said Jane, picking up her darning. 'But he is Simon's godfather by proxy and it is but a matter of him repeating the vows your Uncle Philip made for him.'

Jane had almost convinced herself that she was a fool to believe that Nicholas Hurst would keep his promise. She found it difficult to banish the Flemish woman, who had been his mistress, from her mind or approve of his actions in going in search of her last November. Yet who was she to judge his behaviour, having not always behaved as she ought? But she was not going to dwell on a period in her life that she deeply regretted.

She had heard naught since concerning whether Nicholas had found Louise or not. Before he had sailed for Flanders he had sent her a message, agreeing to be Simon's godfather and suggesting in the meantime that his younger brother act as his proxy, saying he hoped to be with her on the day in March set aside to venerate the Virgin Mary at the very latest. So Philip had taken Nicholas's place at Simon's baptism and his wife, Rebecca, Jane's sister-in-law, had filled the role of her son's godmother.

Due to the children's father, Simon Caldwell, having been killed in an accident the day of his son's birth, Jane and the children were very much in need of a man in their lives, despite most considering her a capable woman—after all, she had kept house for her brother, Giles, after their parents' deaths until her marriage.

It had felt odd at first being a widow and she had found herself wishing fervently that Nicholas Hurst had not gone away. She had thought when he had changed his mind about entering the church, having spent a short time with the Blackfriars in Oxford, that their becoming acquainted could have partly been the reason behind his decision. Then out of the blue he had decided to return to Flanders. It had come as a terrible shock. Especially when Rebecca, who had lived with Jane and her husband, had married Nicholas's brother, Philip, and accompanied him to the king's court at Greenwich.

Sad to say Jane missed Rebecca more than she did her husband. Simon had been a widower and stonemason when her brother had introduced them. Simon had had two young daughters in need of a mother and so her brother had arranged a marriage that was very convenient for both of them. It had worked out far better than she could have hoped, although her husband had spent a large part of his time away from home, working on various building projects. His death had been the result of a fall from scaffolding at a church in Oxford. She had spoken to him often enough about his being too old to do such climbing, but he had not listened.

Of course, his sudden passing had been completely unexpected, taking place as it did the day of the younger Simon's birth. The house in Oxford had become a place of mourning. Her husband had been kind and they had relied upon him in so many ways, to deal with the tasks that fell to a man, especially when it came to dealing with the finances. She could not say that those years married to Simon had been delightful, but she had grown fond of his girls and he had been appreciative of all she did, especially when she had given him the son he had so wanted. He had provided her with all the necessities of life, except that need to be loved. Her husband hadn't had a romantic bone in his body and could not be said to cut a heroic figure. There were times when a woman longed for such attributes in her man, despite knowing there were other essential traits necessary in a husband.

She still had much to learn about the adventurous Nicholas Hurst, but from the moment Jane's brother's widow, Rebecca, had opened the pages of the printed book concerning his travels and read aloud of his adventures to her and the girls, Jane hadn't been able to get him out of her dreams. Not that she had ever revealed how she felt to anyone. The fact that Rebecca had known the Hurst brothers since she was a young girl and had visited their ship-yard at Greenwich meant that she was able to paint vivid word pictures of Nicholas's appear-ance to her listeners. Such descriptions did not appear in his book so were especially appreci-ated by Jane.

The day she had actually come face-to-face with him was one she would never forget. Es-pecially when his behaviour in defending her son lived up to what she had expected of him. Then she had gone into labour, having received the news that her husband was unconscious after a fall.

By the saints, what an experience that had been, what with the famed explorer seeing her in such a state! And yet Nicholas had achieved all that she had asked of him and the three of them had survived the ordeal of childbirth. How had he felt deep inside with her being an-other man's wife? How much had Simon's sud-den death reflected on that memory for him?

One thing was for certain: she had deter-mined he would play a part in Simon's life if it were in her power to bring it about. Hence the reason for asking Nicholas to be his godfather.

A sigh escaped her. How she wished her ap-pearance had been different that day. He could have only compared her unfavourably with the wanton Louise who had been his mistress. Distracted now by the thought of the Flemish woman, she wondered if he had found her. What of the child? Had both been delivered safely from the ordeal of giving birth? If so, had he decided to wed the woman whom he'd felt so passionately about? Her heart ached at the thought.

She squared her shoulders and told herself to believe in Nicholas's promise. He had said he would come. If all was well with him, then God grant that he would be here soon. She would welcome him warmly despite there being still eight months of the mourning period to endure.

Of necessity she'd had to sell the house her husband had left her in Oxford and rent a smaller one here on the outskirts of Witney in order to be able to support herself and the children. She had dared to consider entering the cloth trade, despite it being very much the precinct of men. For that she had been offered assistance by Rebecca's father, Anthony Mortimer.

Just like Nicholas, he was a much-travelled man. Indeed, they had not known of his existence until his sudden appearance a few months ago. He had contacts abroad that he was willing to share with her and she had appreciated the help he had given her so far, but she sensed that was causing him to believe he had more influence and control of her situation than she desired. She suspected that he thought if he were to find her a weaver than she would look upon himself with much favour. Several times he had spoken of feeling lonely and she guessed that he might be looking for a wife to share the house he was having rebuilt at Draymore Manor.

She felt a tug on her sleeve which roused her from her reverie.

'Mama, what if Master Hurst has not changed his mind and intends keeping his promise, but has lost his way in the snow?' said Elizabeth, gazing up at her.

'That is a foolish thing to say,' cried Margaret. 'Master Hurst is a great explorer! He has travelled to the Americas and to the Indies and been all over Europe. He will not get lost.'

Jane's elder son, James, looked up from the wooden-jointed soldier he was playing with and said in a voice that had not so long ago lost its babyish lisp, 'But the snow will cover the highway. His horse might wander off or lose its footing. It'll be dark soon.' Eagerly he added, 'Perhaps he needs a light to show him the way!'

'A light in the window like a beacon leading him here,' said Elizabeth excitedly, gazing at her stepmother. 'Shall I fetch the oil lamp, Mama?'

Jane nodded, glad to be active, which was strange considering how tired she was. She'd risen early that day to go over her accounts and later she had interviewed a man she had hoped would be willing to weave the thread she spun, but without any luck. She found this deeply discouraging and wondered if the time she spent teaching her stepdaughters to spin was just a waste. A depressing thought considering she had been so delighted when she had discovered that she had not lost the skill taught to her by her own mother.

'I deem it would be wiser if we set the lamp in the window upstairs,' said Jane. 'Due to the dip in the street, its light might not be seen if we were to have it down here.'

So a lamp was duly set in the window that jutted out over the ground floor where the family hoped and prayed for Nicholas Hurst's arrival. Jane placed the cooking pot on its chains above the fire and added more onion, beans and turnip to the broth she was making and waited in frustrated silence.

As Nicholas rode on through the falling snow, his head throbbed and his shoulder was aflame with pain. He had to reach Jane—only she could ensure Matilda's survival now. He fumbled inside a pouch at his waist for a kerchief and managed to drag it out and ease it beneath his doublet where the blood still oozed from the wound in his shoulder. Pray God it would stop bleeding soon.

So far he could hear no sound of pursuit, but that did not say he was not being followed. He could make no sense of what had occurred and how Berthe and the other woman had been involved! His mind strayed to that difficult time back in Bruges six weeks ago. After the death of Matilda's mother in childbirth, Nicholas had let it be known that he desperately needed a wet nurse prepared to travel to England and stay there for a year. The woman his Flemish kin had found him had refused his more-than-generous offer to accompany him to England. He had been so relieved when Berthe had come forwards that he had not bothered with references. She had appeared sensible and trustworthy and in desperate need of help herself.

Her story was that her husband had been killed in a skirmish involving the French and the troops of the Holy Roman Emperor, Charles V. The information she had been able to provide about the movements of the Emperor's army had been extremely useful. She had been left almost penniless with her own infant to support after her man's death and soon after her baby son had died. Fortunately she was still producing milk in abundance to be able to give succour to his daughter and she had seemed more than willing to accompany him to the house of Jane Caldwell in England.

Jane! He had to reach Jane.

Was that a light ahead? He pushed back the brim of his hat in the hope of being able to see more clearly and his spirits rose, only to be dashed as the light vanished. He groaned, wondering if he was hallucinating. A wail from the babe that curled next to his heart recalled him to the present and was incentive enough for him to spur the horse on in the hope that he had not imagined that light and that Witney and Jane lay ahead just over the next dip in the white landscape. It would be terrible, indeed, for them to have survived the journey from Flanders, only for them both to perish in this snowy wilderness.

Jane could bear the waiting no longer. The snow had stopped falling and she had an urge to take a walk along the High Street and see if she could see any sign of their expected guest. She would not go far as it would be unwise to leave the children alone for long, despite Mar-

garet being a sensible girl who knew to keep
the younger ones away from the fire and the
cooking pot.

She went out in the gloaming and had just
walked past the Butter Cross when she saw a
rider coming towards her. His hat and clothing were blanketed in snow and the reins lay
slack in his grasp. His shoulders drooped and
his head had fallen so that his chin appeared to
have sunk onto his chest. He drew level with
her and would have gone past if she had not realised with a leap of her heart that it was Nicholas; swiftly she seized the horse's bridle and
brought it to a halt.

'Master Hurst!' she cried. 'What has happened to you?'

Nicholas forced his eyes opened and gazed
down at the woman dressed in black, who
stood looking up at him from concerned brown
eyes, and he felt such relief. 'Jane Caldwell?'
he said, the words slurred. 'It is you, isn't it,
Jane?' He reached down a hand and placed it
on her shoulder.

'Indeed, it is,' she replied, her heart seem-
ing to turn over in her breast when she noticed
that his right cheekbone was bruised and swol-
len. 'You are hurt. Is it that you came off your
horse?'

He shook his head, only to wince. 'No, I was

attacked. The villains would have killed me, but I managed to escape.'

She gasped in horror. 'I thought your enemies had been dealt with!'

Vaguely he realised that she was referring to those who had attempted to kill him in Oxford last year in an act of revenge. Feeling near to collapse, he muttered something in way of reply.

She realised that now was not the time to discuss the matter. 'My house is not far away. I will lead you there.'

He smiled wearily. 'If it had not been for the light, I might have gone astray,' he said unevenly.

Jane wondered if he meant the one that she had placed in the window upstairs and she rejoiced. 'A guiding light was James's idea.'

'He's an intelligent lad,' said Nicholas, forcing the words out.

She nodded, his words pleasing her so much. It was essential that he liked the children and they him. Suddenly she became aware of a bulge beneath his riding coat and that it was moving. At the same time she heard a sound reminiscent of a baby grizzling. 'What is that noise?'

'Noise?' He blinked at her. 'I have been

hearing it for some time and it distresses me. You will help me, Jane?'

'Of course,' she replied, puzzled, thinking that possibly he had a small dog hidden beneath his coat. 'Although I would have thought you'd know there is no need for you to ask such a question.'

'Perhaps not, but it is good manners to do so. The baby...' he said.

'Simon,' she said, reminding him of her son's name, concerned that he might have forgotten it.

'No, it is a girl,' he muttered.

She looked at him askance. 'You have a baby girl concealed beneath your coat? How did you come by her?' Even as she spoke a thought occurred to her and her heart sank.

'It is a long story and it is much too cold out here to tell it now,' he gasped, placing an arm beneath the bulge. He gritted his teeth as pain shot through his shoulder with the movement and he felt blood well up from the shoulder wound.

'Are you all right?' she asked, her eyes widening with concern.

'A blade pierced my shoulder. A mere scratch!' he lied. 'It is more important that Matilda is fed. I thought with you having your son to nurture that you could give succour to her as well.'

Matilda! Jane's disturbed brown eyes met his hazel ones. 'I fear that I must disappoint you. I cannot do what you ask!'

Nicholas looked at her in shocked dismay. 'Never did I think to hear you speak so, Jane Caldwell!'

'Do not take on so,' she cried, hastily seizing the bridle again and hopping to one side so as to avoid the horse's hooves. Her voice dropped. 'It brings a flush to my cheeks to speak of such to you, but I have no choice but to refuse your request because I—I...' She floundered, embarrassed to speak of such a personal matter to a man, yet it was this man who had assisted at the birth of her son. She added in a rushed whisper, 'My milk has dried up and I cannot feed even Simon. No doubt it is due to the sudden death of my husband and all the extra work involved in selling the house. It has been such a worry thinking about how I am to provide for the children, what with trying to find a weaver willing to work with me—a task which appears to have proved beyond even Master Mortimer's abilities so far.' She took a breath, realising she was gabbling to cover her nervousness. 'Now let us not discuss this matter further right now.

We must get you and the child indoors without further ado!'

Mortified and deeply concerned by the mention of Master Mortimer, Nicholas could only stare at her as he swayed in the saddle, clutching his shoulder. 'I beg your pardon. I have no experience of such matters. Does young Simon still live?'

'Aye, I have hired the service of a wet nurse who has ample milk,' she said. 'I do not doubt Anna will be willing to provide for Ma- Matilda, as well, for a small fee.'

He could not conceal his relief. 'You will arrange it?'

'Of course, I would not have any child starve.' She wasted no more time in talk, but swept before him like the galleon he had likened her to when first he saw her, leaving him to follow on his horse.

He swore inwardly, deeply regretting the *faux pas* he had made, and, summoning his remaining strength, told the horse to walk on. He had no idea if there was stabling at this present house of hers. If not, then he would have to find the nearest inn and stable the beast there.

As soon as Nicholas saw the house, which was at the end of a row of terraced dwellings constructed of the local stone, he realised that the knocks he had received had done more than make him dizzy, they had caused him to momentarily forget that Jane's husband had left his financial affairs in a mess. Hence her reason for moving to Witney to a much smaller house than the one he had visited in Oxford. There was no way she would have been able to afford the luxury of her own stabling even if she owned a horse.

She suggested that he ride his mount to the back of the house where there was a garden and leave the horse there for now. 'I will send for Matt, the son of the wet nurse, and he can stable it for you at the Blue Boar Inn.'

As he was feeling extremely weary, Nicholas agreed. He dismounted with difficulty, glad that there was no one there to see him narrowly avoid falling flat on his face. He stumbled to his feet and struggled with the straps of the saddlebags, pain stabbing through his shoulder and down his side and arm like a skewer. At last he managed to complete his task and, not having the strength to throw the saddlebags over his uninjured shoulder, carried them dangling from his left hand towards the rear door of the house.

Fortunately it was unlocked and he pressed down on the latch and entered the building. He found himself in a darkened room and almost fell over the loom that was there, narrowly avoiding bumping into a spinning wheel and several baskets on the floor. Before he could climb the two steps that led to an inner door, it was flung wide from the other side and Jane stood there, holding a candlestick that provided a circle of warm light.

'This way,' she said.

He thanked her and entered the main chamber of the house. Instantly the two girls and the boy who were waiting there rushed over to him. He dropped the saddlebags.

'You've come, you've come,' cried Elizabeth, hugging as far as she could reach of his waist whilst James's small arms wrapped around one of his legs and Margaret stood close by, beaming up at him.

He had never expected such an enthusiastic welcome, although he remembered the children being friendly enough at their first meeting last year. He had been told to tell them stories and had done his best. He thought how different this greeting was from that of his elder brother Christopher's sons and daughter, whom he scarcely knew. They were inclined to be tongue-tied in his company, as if overcome by his presence. He felt tears prick his eyes. If it had not been for Jane ordering the children to allow Master Hurst to warm himself by the fire, he might have been completely unmanned.

She set a chair close to the fire and bade him be seated. On unsteady legs he crossed the floor, hesitating by the cradle to gaze down at the child sleeping there.

'He has grown,' he murmured.

'What did you expect? He is more than four months old now,' said Jane, her face softening.

Without lifting his head, he said, 'I will never forget seeing him born. It was a happening completely outside my experience.'

'That was obvious,' she said unsteadily.

He looked up, caught her eye and she blushed.

They continued to stare at each other, both remembering the forced intimacy of Simon's birth at a time when they were only newly acquainted.

He recalled her cursing him and his rushing to carry out her commands, fearing she might die before the midwife arrived. She had called him a lackwit when he had not reacted fast enough, for Simon's birth had been imminent. When the boy's head had appeared, the ground had appeared to rock beneath Nicholas's feet and he had thought he would swoon. Fortunately her unexpectedly calm voice had recalled him to his responsibility towards both mother and child. He had once seen a calf born and although that experience was definitely different he had managed to react in a way that met Jane's approval.

As for Jane, she was thinking that it was probably best that they had never met before the day of Simon's birth, otherwise she would never have had the nerve to order him around the way she had done. Hearsay was not the same as actually meeting someone face-to-face. Of course, she had known more about Nicholas than he did of her, yet setting eyes on a real live hero was a very different matter from one who lived in the pages of a book and somehow seemed larger than life.

Chapter Two

Jane dropped her gaze and Nicholas forced himself to cross the remaining distance to the fire, wondering afresh what madness had caused him to unburden himself that day of Simon's birth and speak of Louise. He should have kept his mouth shut because it was obvious to him that Jane might find it difficult to accept Louise's daughter in the circumstances. Why had he not considered that as a possibility? Was it because Jane had so impressed him with that maternal side of her nature? He could only pray that his daughter would be able to win her heart as those children in her charge had won his with the warmth of their welcome.

He sank thankfully into a chair. The children followed and stationed themselves with a girl on either side of him whilst James leaned against his knee and fired a question at him.

Jane listened to them talking as she removed her gloves and coat with trembling hands and hung the latter on a peg. She took a deep breath to calm herself, wondering how badly he was wounded and thinking of the baby concealed beneath his doublet. Had *that woman* rejected her daughter or was Louise dead?

Jane took another deep breath and walked briskly over to the group by the fire. 'This will not do,' she said firmly. 'Margaret, you will go to Anna's house and tell her I have immediate need of her. If Matt is there, ask him to come, as well. Elizabeth, you will set bowls and spoons on the table, as well as drinking vessels. James, you will watch the fire and let me know if it needs more wood.'

'And what will you do, Mama?' asked the boy.

Her face softened as she gazed down at him. 'Master Hurst has been wounded and I must tend him.'

The children's eyes rounded. 'Has he been on one of his adventures and had to fight the natives?' asked Elizabeth.

A low chuckle issued from Nicholas's throat, followed by the words 'Not exactly.' He fumbled with the fastening on his coat. 'Although I was attacked on my way here.'

The children gasped. 'Did you manage to kill one of them with your sword?' asked James.

'Hush now! Do not bother Master Hurst with such questions.' Jane shooed away the children and went to his aid. As she undid the fastenings on the sodden garment and set it to dry on a three-legged stool in front of the fire, she noticed a slit in the material. It was sticky and she realised that was where the blade must have penetrated the fabric and the stickiness was blood. She felt slightly faint and for a moment could not move. He could have so easily been killed! The thought frightened her.

'My daughter, Jane,' he reminded her in a gruff voice.

She gazed down at his bulging doublet, feeling quite peculiar, almost envious of the child that lay beneath the padded russet broadcloth so close to his heart. What had happened to her mother? Jane's eyes went to his face and for a moment their questioning gazes locked. Then he closed his eyes and she realised that he was exhausted and she would have to wait for an answer.

She willed her fingers to remain steady as she removed the girdle about his waist that held his short sword and a pouch. She set them aside and began to undo the fastenings on his doublet. The squashed nose of a baby appeared and then the rest of her face. *By my Lady, she is pretty,* thought Jane, a catch in her throat. She touched the child's petal-soft skin with the back of her hand and realised it was not as cold as she feared it might be.

Then she remembered what Nicholas had told her about the child's beautiful mother and struggled with a surge of emotion, thinking again of Louise and resenting the relationship she had shared with this man.

The tiny mouth opened and fastened on the side of Jane's hand and began to suck. She was strangely moved despite knowing in her heart of hearts that she had no desire to give shelter to this child of Louise's.

'It is a wonder you did not suffocate her,' said Jane roughly, undoing the rest of the doublet to enable her to remove the baby, who was dressed in swaddling bands.

She found herself being surveyed by a pair of hazel eyes that were flecked with green and gold, the same as Nicholas's. She told herself that she should be relieved that the little girl had her father's eyes, but her feelings were too confused to feel so. Was that because she wanted to think the worst of Louise, believing that she had lied to Nicholas about the child she carried? Yet as the baby began to cry, Jane's maternal instincts surfaced and she rocked Matilda in her arms.

Nicholas gazed at them both from beneath drooping eyelids. 'I imagined the pair of you looking as you do now,' he croaked.

'Really,' said Jane coolly. 'Is that why you are here, simply because you thought I could take care of your daughter? I had thought better of you, *Master Hurst*. You disappoint me.'

Nicholas shifted in the chair and a spasm of pain caused him to place a hand on his wounded shoulder. 'You misjudge me, *Mistress Caldwell!* I hired a wet nurse for my daughter in Bruges. I came here to confirm the vows Pip made for me by proxy to be Simon's godfather and for no other reason.'

Was he speaking the truth? Disappointed though she was, Jane decided she had to give him the benefit of the doubt. 'Forgive me! For a moment I forgot that you had promised to be Simon's godfather,' she said humbly. 'What happened to the wet nurse?'

'I deem Berthe must have betrayed me,' he said bitterly. 'She was in league with those men who attacked me. As I made my escape I heard her and another woman crying out, "Stop him. He's got the child. Stop him!"'

Jane's head jerked up. 'Why should she do such a thing? Do you think she was put up to it by the child's mother?'

Nicholas sighed, removed his sodden felt hat and fingered where his head hurt. 'Louise is dead,' he said heavily. 'Matilda has no mother.'

Jane could only stare at him. 'I see. I didn't know Louise had died,' she said slowly.

'Why should you? It isn't easy to get a message to someone from abroad, especially during the winter months. Even my brothers were unaware of it. When I visited Christopher, he told me to my face that he considered me a fool for taking responsibility for Matilda.' Nicholas turned the hat between his hands restlessly and then dropped it on the floor and leaned back in the chair, closing his eyes. 'Louise died a couple of days after the birth and she wanted me to have Matilda. I had already decided on that course of action after seeing at close hand what can happen when a daughter is fobbed off as another man's or placed with relatives who have no love for it. That was why I went in search of Louise.'

Before Jane could respond, there was a sound at the front door and Margaret entered with a homely-looking woman wearing a cloak over a brown gown. She stared at Nicholas with a lively curiosity in her large round eyes. 'So you're the famous explorer,' she said. 'I've been hearing about you off and on for the past few weeks.' She folded her arms across her ample bosom. 'About time you arrived—they've all been on pins in this house, thinking you mightn't get here in time for Our Lady's day.' She paused for breath.

'Where is Matt?' asked Jane swiftly.

'He will be here soon,' replied Anna and continued with her former dialogue with Nicholas. 'And now you have come, what's this I hear about you not only being attacked but that you've brought a babe with you that needs suckling?'

Jane said hastily, 'Dear Anna, do not be bothering Master Hurst about such matters now. He is wounded and exhausted and much concerned for his daughter. Here, take the child! I will see that you are paid later.' She thrust Matilda at the wet nurse without waiting to see Nicholas's reaction to the woman who was temporarily to act as mother to his daughter. No doubt the news of Nicholas's arrival would soon be all over Witney. Anna's husband was the local baker and as much of a gossip as his wife. Would the information be spread abroad beyond the town and reach not only the men who had tried to kill him, but also the women who appeared to want the child? It was a puzzle to her.

From a chest Jane took a couple of handfuls of linen bindings and wrapped them in a drying cloth before tucking them under Anna's arm. She wasted no time in seeing the wet nurse out. Then she picked up a candlestick and brought it over to where Nicholas was seated, thinking she would need more light if she was to attend to his wound.

'I hope my actions meet with your approval where your daughter is concerned,' she said briskly. 'Do not mind Anna's tongue. She has a warm heart and, for now, abundant milk. I can reassure you that she is clean and extremely fond of babies, otherwise I would not trust Simon to her.'

'I will take your word for it,' he said, attempting a smile despite his exhaustion.

'I have known her for years,' said Jane, bending over him. 'We were girls together when I lived here in Witney with my parents and brother.' She paused. 'Now shall we remove your doublet so I can take a look at your wound? Did those ruffians rob you at all?'

'No, they did not get the opportunity.' His dark reddish-gold brows knit. 'Although, perhaps I should have not been so trusting of

Berthe. My coin pouch was of late within easy reach of her fingers.'

Jane glanced at the girdle she had laid to one side earlier and crossed to where she had placed it. She picked it up and handed it to him. 'Do you wish to count the coin?'

He weighed the pouch in his hand. 'It is a little lighter than I remember and I did not feel a thing. Fortunately I soon learnt whilst on my travels that it is always wise to have another stash of money concealed somewhere else.'

'You don't think she knew where that was?' asked Jane, wondering how he had come by this wet nurse who was obviously untrustworthy.

'No,' he said confidently.

Jane was glad of that, for she had little coin to spare to pay Anna extra and for any other expenses Nicholas's sojourn here in Witney might involve. She wondered how long he would stay now there was the worry of the attack on him to take into account. She gnawed on the inside of her cheek as she continued with the task of removing his doublet without causing him too much pain.

Once rid of the garment she was able to see more clearly that his fine woollen shirt was more bloodstained than the doublet and that it was unravelling. Obviously the weapon's blade had caught a thread and snapped it. Her heart was in her mouth as she attempted to separate the patch of shirt that was stuck to the wound, for she could feel the tension within him. She decided that it was best if she dampened the fabric and fortunately that did the trick. At last she managed to ease the fabric away to reveal the gash in his flesh into which bits of wool and dirt had been forced. By then he was breathing heavily and his face had changed colour. As for her, the inside of her cheek was raw from chewing on it.

She whispered an apology as she removed the shirt. Now his chest was completely exposed, she could see the scars he had incurred from previous encounters with foes. She felt an unexpected urge not only to wrap her arms around him, but to scold him.

'How many times have you come close to death?' she muttered, straightening up with his shirt clenched in her hand. 'I know of some of your adventures, but not that you had been injured so often.'

'I survived and that is all that matters,' he growled.

'Hopefully you will survive this latest attack on you,' she said tautly before hurrying over to a shelf and removing a bottle of wine from it.

'Can I help, Mama?' asked Elizabeth, hovering about her.

'Fetch me some linen bindings from the chest and another clean rag,' said Jane.

The girl did so and received further orders concerning the supper this time. She went about her tasks as Jane gave Nicholas all her attention once more.

'Do you have any brandy?' he asked in a strained voice, watching her uncork the wine and pour some into a small bowl.

'Aye, as it happens Rebecca's father enjoys the finest French brandy. He brought a couple of bottles when he visited me the other week. Now keep still. I will fetch the brandy in a moment.'

She tipped the cup carefully and watched the elderflower wine that she had made herself the other year wash over the wound just beneath his collarbone. She was aware of the mingling smells of sandalwood, blood, dried sweat and wine and that he gritted his teeth as she swabbed the wound with a clean rag.

'I am sorry if I'm hurting you,' she said hastily. Curling strands of her light brown hair that had escaped from beneath her cap brushed his chin as she lowered her head further.

Nicholas breathed in the scent of camomile and guessed she washed her hair in water perfumed by the dried flower heads. His thoughts drifted back to his boyhood when he had visited his godparents. Sir Jasper had been a prosperous wine merchant with a house in Bristol and another in the countryside a few miles from the port. He remembered a meadow being covered in camomile daisies.

'Do you see much of Anthony Mortimer?' he asked.

Jane moved away and considered her answer as she took a small jar from the stool nearby. 'A fair amount. He is lonely. No doubt he misses the excitement of his old life of travel and meeting people. I am sure you can understand why that should be so, having travelled so much yourself?'

'Not as much as him, I am certain,' said Nicholas, frowning. 'After all, he is much older than I and will surely find it more difficult to settle.'

'Perhaps. When Rebecca's at home, he does spend time in her company,' replied Jane, 'but not as much as he would like. Since her marriage to your brother, she likes to accompany him when he is summoned to court or the king gives him permission to perform for one of his lordly friends at their mansions, castles or palaces.'

Jane began to smooth salve on his wound

and Nicholas felt her breasts press against him. Despite the pain he was in, he was aware of a stirring in his loins and it surprised him. For months he had not been with a woman and had held in his mind the image of Jane as a Madonna: a man did not have sexual desire for such an icon of reverence and worship. It was definitely odd and he knew that he must distract them both from this sudden unexpected yearning of his body. Being a widow, she would know what it signified if she were to become aware of his arousal.

He remembered his younger brother, Pip, wagering that he would never manage to live the celibate life required of priest. Nicholas had determined to prove him wrong. It appeared that his brother was right if the slightest brush of Jane's breasts could create such a reaction in him. He imagined holding their firm roundness, pressing his lips against her soft skin.

He must stop this! He cleared his throat. 'Tell me about this spinning business of yours. Does Master Mortimer take a great interest in it at all?'

'You seem *very* interested in him,' said Jane, frowning.

'My concern is for you. As I've already said, he's not a young man and you have enough on your hands caring for the children and trying to support them and yourself without becoming too closely involved with a man soon to be in his dotage.'

Her eyes narrowed. 'What are you trying to say, Master Hurst?'

'You're no fool, Jane,' he replied. 'You know what I'm talking about.'

'If it is marriage you refer to,' she muttered, a rosy colour flooding her cheeks, 'then I would remind you that it is but four months since my husband died and this year is a period of mourning for me. I am hardly going to encourage Mortimer in such circumstances.'

He had forgotten temporarily about the mourning period, but he did not say so because all of a sudden he felt extremely odd. 'Brandy!' he exclaimed abruptly.

She stared at him and saw that he had gone quite pale beneath his tan. She clicked her tongue against her teeth and hurried away.

He closed his eyes, but despite doing so he could not shut out the scent of camomile that lingered in the air and again was reminded of his godparents and a spring when the tide was high. Sir Jasper had taken him to see the wave that swept in from the Bristol Channel as it fought against the river current. Despite all the wonders he had since seen on his travels, Nicholas had never forgotten the sight of that frightening wall of water advancing towards them and it had haunted his dreams. His god-parents had had no children and the fortune Sir Jasper had amassed had come to Nicholas after the death of his godmother a year after her larger-than-life husband had died. At that time the urge to travel had been strong in him and he had seldom visited his properties. He had put an agent in the house in Bristol and a mar-ried couple in the one overlooking the estuary.

Since Matilda's birth, he had come to the de-cision that he needed to make a proper home for her and it seemed sensible to take posses-sion of his property.

There came the sound of a bottle being opened and liquor poured and then the swish of her black skirts as Jane returned. 'Here you are, Master Hurst,' she said, her voice sound-ing anxious.

His heavy eyelids lifted and he stared at her. 'Why can't you call me Nicholas?' he said fret-fully, taking the goblet from her and downing the brandy in one gulp. 'Tell me, has Mortimer asked you to marry him?'

'What!' Jane returned his gaze with a fro-zen stare. Then she snatched the empty vessel from him and placed it beside the bottle on the table. 'Why do you ask me such questions at such a time? Now, are you ready for me to con-

tinue with my ministrations?' She picked up a
cloth pad and one of the bindings and raised
her eyebrows.

'I am thinking only of your good,' he said.

'I can take care of myself,' she retorted,
pressing the pad on the shoulder wound, aware
that he caught his breath as she did so. 'Hold
this and remain still and quiet.'

He frowned and placed his hand against the
pad, convinced that Mortimer had proposed
marriage to her. 'A woman needs a man, although it is a puzzle to me why you ever asked
me to be Simon's godfather if you do not want
me taking an interest in your affairs,' he muttered. 'Why did you?'

She had no answer to give him to that question that would not immediately result in his
prying even deeper into her reasons for so involving him and could only say, 'It seemed a
good idea at the time.'

'But not now? I admit that I was flattered
when you asked me,' he continued.

'It was not my intention to flatter you,' she
said, binding the pad securely into place. 'Why
is it that you cannot obey a simple command?
You've remained neither still nor quiet when
I requested it.'

Nicholas sighed. 'I am receiving the impression that you believe I have too much of a high

opinion of myself and am no longer suitable to be Simon's godfather.'

'Now you are being foolish. Besides, I'm sure there are lots of people who tell you how brave and clever and marvellous you are,' murmured Jane. 'No doubt some of what they say about you is true, so I still would like you to confirm the proxy promises your brother made on your behalf. I deem it would be good for my son to have such a godfather as yourself as an example of real courage.'

Nicholas groaned. 'You can't really believe all that my brother has transcribed about me from my journals? I would that you didn't set me up as some kind of hero as an example for Simon to follow.'

She remembered afresh their first meeting and chuckled. 'I saw an example of your courage when you braved that cur with a broken arm to defend my James and so did he.'

'That was not heroic. It was damn foolhardiness. I should have grabbed the boy's hand and made a run for it.'

She shook her head. 'I doubt it is in your nature not to make a fight of it when confronted with danger and you must have a certain amount of intelligence to have survived so many adventures.'

'Good fortune had something to do with it,

Jane,' he said, cautiously attempting to move his injured shoulder, only to stifle a groan. 'How about another brandy?' he muttered.

She looked doubtful. 'When did you last eat?'

'Hours ago,' he replied. 'Although what has that to do with anything?'

'Mmm! I suppose it won't do you any harm to become a little intoxicated, but you're going to have to rest that shoulder.' She poured out two small brandies and picked up the thread of their conversation again as she handed one to him. 'I would not deny that fortune plays its part in everyone's lives.' She sipped her own brandy cautiously. 'Although some would say that it is by the grace of God and the prayers of the saints that good fortune also visits us.'

He tossed back his brandy before saying, 'And when life takes a wrong turning do you see the hand of the Devil at work?'

'I would rather not discuss ol' Horny,' she murmured, glancing at the children. 'This wet nurse and the men who attacked you—do you think they will come here?'

Before he could reply they were interrupted by a knock on the door and Margaret hurried to open it. A tall and gangly youth with a shock of flaxen hair stood there.

'Here's Matt,' said Jane, smiling and crooking her finger at the lad.

He came over to them, staring with open curiosity at Nicholas's naked chest with its scars and the bandaging of his shoulder. 'You wanted me, Master Hurst,' he said, giving him a toothy grin.

'Aye, lad. I want you to stable my horse,' said Nicholas, 'and, if you could feed and water him and brush him down and cover him with the blanket after doing so, I'd appreciate that.' He reached for his money pouch and handed several coins to Matt.

The lad thanked him and was about to follow Margaret across the room towards the back of the house when Nicholas indicated he come closer. There ensued a low-voiced conversation between the two males.

Jane overheard but a few words as she emptied the bloodied wine into a slop bucket and so they made little sense to her. She burnt the rags on the fire and then washed her hands before taking up a ladle and stirring the contents of the cooking pot. By the time she returned to Nicholas's side, Matt had left to perform his allotted tasks.

'Sooo,' she said slowly, picking up the goblet containing the remains of her brandy.

Nicholas raised an eyebrow. 'What is it,

Jane? You have a question to ask me? I am also waiting for an answer to the one I asked you.'

'What question was that?' she queried.

'The one you told me I had no business to ask. Does Master Mortimer want you for his wife?'

She sighed exasperatedly. 'Do you not consider him a man who would respect the period of mourning that is customary in my case?'

'So he has not yet asked you. Do you believe he might do so in the future?'

She hesitated and glanced at the children, not wanting them eavesdropping. Nicholas might not be speaking loudly, but even so she did not want the girls in particular overhearing such talk. 'Why must you persist with such questioning?'

'Because it has occurred to me that we could make a match of it,' said Nicholas abruptly, remembering at least three women he had considered marrying in the past, only to discover other men had got there before him. 'Marry me and I swear I will take care of you and the children. You will not have to worry about spinning and where your next penny is coming from if you accept my proposal.'

'And who will take care of you, Master Hurst?' she said faintly, unable to take her eyes from his bruised face. She might have dreamed of his making love to her and she had her hopes, but she had never believed he really could want to marry her. He might not be as handsome as his brother Philip, but she did find him incredibly attractive.

'I will take care of myself, knowing I have a family dependent on me,' he said seriously. 'What do you say?'

She did not reply.

'Mama, are you all right?' Elizabeth's voice seemed to be coming from a distance. 'Is there anything more I can do to help you?'

Jane stammered, 'G-go and see t-to the hens!' She hoped her stepdaughter had not heard Nicholas's proposal because she could not possibly accept. It was too soon after Simon's death and she must honour his memory by adhering to the year of mourning. Besides, there was only one reason he could wish to marry her and that was unacceptable to her. He wanted a mother for Matilda. Yet she was finding it difficult to voice her refusal. She felt as if the intensity of his stare would burn through her clothing and skin to her heart and reveal to him the secret she carried within her. What would he think of her if he knew it? There had always been one rule for men and another for women.

'Well, Jane?' he demanded. 'I mean what I say.'

'Do not rush me,' she said in a low voice.

'You need a few more moments to think?'

'Aye!' retorted Jane. *More than a few moments!* Perhaps he wished to marry her for more than one reason and might want to truly adopt her little family? How clever he was to word his proposal in such a way.

She was reminded of a winter day when she had stood, shivering, outside a church. She had been seventeen to Simon's forty-two years. He had told her to her face that he needed a mother for his daughters and was prepared to accept her without a dowry, her brother having mentioned that it was time she married. She had been glad at the time that Giles had not told Simon that she desperately needed to marry. She had felt terrible at the time. She had wanted to tell Simon Caldwell the truth, but it had taken more courage than she possessed.

It felt odd, thinking about how she had fallen madly in love with Willem Godar, not knowing he was already married. Strangely he, too, had Flemish blood just like the Hurst brothers, but he came from Kent. Once upon a time the very thought of Willem would have filled her with pain and anger, but gradually she had thought less and less about him.

Now Nicholas's proposal reminded her of the foolishness and headiness of being a young girl and in love for the first time. What a fool love made of people. And what would Nicholas think of her if he were to discover the truth? No doubt he would be disgusted. She should be thankful that she was not in love with him, but only lusted after him. No longer in her first bloom of youth, she would not be fooled again by that treacherous emotion. As for Nicholas feeling such an emotion for her—it was not possible! She had never been what some would call desirable as Louise clearly had been, to judge by her daughter, so she could only believe that he wanted to marry her for exactly the same reason that Simon Caldwell had done. So far he had been too clever to say that he wanted to marry her so she could be a mother for his daughter, but she was certain that was the main factor in his proposing to her.

She did not utterly hold that against him and she would be lying to herself if she pretended that she would not enjoy being the wife of an heroic, rich explorer. Yet something inside her rebelled against the very idea that he saw in her only that maternal aspect of her femininity.

Yet if she turned down his proposal, no doubt there would be other women who would leap at the chance of becoming his wife. Oh,

Holy Mother, she certainly did not want him marrying someone else! He would be such a catch for a woman in her position. So why be churlish and hesitate to give him the answer he obviously wanted?

'What do you say, Jane?' he rasped. 'It is important that I have your answer now.'

His tone of voice stung her and she reached for the brandy and poured a little more in her cup and gulped it down. It gave her the courage to look him in the face. 'You're unreasonable,' she gasped. 'Expecting me to give you an answer just like that.' She snapped her fingers. 'I have already reminded you that I am still in mourning.'

His mouth set firm. 'I have not forgotten! I was there with you the day your husband died.'

'Then can you not be patient?'

'Not when I am aware that Rebecca's father is taking an interest in you. Now Berthe has betrayed me, I need a woman who will be part of Matilda's life for as long as it is necessary, which made asking you to be my wife more difficult than you can ever understand.' He seized her hand and pressed it against his bare chest. 'Can you feel my heart beating? It took much for me to propose to you a few moments ago. I realise now that I made a mess of it. For that I ask your forgiveness.'

Chapter Three

Jane's fingers shifted beneath his hand. It was true she could feel his heart pumping and it gave her a peculiar but exciting thrill to know that she could affect him in such a way.

'This is foolishness,' she said breathlessly, 'and yet you are so clever. No doubt you are practised in the art of persuading women to do what you will. But how can you talk of marriage when you have only just arrived here, wounded and exhausted? Marriage is a serious matter and needs much consideration before a decision can be made.'

Nicholas gave her a weary look, but there was also a hint of bewilderment in his hazel eyes as he released her hand. 'If there is one thing I have learnt on my travels it is that one has to seize the moment as it might never come again. Ask yourself a question: If I were to die, would you be filled with regret?'

She felt threatened again by the very idea of his dying. 'How dare you ask me such a question? Most likely you have put it to me so as to rouse my pity because you are wounded.' She took a deep breath. 'Why should you die? I have tended your wound and I have a certain skill when it comes to healing. You must give me more time to consider your proposal. At least a month,' she added wildly. 'After all, you have been hit on the head and might not be in full possession of your wits. It could be that you will change your mind.'

He looked taken aback. 'I assure you I am not out of my head. You'd be better accepting me this very moment. I cannot understand why you hesitate. I thought you a woman of sense. Am I so physically unattractive? Am I poor? No, I am well able to support you and the children in comfort. I have two houses and you can choose to live in both or either. You can throw out all the furniture and purchase new. You and the children will be able to dress in a grand style.'

She felt a flash of annoyance. 'What is wrong with the garments we are wearing now? You think to persuade me with your wealth and your appearance. I tell you such things do not impress me.'

'Which would make me admire you all the more, Jane, if I believed it to be true,' said Nicholas with a wry smile.

His arrogance almost took her breath away. 'How dare you,' she cried. 'I would not marry you if you were the last man on earth.'

'Mama, you're shouting,' said Margaret.

Jane whirled round and stared at her stepdaughter. 'Go and have your supper and serve the others,' she snapped. 'Master Hurst and I will eat later.'

Margaret nodded; her eyes were alight with interest as they darted from Jane's face to that of their guest. 'Master Hurst is not the last man on earth,' she stated. 'But if he were, it would be sensible of you to marry him.'

Jane barely managed to control her emotions. 'You should not be listening. Go and have your supper,' she repeated. 'Now!'

The girl went.

Jane turned back to Nicholas, but this time she had the sense not to meet those eyes of his. 'Now see what you've done?' she whispered, dropping her gaze, only to find herself staring at his bare chest. The urge to touch it was overwhelming.

'Consider the pleasure you'd have in choosing new materials and clothing yourself and the children in colours that lift the heart and spirits and made you want to dance and sing,' whispered Nicholas insidiously, reaching for the brandy.

She placed a hand on the bottle. 'I know why you are like this. You're intoxicated.'

'I deny that,' he said, wrenching the bottle from her grasp.

She tried to wrestle it from him and managed it. She could not resist looking at him with a hint of triumph, only to see he was looking wan. Nevertheless he staggered to his feet and again her eyes were on a level with his chest. She could not have been more aware of his maleness at that moment than if her body had been joined to his. The mingled scents of sandalwood, salve, dried sweat and brandy filled her senses yet again and she had an urge to press her lips against his skin; her fingers wanted to twist the curls of his chest hair and hold tight. A shiver went through her as she recalled the ugliness of the wound she had just bound and she prayed that it would heal.

'Forgive me, Jane, for teasing you,' he said, lowering his head so that his lips touched her left ear. 'Accept my proposal and I swear I will not rush you into marriage. I am persistent because I truly believe that we will be good for one another and the children.'

'You are being presumptuous, Master Hurst,' she said unevenly, unable to resist touching the spot that his lips had saluted, but she did not meet his gaze. 'What does a man who has spent his life going hither and thither wherever he wished know about fatherhood and living in a family?'

He looked hurt. 'Obviously you disapprove of my past way of life, but I can change.'

'You believe I wish to change you?' she found herself blurting out.

He looked surprised. 'Aye, surely you would want me to stay at home with you and the children?'

'I wonder if that would be expecting too much of you?' she said frankly. 'Despite your having the best of intentions. Tell me about your mother. What did she think about your travelling?'

He fell silent, gazing down at the graceful line of her neck as she placed the brandy bottle on the table. Then he took a deep breath and said, 'I know she worried about me, but she never tried to persuade me from following my dream. She had imagination,' he said softly. 'She was the one we boys went to when Father was overbearing and gave us a beating.

She encouraged Pip in his storytelling. I still miss her. One day I went away and when I returned she was no longer there. I'll always regret...' His voice trailed away.

But Jane could guess what he regretted and that he did not wish to speak of it, so she remained silent.

Nicholas kept his head down, blinking back tears. He felt Jane understood how he felt. If she did eventually accept his proposal, he believed that she would be an excellent mother and wife, faithful to him and caring of her children. But perhaps she was right and he would be unable to be either the husband she wanted or the father the children needed. He would fail them and they would turn against him. Suddenly that faintness he had experienced earlier came over him again and he staggered and caught his shoulder on a carved knob on the back of the chair. He gasped in pain.

'Are you all right?' asked Jane, instantly going to his aid and helping him into the chair.

'Brandy,' he whispered.

She hesitated before saying, 'Have you not had enough? I have a fear of drunkards.'

'Do you want me screaming with pain, woman?' he roused himself to ask savagely.

His tone of voice caused her to tremble. 'I—I find it difficult to imagine you—you screaming, Master Hurst. You're a hero. I have heard the truth from your own lips each time Rebecca told us a tale of your adventures.'

'You should not believe all that you hear, Jane.' His eyes darkened. 'It was my brother's intention that the readers of my first book believe me a hero when he edited my journal for the printing press.'

Jane sighed. 'You would do well not to disillusion me if you wish me to marry you. The feminine within me demands heroics as well as dependability in a husband and father.' Instead of brandy, she poured some of the elderflower wine into a goblet and handed it to him. He took it. She touched his shoulder lightly and felt a quiver run through him. 'I have no wish to hurt you.'

'I am relieved to hear it. I ask that your touch remains as gentle as possible even if you do not wish to be my wife.' He grimaced and drank the wine down before resting his head against the back of the chair.

'I will get you some food,' she said.

He thanked her and closed his eyes, trying to convince himself that surely a sensible woman such as Jane would see the advantages of a match between them despite his shortcomings. Suddenly he felt incredibly tired and tumbled into oblivion.

Jane watched his body slump like a sack of grain and heard the rhythm of his breathing change. She should have fetched him some food earlier, but she would not wake him now so he could eat. Best he rested. It seemed that the brandy and wine had done their work. What would Anthony Mortimer think if he knew that she had been dosing Nicholas with his best liquor? Not that she had any intention of informing him of the fact, although perhaps he would notice the level in the bottle had dropped. Hopefully he would not think that she had taken to drink because he could not find a weaver willing to work with her. Of course, if she accepted Nicholas's offer of marriage she would not have to worry about weavers or what Anthony Mortimer thought of her.

A sigh escaped her and she walked over to the children and told them they must be quiet so as not to wake Master Hurst. She was aware of the girls' eyes on her and wondered if Margaret had told her younger sister about the conversation she had overheard. How would they feel if she did marry him so soon after the death of their father?

She turned back to Nicholas, noticing how the bandage on his shoulder showed up so white against his tanned skin. There must have been occasions when the heat had been so intense where he had travelled that he had stripped off his shirt. She watched the rise and fall of his chest. Such a chest! Strong and broad with just a sweep of fine reddish-golden hair forming a V to the waist of his hose. She was aware of a heat building inside her feminine core such as she had never experienced with her late husband.

One of the girls spoke and Jane looked up and realised her stepdaughters were still watching her. She felt her cheeks flame despite knowing they could not possibly know what she was thinking. She should be ashamed of herself. 'A blanket,' she said brightly. 'Master Hurst will catch a chill if he is not kept warm.'

She hurried over to the other chest where she kept sleeping pallets, as well as blankets. From its interior she removed what she needed and returned to Nicholas. As she did so it occurred to her that as far as she was aware her stepdaughters had never seen a man half-naked before. Their father had not been one to bare his flesh, even in her company, but it was too late now to tell them to avert their gaze. Suddenly she remembered the classical naked sculptures in the garden of the house in Oxford that her husband had chiselled out himself. She had voiced her disapproval because of his daughters, but he had told her it was art. At the time she had thought how contrary men were. Yet, so many considered contrariness a failing in women.

She unfolded the blanket and tucked it about Nicholas, wondering what to do about their sleeping arrangements. Propriety insisted that he remove himself to the inn. Yet she was not of a mind to wake him and insist on his going there. Neither did she think it would it be right for him to do so on the morrow in his wounded state.

Upstairs there was a large bedchamber and an adjoining smaller one. She and the children normally shared the double bed in the larger room, but during the worst of the winter weather when ice had frosted the inside of the windows and their breath turned to mist, they had taken to sleeping on pallets downstairs in front of the fire. She did not like doing so, but common sense told her that it was the sensible move to make if they were to survive the winter without succumbing to severe chest ailments. She had been considering moving upstairs the last few days, but then the snow had arrived. Hopefully it would go as suddenly as it had come.

The children had finished eating their supper and now Jane ate some bread and broth. Then, with their help, she removed pallets and

blankets from a chest and settled them on the
floor a safe distance from the fire. After saying
a prayer with them, she waited until they were
asleep before removing some coins from a jar.
Then she put on her coat and left the house.

The storm seemed to have passed and the
snow was turning to mush underfoot. She
could see stars twinkling overhead, although
the moon had not yet risen. Anna lived but a
short distance away up the High Street with her
baker husband, toddler and five older children,
so it was only a matter of minutes before Jane
was knocking on her front door.

She refused Anna's invitation to come inside, saying, 'I must get back as soon as possible. You managed to feed Master Hurst's
daughter without difficulty?'

'Aye. She is only tiny and does not need as
much milk as Simon. My son is almost weaned,
so it is fortunate for her that I have been feeding Simon, otherwise my milk would have
dried up. As it is, only our Lord knows how
long I will be able to feed Simon and this new
little one.'

Jane looked at her in dismay and then suddenly thought of Tabitha, a nursing mother and
wife to Ned, one of Philip's troupe of travelling players. For a short while Tabitha had
helped Jane in the Oxford house towards the

end of her pregnancy while Rebecca was away. If the worse came to the worst then perhaps Ned could spare Tabitha if she was able to feed Matilda? She would keep it in mind.

'It has occurred to me,' said Anna, 'that the little one will need a feed during the night and at first light. I suggest that I keep her with me until morning.'

Jane agreed. 'I will not bother asking Master Hurst as he is fast asleep in the chair. I doubt he will stir until morning. I deem he is not well enough to be moved to the inn.'

Anna gave her a look that spoke volumes and Jane flushed as she pressed the coins she had brought into Anna's hand, adding, 'I will bring Simon to you in the morning and collect Master Hurst's daughter then.' She wished her a good night before hurrying back to the house.

She was relieved to find Nicholas still sleeping, although she thought he looked uncomfortable and would awake with a terrible crick in his neck if he remained in such a position. She fetched a small cushion and managed to ease it beneath his head without much difficulty.

He muttered indistinctly and opened his eyes. She held her breath as he smiled up at her, seemingly instantly recognising her. Then his eyelids drooped. Impulsively she dropped a

kiss on his head. His smile had been so warm
and friendly that she was oddly affected by it.
She lingered for a while, considering his proposal and what he had said about her having
a choice of two houses in which to live. That
he had two homes was news to her. However,
it would mean another move for the children.
Was that fair on them when they had only recently left the home that had been theirs since
their births and were just settling down here
in Witney?

She continued looking at him as she hung up
her coat, wondering if he would do as she asked
and wait a month before broaching the subject
of marriage again. Then she bolted the front
door before going into the workroom and making sure the door to the garden was locked as
well. After placing a log on the fire that should
smoulder for hours, she unrolled her own pallet
and, wrapping a blanket around her, lay down
to sleep. She had much to ponder on, but was
so tired that she was asleep in no time.

It was discomfort and pain in his head and
shoulder, as well as the noise of a woman hushing a crying baby, that woke Nicholas. For a
moment he believed himself back at Louise's
house in Flanders and then the events of yesterday flooded in. Somewhere a cockerel crowed

and then another and another. He forced open his eyes and looked about him.

'Jane, is that you?' he asked in a low voice.

In the pearly-grey light coming through the window he saw a woman's head turn and then she tiptoed over to him. He thought he remembered Jane placing a cushion beneath his cheek. Had he dreamed that she had also pressed a kiss on the sore spot on his head? If so, that raised an interesting question.

'I'm sorry to wake you,' she said. 'How are you feeling this morning?'

He shrugged. 'I had intended spending the night at the inn in order to protect your reputation, but...'

'You were exhausted and who is to say that your enemies might not have found you there?' she said hastily. 'I fear you must have been uncomfortable.'

'I've spent nights in worse places,' he said, easing his neck and slowly rolling his head before drawing the blanket over a naked shoulder. 'What are you doing?'

'I'm taking Simon to Anna. I left your daughter with her last night and will bring her back with me.'

'The nightly feed!' he exclaimed, grimacing with pain as he eased himself upright. The movement resulted in the blanket slipping down again and revealing his chest. 'I had given no thought to it since coming here and I forgot Anna needed paying despite remembering to pay her son.'

'I have paid her,' said Jane, wondering if he had a spare shirt in his saddlebag. 'Rest now. The children are sleeping down here as they have done most of winter. I must make haste, for Simon is hungry.'

He smiled. 'I will not delay you and will reimburse you when you come back.'

Jane nodded and hurried from the house.

Nicholas rose from the chair and, avoiding the sleeping children, picked up his coat from the stool where it had been drying. Leaving the blanket on the chair, he swung the garment with difficulty about his naked shoulders and went through into the rear chamber where he was able to make out shelves, as well as a spinning wheel, a loom and baskets of raw wool and thread. He drew back the bolt and lifted the latch, wondering if Jane had come to a definite decision yet regarding his proposal.

He went outside into the garden and found to his relief that most of the snow had already melted and that the sky was free of cloud. There was an apricot-and-silver glow in the east and the scent of spring in the air, as well as the tantalising smell of baking bread. His

stomach rumbled, reminding him that he had
not eaten since midday yesterday.

For a short while he lingered, gazing down
the garden over a vegetable patch and herb garden to a couple of fruit trees and what must be
a hen house; he could hear the fowls clucking
sleepily and unexpectedly was reminded of the
woman's voice he had thought he had recognised as he made his escape yesterday. If he
was right, then it surely meant that she was
behind the attack and had hired the men. And
what of Berthe? Why should she have decided
to make an enemy of him? It was troubling that
she knew his destination was Witney. Maybe
he should prepare for unwelcome visitors? He
frowned, thinking that perhaps he should get
in touch with the constable of the shire. He'd
had dealings with him last year after the attempt on his life in Oxford.

He returned to the house. Despite a throbbing head, an extremely stiff and painful shoulder and various aches and pains in other parts
of his anatomy, he managed to steer around
the sleeping children to the fire. He split the
smouldering log with a poker and added some
faggots of firewood. Then he poured the remains of a jug of ale into the pot containing
what appeared to be barley broth and hung the
pot over the fire.

Whilst he waited for the food to warm, he took a knife from the table and cut the stitching in the hem of his riding coat. He removed a narrow oilskin package and a strip of folded soft leather containing several gold coins. Placing them on the table, he stared down at them. He would need to change one of them for coins of a smaller denomination if there was not enough in his pouch to pay Anna and to reimburse Jane.

Was there a goldsmith or banker in Witney? If so, he would be able to produce proof of his identity and avail himself of more coin if necessary. He wanted to hold on to a couple of the gold coins to give to his younger brother. The other year they had made a wager as to which one of them would marry first. Nicholas smiled at the memory, for he was extremely fond of his actor-and-playwright brother and prayed that he would soon return to Oxford so he could discuss with him not only yesterday's events, but also his plans for the future.

He rose and went over to where he had left the saddlebags and removed thread and needle from a leather container and returned most of the gold coins to their hiding place. He kept out the package and sewed up the hem of his coat.

By the time he had accomplished his task, he was feeling faint again, so rested for a while be-

fore getting to his feet and going over to stir the
broth and remove it from the heat. The room
was getting lighter by the moment, so he had
no difficulty in seeing his way about in his
search for an eating bowl. He wondered when
the children would wake. He would appreciate
silence for a little while longer, at least until
Jane returned.

But it was neither Jane nor the children who
disturbed the peace as Nicholas sat down to
break his fast, but the sound of the back-door
latch being lifted that instantly alerted him to
an intruder. A voice called out a greeting. He
was on his feet in moments and hesitated before seizing the poker, then made his way into
the back room where he came face-to-face with
a man.

He had grey eyes in a strong-boned face and
Nicholas thought he looked vaguely familiar,
but could not put a name to him. 'Who are
you?' he demanded.

The man stared at the poker in Nicholas's
hand. 'I might ask you the same question, except I know who you are.'

Nicholas's expression hardened. 'Do you,
indeed? Make yourself known, man, before I
use this!'

The intruder removed his cap and smoothed
down the black hair that fell to his shoulders.

'I am the weaver, Willem Godar. Is Mistress Caldwell within?'

'Willem! That is a Flemish name,' growled Nicholas, his fingers tightening on the poker, 'and so is Godar.'

'Aye, but my family have lived in England for years and I was born over here.' His eyes narrowed and he pursed his lips. 'If I am not mistaken, you are the renowned explorer, Nicholas Hurst.'

Nicholas questioned whether that was a note of amusement or derision in the man's deep voice. He had an accent which was not from this part of England, but one that was familiar to him. *Kentish!* Nicholas kept a firm grip on the poker and drew his coat more tightly about him. 'How do you know me?'

'I was born in Tenderden, not far from Raventon Hall. I remember seeing you on a couple of occasions when you visited Sir Gawain and Lady Elizabeth. I was amongst those who helped search for the murderer who killed his first wife. You were there then.'

Nicholas remembered the occasion. There had been a time when he had wanted to marry Elizabeth. He told himself that it was highly unlikely that Godar and Berthe could have met before and be in league with each other.

'All right, I accept that you've seen me before, but what are you doing here in this house? Mistress Caldwell made no mention of expecting a visit from you.'

'I heard she was in need of a weaver and so I decided to come and see her,' said Willem. 'I have been to this town before and liked it.'

Did you, indeed? thought Nicholas. 'Who told you she was in need of a weaver?' he asked.

Willem rested a shoulder against the wall and folded his arms across his chest. 'Sir Gawain Raventon was my informant.'

Nicholas lowered the poker, thinking that Rebecca must had been in touch with Elizabeth and told her about Jane's difficulty in finding a weaver. Even so, for this man to travel such distance from his home town, to work for a woman, surprised Nicholas. As did the earliness of the hour he had called and his entering by the back door. His suspicions resurfaced.

'When did you arrive in Witney?' asked Nicholas. 'And what was your route?'

'I came north with Sir Gawain to Oxford. He wished to visit his printing works and bookshop on Broad Street.'

Nicholas frowned. 'I was there yesterday and there was no mention of Sir Gawain visiting the premises.'

Willem shrugged. 'Maybe he wanted to

catch his workers unawares. What hour were you there? We did not arrive until after noon. By the purest chance a man called Mortimer was in the shop, purchasing a copy of your latest book. Sir Gawain suggested that I accompany him to Minster Draymore, which is but a short distance from here.'

'So you spent the night at Mortimer's manor house?'

Willem grimaced. 'Despite the unexpected blizzard, he told me that it was not fit for visitors, although he planned staying there himself, so I found lodging in Minster Draymore.'

Nicholas nodded, thinking what he had to say sounded feasible. 'Where is Master Mortimer now?'

'I presume he is still abed. When I saw the weather was clearing, I decided to make my way here without bothering him.'

Nicholas stared at him pensively. 'Does he know your purpose in coming here?'

'Aye, Sir Gawain told him.' He smiled. 'I received the impression the news did not please him.'

'That doesn't surprise me,' said Nicholas drily. 'It is a wife he wants, not Mistress Caldwell having another man to turn to.' He paused, for his coat had begun to slide from his shoulders and he hoisted it back in place again with a wince. 'Tell me, Master Godar, why come here when Tenderden is famous for its broadcloth and you are at home there?'

'You ask a lot of questions, Master Hurst,' drawled Willem, 'and I don't see how that is any of your business.'

Nicholas's eyes narrowed. 'Fair comment! Perhaps you would not mind telling me if you are married?'

He hesitated. 'My wife died recently.'

'My condolences. Do you have children?'

'Aye, although again I do not see what business that is of yours, Master Hurst.' Willem frowned. 'I would ask you another question despite you did not answer my last one! Why the bandaged shoulder? How did you come by it?'

'I was attacked on my way here,' said Nicholas, his expression hardening. 'Now, if you can explain why you didn't knock on the front door, but sneaked in the back way?'

Willem's eyes flashed with annoyance. 'I did knock, but received no answer, so I came round here and found the door unlocked.' He paused. 'Have you reported the attack to the constable? If I did not mishear Sir Gawain yesterday, then you were attacked last year in Oxford, as well as in London.'

'So you were discussing me,' said Nicholas, frowning.

'Only because of your book. Will you be staying here long?'

'Until this latest attack is dealt with I will be remaining in Witney.' He thought that Godar looked none too pleased with that news.

'How many of them were there? Were you robbed?'

'Fortunately I managed to escape with my possessions intact as there were only two men.'

'Then you were fortunate.' Willem walked over to the loom and gazed down at it. Watching him, Nicholas experienced a flash of anger. It seemed to him that this weaver was making himself at home much too early. He wished he could kick him out, but sensed the weaver would not be so easy to get rid of and had a strong feeling Jane would resent him taking charge in such a fashion.

As if aware of Nicholas's eyes on him, Willem turned and met his gaze. 'Perhaps Oxfordshire isn't the safest of places for you, Master Hurst? Do you think the two attacks are in any way connected?'

Nicholas shrugged and a flash of pain crossed his face. 'Unlikely, although I didn't believe myself to have so many enemies.'

There was a long silence.

Willem hesitated before saying, 'Mistress Caldwell…?'

'She has gone to the bakery and should soon return,' said Nicholas. 'Perhaps it is best that you remain in here whilst you wait. The children are asleep in the other room.'

Willem nodded and went over to one of the baskets and fingered the wool. Nicholas decided to leave the weaver to his own devices, wondering what else he might have discussed with Sir Gawain. He doubted the knight had mentioned the names of the men involved and the reason why they wanted him dead.

He checked the contents of the pot and ladled out more broth for himself and then sat down at table, wondering whether Jane would welcome Willem Godar's offer to weave for her. If so, would that mean she would give him a definite nay to his proposal?

Hell, he wished the weaver had not chosen today to arrive. Conscious of his aching head and painful shoulder, he closed his eyes and went over yesterday's attack on him. He thought of Berthe and how she had seemed genuinely fond of Matilda. Could it be that her grief for her husband and baby had overturned her mind and she had decided that she must have a baby to replace the one she had lost? But why wait until they arrived in England to abduct his daughter? She could have taken her any time. It didn't make sense!

His thoughts drifted to his conversation with Willem Godar and he wondered whether Mortimer would be Jane's next visitor. He was still a bit of a mystery to Nicholas. After an absence of twenty years, the older man had returned to England a rich man in search of the woman he had loved and the daughter he had left behind. Anthony's twin brother had tricked that woman into marrying him and Rebecca had been reared as his daughter. He had come to work at the Hurst family shipyard every summer and that is how Nicholas and his brother knew her. It was because of Anthony Mortimer's actions in seeking out his daughter that Nicholas had decided to return to Flanders and take responsibility for his own child. He sighed, considering that despite the emotional turmoil of what had taken place in Bruges, he did not regret any of his actions.

He yawned and was on the edge of falling asleep when a noise close by disturbed him. Fully awake now, he became aware not only of the faint clacking of the loom in the other room, but that he was being watched by Margaret, Jane's elder stepdaughter.

'It wasn't a dream after all and you are here,' she said.

He returned her smile and pinched his wrist. 'Well, I'm certainly flesh and blood.'

She laughed and cocked her head to one side. 'What is that clacking noise?'

Nicholas wished that Willem Godar was a dream. 'A weaver has come to see if your mother wishes to avail herself of his services.'

Margaret's eyes rounded. 'I wonder what she will say to him! I will have a peek at him in a moment.' She pushed back the blanket and stood up in her chemise. Nicholas looked away and only faced her when she spoke his name. She was rolling up her pallet. 'How is your shoulder today, Master Hurst?' she asked politely.

'Better than yesterday, thank you, Margaret,' he replied. 'And how are you feeling this morning?'

'I'm pleased you are here and that you remember my name. Master Mortimer gets our names muddled up,' she said, looking chagrined. 'Perhaps it is because he is old like my father was. You're not going to die, are you, Master Hurst? You're not as old as either of them.'

'I certainly hope to live a lot longer,' said Nicholas, unaccustomed to such conversation, but wanting to reassure the girl.

'Mama says that when you are properly Simon's godfather it will be as if you are one of our little family. Does that please you?'

Had Jane really told Margaret that? The thought warmed him and he said, 'It pleases me very much.'

'Good!' Margaret sighed happily. 'I am hoping that Mama will say that we can have a small feast to celebrate your being here.' She smacked her lips. 'Maybe she will kill one of the hens. It will make a change from fish or cheese or just vegetables and barley as is customary during Lent. Although one less hen will mean less eggs once they start laying again. Still, the hens are sitting on eggs and so there will be chicks in the hen house that will grow into more hens.' She beamed at him and skipped over to the window and climbed onto the seat beneath. 'Most of the snow has melted. Good. I will go and tend to the poultry as that is my first task of the day. Oh, and here is Mama with the bread and ale and Simon or...' She scrambled down and looked into the cradle before turning to Nicholas. 'Perhaps it is your baby because there are no babies here?'

Nicholas agreed that it most likely was his daughter, Matilda. He forced himself to walk over to the front door and opened it and smiled down at Jane. 'May I help you?'

She frowned up at him and hesitated before carefully placing his daughter in the crook of his unaffected arm. 'You should be resting.

Matilda is fed and changed. I notice you still have no shirt on. Is there one in your saddle-bags?'

He nodded, gazing down at his sleeping daughter.

'Good. You really should be resting.'

'I will rest soon enough.' He kissed Matilda's cheek before carrying her over to the cradle and placing her down.

'Have you eaten?' asked Jane, thinking that he really did look drawn and weary.

'I was about to do so when we had a visitor and Margaret woke up,' he replied.

Jane looked startled. 'A visitor?'

'Aye, can you not hear the loom clacking? The man says he has come from Kent with Sir Gawain. His name is Willem Godar.'

Chapter Four

Jane stiffened and stared across the room to the door of the workroom as if in a trance. *No, no, no!* she thought, hoping her face had not changed colour. 'How is it that Sir Gawain has involved himself in my business?' she cried, scowling.

'Presumably Rebecca wrote to his wife about your need for a weaver. They are numerous in that part of Kent.'

'Of course, that will be it! Beth and Rebecca will want to help me,' she said, wishing they had not interfered. Slowly she walked over to the table and placed the bread and jug of ale down, hoping against hope that Willem had not mentioned to anyone what they had once been to each other.

'His name is Flemish, quite a coincidence, considering I've not long returned from that country,' said Nicholas.

'Aye, but there are any number of Flemish weavers and brewers in England these days,' she said brightly.

'I would not deny it,' said Nicholas, his gaze intent on her face. 'Even so, perhaps you'd like me to speak to Master Godar on your behalf? He's made himself very much at home, which I found irritating. Apparently he knows Witney, having visited here in the past.'

'Most likely he came to one of the fairs,' said Jane hastily. The last thing she wanted was Nicholas present when she confronted Willem. 'I will speak to him myself. It could be that I will remember him when we come face-to-face.'

'If that's what you wish,' said Nicholas politely.

She could tell he was disappointed by her answer. Oh, why did Willem have to arrive now, making her life even more complicated than it was already? She glanced at the door to the workroom, which had been left slightly ajar. The clacking of the loom was momentarily silenced and she could hear Margaret talking to Willem. Pray God he did not say anything amiss to her.

Nicholas's eyes had followed Jane's. 'Perhaps you would just like me to be there?'

Jane's heart sank. 'No, I will manage! I—I thought that perhaps you could go upstairs and change into a clean shirt. You are not looking your best.' She did not wait for his response, but hurried over to the workroom.

Nicholas made no move to do what she suggested and heard her tell Margaret to go and see to the hens before firmly closing the inner door. He was disappointed that she had turned down his offer. It was his belief that a woman needed a man at such times, but obviously she was of the opinion that his appearance set him at a disadvantage in front of the weaver. It could be that the well set-up Willem Godar was a man with whom she could work in tandem. Especially as he had the backing of Sir Gawain and no doubt would have Beth's and Rebecca's approval, too.

Or was he reading too much in Jane's act of independence than was there and he had no cause to worry? She might yet consider accepting his proposal if for no other reason than for the sake of the children.

On the other side of the door Jane was confronting Willem. 'Why have you come?' she asked angrily.

He looked surprised. 'Sir Gawain spoke of you being newly widowed and needing a weaver, so I thought that fate was conspiring for us to be reunited.' He moved away from the loom towards her with a hand outstretched.

She was tempted to back away from him, but instead stood her ground, folding her arms across her breasts. 'What of your wife?' she asked scornfully.

He smiled. 'I'm a widower. I tell you, Jane, in all the years since we last met I've never forgotten you and look upon the time we spent together with great fondness.'

'Well, that is more than I can say myself.' Her eyes glinted. 'You think you can come here uninvited and believe I will feel the same about you as I did when I was a young girl?'

He shrugged. 'No, I accept that although you were in love with me then, time changes us all. You have matured into a fine-looking woman so I will be honest with you. I wish to leave Tenderden and I have need of a helpmeet.'

She stifled an hysterical laugh, marvelling that she should have three men interested in her. 'You have come here believing I will marry you? Perhaps it is that you have children needing a mother?'

He nodded. 'There are the boys, of course.'

His answer was as she expected. 'How many?'

'Four.'

His reply almost took her breath away. *Four!* He must really believe she was desperate. What had Sir Gawain told him of her situation? Whatever he had said she was so glad that Nicholas's arrival meant that she could throw Willem's proposal back in his face.

'You've had a wasted journey,' she said coldly.

Willem scowled. 'No doubt Master Hurst is the reason for your change of heart?'

She hesitated. 'What did he tell you?'

'What does it matter what he said? It was enough that there was that about his manner that reminded me of a dog protecting a bone.'

She gasped, indignant that Willem should describe her as a bone. 'You will go now,' she said, pointing to the door.

He smiled. 'Don't be a fool, Jane. Nicholas Hurst isn't the kind of man who will ever settle down.'

'That is none of your business.'

'I see that I am right. You think that he will marry you.'

She tilted her chin. 'He has asked me to marry him.'

Willem gave a low whistle. 'Has he, in-deed—I wonder why?'

She swore. 'You insult me. You speak as if no other man would find me comely.'

Willem's eyes narrowed. 'I didn't say you don't have your attractions, Jane. I deem you haven't told him about us, though.'

'I put you out of my mind once you were out of my life,' she lied.

'But now I'm back.' He moved over to the loom and patted it. 'You have good taste. It is a far better loom than the one I have in Ten-derden. Was it your father's? I remember you telling me that he was a master weaver.'

'Never mind the loom,' she snapped. 'I want you out of here.'

Willem glanced at her. 'Is that because you've had an offer from Master Mortimer, too?'

Willem's words startled Jane. 'How do you know about him?'

'I travelled from Oxford in his company. I can't see him being happy if he knew you'd had an affair with a married man.'

'Are you threatening me?'

'Both are rich men and I could do with more money to invest.'

'I would rather die than ask either of them for money for you.'

He looked surprised. 'Fierce words, Jane. Why such antagonism? You were a willing partner in our affair.'

She could only stare at him because she had no intention of telling him that the reason she felt so strongly was because after he had left her within weeks she had discovered she was with child.

He rasped his fingernails against his jaw. 'To be honest, I have no quarrel with Master Hurst if you decide to marry him, but I cannot see him setting up home in this house with you. I, on the other hand, would be content to take over the lease from you for old time's sake. I see that you have thread to spin. I would like to go into business here and no doubt there are other spinsters in the town.'

She knew what he said about Nicholas wishing to make a move was true and that she would need someone to take over the lease, but did she really want to sell it to a man who had deceived her and worse? 'I'll think about it,' she said coldly, 'although my answer is unlikely to be aye. I despise you for not being honest with me.'

'I knew you still had feelings for me.' He grinned and took a step towards her.

'You are presumptuous. There is an inn where you can stay. Leave the way you came in.' She opened the inner door and closed it firmly behind her.

Nicholas glanced up as Jane entered the room, but could not read her expression. 'So what have you decided?' he asked.

She did not immediately answer because she was unsure what to say, but, noticing that he was still half-naked, asked, 'Why have you not put on a clean shirt? You agreed that you have one.'

'Of course I have one,' he said, running a hand through his hair. 'But James and Elizabeth woke up and distracted me.'

Only now did she notice the two younger children sitting close to him and watching them. 'Get dressed, you two,' she ordered.

They scampered over to where they had left their garments.

'Well?' asked Nicholas.

She hesitated and then took a deep breath before saying, 'I should tell you that Master Godar and I have met before, but I never expected to see him again.'

Nicholas stiffened. 'Was it a long time ago?'

She walked over to the fire, avoiding meeting his eyes. 'It was at Witney Fair several years ago. I can't remember exactly when.' She toyed with the ladle in the cooking pot. 'I've told him that he must put up at the inn. I will not have him here.'

'Of course not.' He was tempted to ask if there had been anything of a romantic nature between them, but part of him would rather not know. Instead, he said in a cool voice, 'No doubt you'd prefer it if I stayed at the inn, as well? If so, I'll need to change a gold coin. Is there a banker or a moneychanger in the town?'

'You have gold on you?' she asked, distracted from worrying about what Willem might tell him.

'Aye. The coins were sewn into the hem of my riding coat. Two of them I won from Pip in a wager.'

She could not resist asking, 'What kind of wager?'

'Which one of us would marry first.'

Her curiosity intensified. 'When did you make this wager?'

'On the isle of Rhodes. It was before I met Louise and my brother was re-acquainted with Rebecca.' He took out two of the coins and tossed them in the air and caught them.

Watching the gold glitter, Jane was for a moment envious, not only of his wealth, but that he had visited places that she could only dream about. A sigh escaped her. 'You surely must have wished yourself there when you were caught in the blizzard yesterday.'

'If I had thought of it, aye.' He shifted abruptly in the chair and drew in his breath with a hiss and put a hand to his shoulder.

Immediately Jane forgot everything else but his wound. 'Here, let me look at the binding.'

He pushed back his coat and she clicked her tongue against her teeth as she saw a streak of blood on the fabric. 'You have been doing too much, too soon! I knew you should rest. I must tend to this immediately.'

He grabbed her wrist. 'No, it can wait. We have other far more important matters to discuss.'

She gazed into his face and saw the determination written there. 'How could anything be more important than your healing?' she blurted out.

Her words affected him deeply. 'I believe you mean that, Jane.'

'Of course I do.'

'I'm touched.' He stroked the palm of her hand with his thumb and the movement proved oddly sensuous. Suddenly she felt breathless and excited at the same time. 'Please, stop that?' she asked, a catch in her voice.

'Then agree to marry me,' he murmured. 'And before you make the excuse again that it is only four months since your husband died, I tell you now that I am certain he would understand your need to provide his offspring with a father as soon as possible.'

She glanced at the children. Nicholas might not be speaking loudly, but even so, she did not want Elizabeth in particular hearing such talk.

'I do not doubt it,' she said in a low voice. 'Simon was a good man and if the roof had not been damaged by a tree in a storm last autumn and it was costly to repair, then he would have left me and the children in a better financial position. Yet he abided by certain rules and so do I.'

'You mean you are prepared to wait until the year of mourning is over? What if there was to be another attack on my life? What if this time my enemies succeeded in their aim? As Simon's godfather, it will be my task to provide him with all that is necessary for him to live a good life. That means if I am not alive then I must advise you now that when you remarry you must not marry Mortimer or Godar. One is old enough to be *your* father, never mind my godson's, and the other I don't trust.'

His choice of words baffled her. 'I know what is wrong here. It is that you are accustomed to getting your own way and you want everything settled good and tight for your daughter's sake. I do not believe you will die. After so many adventures, you're too stubborn to give in to death as your being here testifies. Rather, it is more likely that Master Mortimer will die before you.' Her eyes sparkled. 'Thinking of it seriously, I deem that if I married a much older man, such as Rebecca's father, then I could be a rich widow in no time at all.'

Nicholas glowered at her. 'But no doubt you would earn every penny of his fortune if you were to be his wife and then widow.'

'What are you saying?'

'At his age his health could soon disintegrate and he might not die as quickly as you would like, but simply be an invalid for years. Whilst he could afford to hire a woman to nurse him, I deem you have a strong sense of duty and would feel compelled to care for him yourself.'

'I am not as self-sacrificing as you believe me to be, *Master Hurst*,' said Jane. 'Nor as mercenary, otherwise I would have accepted your proposal immediately.'

'Then perhaps you will change your mind and not marry either of us, but Master Godar instead? He could make you the perfect husband if you want to be a weaver's wife for the rest of your life and wish the same for your sons.'

'Oh, why are you saying this?' hissed Jane.

'As if I would marry Master Godar, even if he wished to marry me. He just wants to resettle and Witney would suit him.'

'Perhaps,' said Nicholas doubtfully.

Jane groaned, wishing fervently that her past had not come back to haunt her. How could she ever tell Nicholas the whole truth about the events that she so regretted?

'I am telling you the truth,' she said with a sigh, lowering her gaze, only to find herself staring at his bare chest. The temptation to throw herself at it so overwhelmed her that she had need to take a deep, steadying breath and turn her head away. 'In all this, I feel you are not taking into consideration my duty to the children,' she murmured. 'As it is, if you truly plan to take your duty as godfather to Simon as seriously as you appear, then I must heed your advice. Yet I am remembering that not so long ago your mind was set on taking holy orders, only to alter your decision and return to Flanders in search of your mistress.'

'You know the reason why I did so,' said Nicholas, suddenly weary.

'Aye, but if she had not died would you be here now?' blurted out Jane.

The question took him unawares and he needed all his self-control not to show any reaction. Sensing that now was not the time to be completely honest with her, he said mildly, 'What is the use of asking me such a question? She did die and I am a changed man.'

'You mean that your feelings for her are dead as is that urge to explore the world?'

'Aye,' he said firmly.

She stared at him, not utterly convinced.

He leaned towards her. 'You must believe me, Jane. I desire nothing more than to live peacefully here in my own country and make a home for you and the five children. I have it in mind to found a shipbuilding business of my own. I want to construct a different kind of ship from those which my father and then my brother Christopher specialised in over the years. Their design has not altered in all that time and I consider that lacks foresight.'

She stared at him, open-mouthed, and then blurted out, 'You would have us live near the sea? I have never lived on the coast and neither have the children. It would be a tremendous upheaval for them. We have not long moved here. I do not consider it fair that they should have to cope with another move so soon.' Agitatedly she moved away from him, picked up the ladle and stirred vigorously the little of the broth that remained in the pot. 'No, Nicholas Hurst, I cannot give you the answer you want.'

'Then so be it.' Nicholas pushed himself out

of the chair. 'I hope you don't live to regret it. I'm off.'

The ladle slipped from Jane's fingers and fell into the pot, splashing her gown. She turned on Nicholas. 'Now see what you have done with your impatient ways?' Picking up a cloth, she attempted to mop the spilt broth from her gown, but only succeeded in making the damage worse. 'You will drive me into doing something foolish if you continue in this vein,' she said, exasperated.

'My offer still holds good,' said a voice from the other doorway, sounding amused.

Both Jane and Nicholas turned and stared at Willem, wondering how much of their exchange he had heard. She took a deep breath and said coldly, 'What are you doing here? Should you not be visiting the inn and reserving yourself a bedchamber?'

'Plenty of time for that,' he said. 'Right now I want to discuss the wool you use for spinning thread.'

She scowled at him. 'I do not wish to discuss it. I want you to leave.'

'Come on, Jane,' he said in a wheedling tone. 'What harm will it do to talk? I would like to use your loom and see if it suits me.'

Nicholas drew in his breath with a hiss. 'Is

there some fault with your hearing, Godar? Mistress Caldwell asked you to leave.'

Jane thought, *Men—always having to take over.* 'I can speak for myself, Master Hurst, thank you very much,' she said tersely.

Nicholas's lips tightened and he went over to where he had placed his saddlebags, removed a shirt, snatched up his doublet and, with his coat slung over his shoulders, left the house by the front door.

Jane stared after him, dithered, worried that she had deeply offended him, and after a few moments followed him outside. To her astonishment he had tossed off his coat, so exposing his upper torso for all to see. 'You cannot do this!' she whispered. 'You are not in an alien land now. This is England!'

'Pretend you do not know me,' said Nicholas, dropping his doublet on the ground and shaking out the shirt.

She watched him struggling with the garment, itching to assist him, but sensing he would refuse her help. 'Is this the way you behaved in *that woman's* company?' she blurted out.

'By *that woman*, I presume you mean Louise,' said Nicholas through gritted teeth, managing at last to drag on the shirt. 'I would prefer it if you kept her out of our conversation. So she was not as honest with me as she should have been, but she had her reasons and more often than not behaved circumspectly.'

Jane was so taken aback by his defence of his late mistress that she could only stare at him. Then, seething and near to tears, she turned on her heel and went back inside the house.

Nicholas swore and snatched up his doublet. Why had he said that? Was it because he'd been unable to tell her the truth earlier about Louise? Well, it was too late now to recall his words. There were matters he had to see to this morning. He set about donning his doublet, but found it more of a struggle than he had done with the shirt. His shoulder was aflame and he had no choice but to pause to catch his breath and lean against the wall of the house.

'What are you doing outside Mistress Caldwell's house, half-dressed, Master Hurst?' asked a voice he recognised.

Nicholas's heart sank and, lifting his head, he stared at Anthony Mortimer. He wished the man a thousand leagues away and would have liked to pretend he did not know him, but that would not be polite. 'I have been visiting Mistress Caldwell and the weaver, Master Godar, has arrived, so I decided to leave them alone to discuss business,' he replied heavily. 'Good day to you, Master Mortimer.' He turned his back on him and began again his struggle with his doublet.

'You are behaving very strangely,' said Anthony, dismounting.

Nicholas did not ask what he meant by that, stumbling against the wall of the house. He rested his aching head against the pale yellowish stone and closed his eyes. 'I was attacked on my way here yesterday,' he said in a muffled voice.

'God's blood! Where was this? What time of day? Did the rogues get away with much?'

'No, I managed to escape before they could rob me, but their intention was to kill me and abduct my daughter.'

'Your daughter!' exclaimed Anthony.

'Aye, but she can be of no interest to you. Do not let me delay you from going inside, Mortimer.'

'Allow me to help you!' Anthony clapped a hand on his shoulder.

Nicholas stifled a cry and shrugged him off. 'I would rather manage alone,' he said through gritted teeth.

The older man said irascibly, 'Don't be a fool, man.'

'You'll understand if I insist on your not touching my shoulder again when I tell you I was stabbed there,' said Nicholas.

Anthony swore. 'I presume Mistress Caldwell knows of this?'

'Of course, she tended me.' Nicholas's head was swimming and he wished Mortimer would leave him alone.

The older man frowned. 'You spent the night here?'

A faint smile flitted across Nicholas's face and an imp of mischief caused him to say, 'In her bed.'

'Surely you jest!' said Mortimer.

'Now who's being the fool, man?' muttered Nicholas, closing his eyes. He heard the front door creak open and then close.

Nicholas remained where he was, trying to gather his strength before making another attempt to shrug himself into his bloodstained doublet. This time he succeeded but the effort so exhausted him that he slid down the wall until he was sitting on the ground and there he remained.

After what seemed an age, he noticed a woman approaching, carrying a baby, and realised it was Anna. He remembered that he needed not only to reimburse Jane for the money she had already paid out to the wet nurse, but also that he would need to pay Anna for her further services. In any other circumstances he might have asked the wealthy Mortimer if he could exchange a gold coin for ones of smaller denomination, but their exchange made that difficult for Nicholas to approach him with such a request.

As he watched Anna pause and begin a conversation with a woman crossing the road, it occurred to him that she might also be acquainted with Willem Godar. He wondered what the two women were talking about—no doubt he and Jane were definitely a subject for discussion.

He waited a little longer before deciding it was time he made a move and, placing his hands on the wall behind him, he managed, not without some difficulty, to slowly climb the wall with his hands until he stood upright. Then, breathing heavily, he staggered towards the door, knowing that now was not the right time after all to go in search of smaller coinage. He managed to slip inside the house, remembering to leave the door ajar for Anna to enter.

Mortimer was sitting in the chair Nicholas had vacated earlier whilst Jane stood beside it. From her expression whatever he was saying did not please her. Nicholas groaned inwardly. Had Mortimer repeated their conversation? Why had he felt the need to annoy the old man? Of course, he could be mistaken and Mortimer was questioning her about Master Godar.

Nicholas cleared his throat and Mortimer's

voice trailed off and he stared in his direction. Jane lifted her head and he could sense her annoyance from across the room. He staggered towards them. 'I beg pardon,' he said. 'I don't know what got into me, Jane.'

Her hand fluttered to her breast and then she took a deep breath and hurried towards him. 'You'd better sit down before you collapse.'

'I will sit at the table,' he said. 'Anna will be here shortly with Simon.'

'What's that about Simon?' said Mortimer, sounding surprised. 'He's here in the cradle.'

'That's my daughter,' said Nicholas, lowering himself carefully onto the bench beside James and leaning on the table. 'Her mother is dead.'

Mortimer pursed his lips. 'I seem to recall a mention of your returning to Flanders in search of a mistress. Wasn't she the cause of all the trouble that resulted in the attack on you last year in Oxford?'

Nicholas nodded and realised that was a mistake. He was feeling extremely dizzy again. When Jane spoke, he struggled to understand what she was saying. Could it be something about not speaking ill of the dead? Surely not! Not when he knew that Jane would probably like to say a lot of uncomplimentary things about Louise. He thought Mortimer was saying that she was extremely tolerant and then he began to talk about some travellers who had asked for shelter. Nicholas opened his mouth to ask how about a brandy, but no sound emerged.

Jane was staring at him. 'Perhaps Master Hurst needs a brandy.'

'I think that might be a mistake so early in the morning,' said Mortimer firmly. 'I suggest that he finds lodgings at the inn. He certainly should not stay here another night.'

'In his present condition he presents no threat to my virtue,' said Jane confidently.

'Even so you must consider your reputation, Jane,' said Mortimer.

She made no comment, pouring liquor into a goblet and carrying it over to Nicholas to place it in front of him on the table. 'You're looking dreadful,' she said in an undertone. 'I think you should be in bed and so I will get rid of Master Mortimer and Master Godar immediately and help you upstairs.'

'There is no need, Jane,' he muttered, reaching for the goblet. 'I will do fine here.'

'I have no intention of discussing this matter further with you,' she said, turning away from him.

Nicholas downed his brandy and felt even more light-headed. 'Perhaps it's food I need,' he muttered.

'No doubt there is truth in what you say,' said Jane, having heard him. 'You fell asleep last evening before I could bring you food. Perhaps you would like to share breakfast with the children. Master Mortimer will be leaving soon.'

Mortimer said grimly, 'I can see you are determined to help Master Hurst.'

'She is trying to make the best of a difficult situation, Master Mortimer,' said Nicholas. 'It's her maternal instinct no doubt coming to the fore. Jane would find it difficult to turn anyone away who was in need of help.'

'I know she has a kind heart,' said Mortimer. 'That is why I would speak to her about two travellers who sought shelter at Draymore Manor yesterday.'

But Jane was only half-listening and as for Nicholas, he was suddenly aware that James and Elizabeth were staring at him anxiously. He attempted a smile, but it proved difficult. His shoulder was throbbing and his head felt even more peculiar. Then all the strength seemed to drain from him and he felt himself slipping.

'Mama!' shrieked James.

Jane whirled round and rushed over to the table. She straddled the bench the other side of Nicholas and managed to prop him up with her body. At that same time Willem came in from the other room and Anna entered the house. 'Oh lor', what's happening here?' asked the wet nurse.

Willem wasted no time going to Jane's aid, whilst Anna placed Simon in the cradle before hurrying in his wake. 'Men, what would you do with them?' she muttered to Jane across Nicholas's prone body. 'I saw him outside and it was clear as daylight that he was not fit to be out. What was he thinking of?'

'Money,' gasped Jane, her heart thudding. 'He wanted to make sure you were paid and needed change.' She was scared silly that even with Willem's help, she was not going to be able to prevent Nicholas from sliding onto the floor. What if he were to crack his head open on top of the injury he already had?

'Here, get out of the way, Jane,' said Anthony.

Jane did not immediately release her hold on Nicholas. Only when she was absolutely certain that the older man had a proper grip on him did she do so. Once the two men were bearing Nicholas's weight, Jane asked them to carry him upstairs and place him on the bed.

Anthony stared at her. 'Do you know what you're saying? We could lay him here on the table if you want to have a look at his wound.'

'She will need the table,' said Willem. 'He is best upstairs where he can rest properly and Mistress Caldwell can attend him.'

Jane could not but be grateful for his support despite still being extremely annoyed with him. 'That is my thought exactly. Master Hurst is accustomed to having his own way and so is best out of the way upstairs. The children and I have been sleeping down here on pallets during the winter and still do so.'

'So be it, then,' grunted Anthony.

Together, the two men managed to carry Nicholas upstairs where they placed him on the bed in the front bedchamber. Jane was fast on their heels, having removed bed linen and a blanket from the chest. She planned to return downstairs to sort out fresh bindings and salve later. The bed took up most of the space in the room, so with the two men standing there, getting their breath back, she had difficulty squeezing past them to the bed.

'Thank you, Masters,' she said, spreading the blanket over Nicholas and thinking she would make up the bed properly later. He groaned and stirred, but his eyelids remained closed. 'You fool!' she whispered, feeling a dampness behind her eyes.

Willem touched Mortimer's sleeve and made for the door. Anthony hesitated, but Jane turned and said, 'You can do no more here and I will need to go downstairs to fetch all that is necessary for me to redress his wound. It would be best if you were both out of the way.'

On hearing those words, Anthony followed Willem downstairs with Jane bringing up the rear. Willem did not immediately return to the workroom, but sat down in a chair by the fire, whilst Anthony excused himself and left. It was a relief to Jane to see that the children had nearly finished their breakfast and that Anna had remained with them.

'How does Master Hurst fare?' she asked.

'Hopefully he will soon regain consciousness, but I am going to need more bindings,' said Jane. 'I will have to cut up an old drying sheet.'

'Let us pray he soon recovers,' said Anna, getting to her feet. 'If you can manage, I will go now and come back later.'

As soon as the door closed behind their neighbour, James said, 'Is Master Hurst going to die, Mama?'

'Of course not,' said Jane fiercely, flinging open the chest. 'But you are all going to have to be good and of help to me.'

'What can we do?' asked Margaret, getting to her feet.

'You can go and see if any stinging nettles

are coming through the earth behind the hen coop. If so, gather some, but make sure you wear gloves. I will blanch them and mix them with a little honey and wine to make fresh salve. Elizabeth, you can clear the table and clean the bowls and spoons.'

'And what will I do, Mama?' asked James.

'You will go upstairs and if Master Hurst is awake, come and tell me straight away.'

He nodded vigorously and tiptoed upstairs.

Jane glanced at Willem and saw that he had moved away from the fire and over to the table. He had hold of something and was turning it between his hands. She had hoped he would leave for the inn, but it appeared he was determined to linger. Surely common sense would have told him that he was best out of the way? She felt that she could not tell him to get out again after he had helped her with Nicholas. Well, she would just have to ignore him and collect together all she needed and carry them upstairs. To her surprise as she did so, not only did he make no comment, neither did he even look her way. His attention appeared to be on a package he held in his hand. She didn't remember seeing him with it earlier and frowned.

She was still frowning as she went upstairs to find her son sitting cross-legged on the bed, his gaze fixed on Nicholas's face.

Chapter Five

'He hasn't opened his eyes yet,' said James.

Jane found that worrying. Surely Nicholas should have recovered from his swoon by now? Then she noticed his position had shifted so that he was lying on his uninjured side. Maybe he had been so exhausted by his efforts to make himself more comfortable that he had lost consciousness once more. She placed the back of her hand against his forehead and found it hot, but not afire. Perching on the side of the bed, she was in a dilemma about what to do next. If he had been awake, then she would have attempted to remove his doublet.

She touched the fresh bloodstain on the material. It was drying, which hopefully meant the wound had stopped bleeding and the blood had begun to clot. She felt the shirt beneath and wished that he had thought what he was about before putting on a fresh garment because this one was bloodstained now and she needed to remove it straight away if she was to get the bloodstain out. Hopefully he had another shirt in his saddlebag. She undid the top of the garment and slipped her hand inside and pressed down gently on the bandage and was relieved when no blood welled up. Perhaps it would be wisest to let him rest undisturbed for a while?

She sat there, gazing down at him, absently caressing his bare shoulder. She could only think it was devilment that had caused him to tell Anthony Mortimer that he had slept in her bed. Well, he had begged her pardon, so she must forgive him. Suddenly she noticed a smear of blood on the pillow. At the same time she heard the sound of a fretful baby.

'Simon's crying, Mama,' said James, his eyes bright as he gazed at her. 'Shall I stay here while you see to him?'

Jane nodded. 'Let me know when Master Hurst wakes.'

She went downstairs and found that Elizabeth had lifted Simon from the cradle and was hushing him. Jane took him from her. Noticing that Willem was no longer in the room, she was relieved and asked where he had gone.

'He left,' replied her stepdaughter.

'Did he have anything to say before he went?'

Elizabeth shook her head. 'But I noticed that he left behind that package on the table.'

Cradling her son in the crook of her arm, Jane went over to the table and picked up the package.

'I saw Master Godar open it out and inspect the contents out of the corner of my eye while I was cleaning the bowls,' said Elizabeth.

Jane frowned. 'Are you certain?'

Elizabeth nodded. 'The wrappings were on the table.'

Jane took a closer look at the oilskin wrapping and the wax seal. It appeared undisturbed. She touched the edge of the wax with a fingertip and found it warm and slightly soft. There were minute fragments of hard wax on the table. She pursed her lips before going over to the saddlebags and searched for a shirt and was relieved to find one, along with clean hose and swaddling bands for Matilda. There were also several drying cloths as well as toiletries.

At that moment there came a shout from above and Jane wasted no time hurrying upstairs with Elizabeth following closely on her heels. Nicholas was still lying on his side, but had managed to prop himself up on one elbow.

As she entered the bedchamber, she heard him say, 'You must ask your mother about that first.'

'What must he ask me?' said Jane, relieved beyond measure that Nicholas had recovered consciousness and was able to have a conversation with her son.

Nicholas gave a wry smile. 'If I don't die, James wants me to be his godfather as well as Simon's.'

Jane shook her head at the boy. 'What are you thinking about, young man? You have a godfather!'

'But Uncle Giles is dead, so he is of no use to me,' complained James.

'Of course he is of help to you,' said Elizabeth, leaning over the foot of the bed and staring disapprovingly at her half-brother. 'He was a good man and so he is with the saints in Heaven where he can intercede for you. You should not have bothered Master Hurst with your selfish desires—or at least not until he is feeling a lot better.'

James gave his mother a wide-eyed stare. 'But I wasn't being selfish, Mama. Master Hurst has no son and I thought two godsons were better than one.'

His answer was so reasonable that it caused Nicholas to chuckle and Jane to hide a smile. 'Enough, both of you children,' she said. 'Master Hurst must rest. As it is we'll have to postpone the ceremony in church until he is better. Now go downstairs and into the garden and see how Margaret is faring with the nettles and the hens.'

Reluctantly the two children departed. Jane was left nursing a fretful baby and with a prospective husband whom she had quarrelled with in need of her attention. 'Children,' she said, rolling her eyes.

'Aye, children,' murmured Nicholas, cautiously pushing himself up further on his elbow. 'So what next, Jane?'

'You will stay in bed and do as I say if you have any sense at all,' she chided. 'I have heard Rebecca and Philip both speak of you as being clever, so now prove it to me. If you were to die due to your own foolishness, it would upset the children and they have had enough sadness in their lives.'

'You were convinced earlier that I would not die,' said Nicholas, his gaze locking with hers. 'Have you now changed your mind?'

She shifted the grizzling baby to her other hip and said earnestly, 'I need you to be sensible. No more leaving this house until I say so.'

'I am at your mercy and will do exactly as I am told,' said Nicholas, giving her a smile of

such charm that she could not resist returning
that smile—and she so wanted to kiss him!

'I will take you at your word.'

'Good. Now tell me, what is wrong with
Simon?' he asked.

'I deem he is teething. James had a first
tooth before he was five months old, which is
early so I was told by other more experienced
mothers. It is possible Simon is going to follow suit.'

'How long will this process take?' asked
Nicholas, eyeing the whingeing child with trepidation. 'It is a fact of life to which I have never
given any consideration. The necessity of having a tooth drawn, aye, but...' He paused, staring as she offered her knuckle to Simon, who
gnawed on it. 'Doesn't that hurt?'

'Not really.' She glanced at him. 'I do have
a sheep's-horn teething ring in the chest downstairs, so will root it out.'

Nicholas looked thoughtful. 'I never realised
there was so much work involved in tending
babies. You are going to need help, Jane. You
can't take care of me, five children and the
house. Here, take this gold coin.' He produced
it from inside the sleeve of his shirt. 'See if
you can exchange it, so you can hire a girl to
help you.'

'I will do nothing of the sort,' she said

roundly. 'I have two stepdaughters old enough to help in the house as well as having Anna taking care of the feeding and changing of the babies. Besides, if word gets around that I have a gold coin to change, then no doubt every thief in the neighbourhood will think there could be more on the premises. The news of your arrival has already spread in the town.'

'Then the sooner I speak to the constable the better,' said Nicholas grimly, resting back against the pillow. 'Can you get a message to him?'

'I will speak to Anna's husband. I am sure he'll know the quickest way to get in touch with the constable. If Anthony Mortimer had not left so soon, I could have asked him.'

Nicholas looked surprised. 'Are you saying that Mortimer has left you alone with me?'

She nodded. 'I doubt I will ever be in a position where I am his rich widow now after what you've said to him.'

His eyes gleamed. 'I would be lying if I didn't say I am glad.'

She looked at him disapprovingly. 'But it was wrong of you to behave the way you did. Going outside half-naked and telling him that you had slept in my bed. Have you no thought for my reputation?'

'I could have slept in your bed without you

being in it,' retorted Nicholas, his eyes twinkling. 'Anyway, you must tell Anna that I have asked you to marry me, so that should take care of your reputation.'

'I should have known you'd say that,' said Jane tartly. 'Now I need to look at your wound and I suspect that blow you had to the head has affected your wits.'

He said ruefully, 'Maybe it did, but I still want you to marry me, Jane. Do say aye!'

'You are still determined, despite knowing so little about me and my having four children to support?' said Jane in a wondering voice.

He met her gaze. 'What more is there to know? Is it to do with Godar?'

Her stomach seemed to flip over like a collop on Shrove Tuesday and, without a word, she left the bedchamber.

She found Margaret placing the nettles in a pot of water and hanging it over the fire. 'Good girl,' she said. 'You're a great help to me.'

Her stepdaughter smiled and skipped away.

Jane's head buzzed with all kinds of thoughts after her exchange with Nicholas and determinedly she attempted to empty her mind, knowing she would end up with a megrim if she continued the way she was.

It was some time before she returned upstairs. She found Nicholas in exactly the same position that she had left him, but noticed his boots on the floor. She was about to scold him for not taking things easy, when he muttered, 'Don't say it, Jane. Be glad I eventually noticed the mess I was making of your mattress and removed them.'

'I only hope you haven't set your wound bleeding again.' She nudged the boots aside with her foot, torn to whether she should bring up the subject of Willem or not.

'I would have much preferred not to put you to any more trouble,' he said.

Her gaze washed over him. 'I feared you might have cracked your head on the floor when you swooned.'

His brow furrowed. 'Last I remember was sitting at the table with James.'

'Aye, he called for help as soon as he realised you were in difficulty. I hope you didn't take seriously that nonsense about you taking on the role of his godfather.'

Nicholas rasped his unshaven jaw with a thumbnail. 'I've already made my feelings clear about playing an important part in Simon's upbringing, I'm prepared to do the same for James. I returned to England with the notion of helping you and the children, but instead our roles seem to be reversed at the moment.'

'You're not to blame for that and it is of help

to me now your being up here. You will not be able to wander off so easily.' She smiled, hoping he understood why she said those words. 'I need you to sit up.'

'You'll have to help me to do so,' he warned.

'Of course.' She took his hand and drew his arm about her neck and managed to hoist him higher against the pillows. He helped by pushing with his feet against the board at the foot of the bed. Breathing heavily, she was about to detach herself when she felt his lips brush her cheek.

She turned her head swiftly, her mouth forming a surprised O, and found his face only inches away. It seemed inevitable that their lips should meet. The kiss seemed to go on for ever until at last Jane managed to tear her mouth away from his and get to her feet. She was all of atremble and knew she had to put some distance between them. Going over to the window, she gazed out.

Nicholas said hoarsely, 'Admit, Jane, that you enjoyed that kiss!'

She made no answer.

'I don't want to marry you simply because it would be convenient for both of us, my dear.'

She took a deep breath and faced him. 'Did you ask Louise to marry you before you shared a bed with her?'

His eyebrows snapped together. 'Why must you again bring Louise into the conversation?'

'Because she was your mistress and you had a child with her,' cried Jane, slapping the foot of the bed. 'I want to know if you would have married her if she had not already been betrothed.'

'Why do you need to know? Do you have a problem accepting Matilda because she was conceived in what you regard as carnal sin?'

'Matilda is only a baby, I would not lay her parents' fault on her shoulders whatever the church teaches,' she said in a low voice. 'Besides, it says in Holy Writ that all sin and fall short of the glory of God!'

The muscles of his face relaxed. 'Aye, and those who are supposed to set us an example are no exception. Royalty have mistresses as do many a nobleman. They sin and go to confession, pay penance and are forgiven. More often than not, they sin again. If it would make you feel any better, I did ask Louise to marry me, but she told me her uncle would not agree to her marrying an English wanderer.'

'Yet you shared her bed!' said Jane, shaking her head as if unable to comprehend his actions.

Nicholas gazed at her thoughtfully. 'Were

you ever passionately in love with your husband, Jane?'

She flushed. 'You ask that as if you don't believe I know what it is to feel passion.'

'I'm curious, that's the reason I ask.'

'No,' said Jane regretfully. 'I felt affection for him because he was kind to me, but that is all.' She squared her shoulders. 'Anyway, what does it matter? I suspect the point you are trying to make is that when one is passionately in love, one can be forgiven for not controlling one's lust.'

'It's certainly more difficult than when one simply feels affection. What about Godar? He's a well set-up fellow.'

She stiffened. 'Appearance is not everything as I'm certain I've said before.'

'Were you ever in love with him?'

Her heart began to pound and she sought frantically for an answer. 'I was only a girl. What did I know about love?' She sighed. 'I should not have succumbed to temptation and returned your kiss and we wouldn't be having this conversation.'

'But you did and we both enjoyed the experience.' His tone was light despite his conviction that she was avoiding giving him a direct reply to his question.

'I admit nothing,' she said firmly. 'Now let us drop the subject.'

His eyes narrowed. 'Why? I can't believe that I am embarrassing you. It is not as if you are a maiden.'

'I should think you above any other man alive should be aware of that,' said Jane waspishly, picking up a pair of fabric shears from amongst the paraphernalia she had brought up with her. She avoided looking at him as she began to cut the drying cloth into strips, knowing that sooner or later she was going to have to go over to the bed and tend to his wound. Somehow she did not think he would kiss her again and yet the memory of that meeting of lips still lingered, causing her whole body to ache pleasantly.

Watching her from beneath his half-closed lids, Nicholas wondered what she was thinking about as she snipped the fabric. Had she been a maiden when she married? It would explain her reluctance to answer his question if she had succumbed to temptation where Godar was concerned. The question was whether he had been married at the time and whether she had been aware of it or not? He wanted to trust her, believe that when they knew each other better, they could bare their souls to each other. Was he expecting too much? Maybe he did and perhaps that was because what had followed after they first came face-to-face had been so out of the ordinary.

He recalled the painful labour involved in her giving birth again. He would like a son of his loins, but it had been difficult seeing her suffer. But if she agreed to marry him and was willing and desired more children, what then? He would like to make love to her, no doubt about that now.

His mind drifted and he pictured the pair of them sharing the great carved oaken bed in his godparents' bedchamber. Somehow he must persuade Jane that she and the children would enjoy living near the sea. She was bound to like both houses, especially the one outside Bristol which his godfather had built to escape outbreaks of the plague in the port. He would buy a new feather mattress and refurbish the bedchamber in such a way that it would enchant her. He would purchase damask fabric from the East for hangings and bedcovers. She would be clad in fine silk that would reveal the shape of her breasts, hips and belly. Almost he could feel the fabric sliding between his fingers and the texture of her skin beneath his lips.

'Have you fallen asleep, *Master Hurst*?'

He started almost guiltily at the sound of

her voice and his daydream evaporated and he opened his eyes. 'Why do you persist in calling me *Master Hurst* in that tone of voice when I call you Jane? I insist that you call me Nicholas.'

'*Insist!*' She arched her eyebrows and surprised him by saying, 'Then Nicholas it will be. Annoyingly you could have ruined another of your fine shirts, but perhaps if I cut out the bloodstained patch and take part from the tail, I will be able to mend it so it will be barely noticeable. Now you must keep still and not flinch if I touch your skin with the shears.'

He grinned. 'You alarm me, Jane! Please, don't wave them about.'

She said drily, 'You don't have to worry. I have no intention of…' Her voice trailed off, shocked that she had been about to say *making a eunuch of you.*

His hazel eyes flared wide and he grinned. 'God's blood, Jane, I'd like to know what your intentions are, not what they are not.'

The colour rose in her cheeks. 'I was going to say I have no intention of hurting you.'

'Hmmm, that is a relief to me, although why you almost bit your tongue off to prevent yourself saying so is a mystery to me.'

Jane sensed he knew what she had been about to say and decided it was best if she kept her mouth shut and her wayward thoughts under control. She wormed the point of one of the blades into the weave of the shirt and proceeded to cut out the bloodstained patch of linen. She sliced through the bandage and then, putting the shears to one side, dampened the binding until she was able to peel the fabric away.

She was relieved to see that there was only a slight swelling about the wound, although further cleansing was necessary. As she wiped away some streaks of dried blood from his chest, she noted again the different shaped scars there. One in particular fascinated her, for it was low down and so long and jagged that she could not resist running the tip of a finger over it.

'I received that from a charging boar during a hunt with my Flemish kin,' said Nicholas, a hint of breathlessness in his voice. 'I was fortunate to escape being disembowelled.'

She shuddered. 'I've never been on a hunt.'

'It's not a sport for women, although Louise—' He stopped.

'Although Louise hunted—is that what you were going to say?' Jane pressed her lips together as she carried on tending his wound.

'Aye.' He hesitated before adding, 'She was a veritable Diana, foolishly so.'

Was Nicholas actually making a criticism of that woman? She dabbed his skin dry, longing to ask what Louise had done that he considered stupid, but thought it wiser not to refer to her again. Instead she asked, 'Who's Diana?'

'A mythical goddess of the hunt. She was the sister of Apollo, a god of healing amongst other things.'

Jane frowned. 'Apollo I have heard of because my husband, Simon, had a fondness for pagan male statuary. There were several such he sculptured himself in the garden of the house at Oxford. I admit I did not approve, considering them unsuitable for a home in which there were young girls. But they fetched a fair price after he died and so I was appreciative of his skill as a stonemason and sculptor. The girls likened the face of one of them to your brother Philip.'

'I have to admit that Pip is the handsomest of the three of us Hurst brothers,' said Nicholas, putting a hand to his injured shoulder.

'Please, don't do that,' said Jane, removing his hand and inspecting it before placing it on his chest. 'You are not so bad-looking,' she added, a hint of humour in her voice as she continued her task. 'And is it not better that a person is good inside than just fair of face? Not that I would dispute your brother's generosity and kindness to people,' she added hastily. 'I was glad when he married Rebecca, although I miss her company still. It's not at all the same sharing a house with just the children.' She began to apply the salve which she had made using the boiled stinging nettles and then covered the wound with a clean rag and bound it.

'I have a widowed aunt who might suit you if it's a woman's companionship you want and not a husband's?' he teased.

'Really, Nicholas, I would find my own female companion if that was what I needed.' Her fingers quivered as she finished bandaging his shoulder. 'Now I must have a look at your head.'

Once that was done, she reached for the shirt she had taken from his saddlebag. As she helped Nicholas on with it, he caught hold of her hand and, lifting it to his lips, kissed it. 'You're a good woman, Jane.'

She coloured and snatched her hand away. 'I told you that you don't really know me.'

'Help me to know you better,' he said seriously. 'What is it you think I need to know?'

Jane stared at him and still hesitated to tell him what so bothered her. Her heart raced and she felt quite sick at the thought of how he might react. Then she knew what to say. 'I once hit a man with a hoe, but I learnt my lesson and was careful not to give way to my anger to that extent ever again.'

He was astounded. 'Who was he?'

'No one you will have heard of. He was a bully and a cheat. I vowed never to be deprived of my freedom again.'

'You were locked up?'

'He lied about me on more than one occasion and men in power are more likely to believe other men than women.'

Nicholas swore softly, wanting to meet this man. 'Is he still alive?'

She smiled. 'No, fortunately I was not the only one who despised him. He came to a sticky end—he was stung to death by bees when he would have stolen honey from a beekeeper's hives.' She moved away from the bed. 'Now you must rest. I will bring you up some food soon.'

He leaned back against the pillow. 'I would that you would tell me more of your story, Jane. As for you ever losing your freedom again, I vow it will never happen.'

'I would rather that you vowed if aught were to happen to me, then you would make certain the children were kept safe from such men.'

'I swear I would do all that is in my power to ensure their safety and their freedom. And I will keep my word even if you decide not to marry me, but I think you will despite being far too good for an adventurous wanderer like me.'

Jane felt almost swamped with guilt, but still she could not speak of that which she was ashamed. 'I have told you that I am no saint!'

'In that case we shouldn't fare too badly.'

The intensity of his gaze caused an aching sensation in her gut and she longed to throw herself on him and be held tightly in his arms. 'I must go,' she muttered.

'I will not keep you,' he said.

She thought he sounded disappointed, so she kept her eyes down as she gathered the soiled cloth and bindings as well as the shirt she had cut and hurried from the bedchamber.

There was no sign of the girls or James in the room below and only Nicholas's daughter lay sleeping in the cradle. At least she was not a crier, thought Jane, gazing down at the child for a moment. Then she went over to the fire and dropped the soiled materials into its glowing heart.

She stood there, thinking over what had taken place upstairs. She really would be a fool not to marry him. He need never know the whole truth about her past. She had to do what was best for the children. No doubt they would soon become accustomed to living by the sea and they liked and admired him.

Suddenly she became aware of singing and realised it was coming from the workroom. She opened the door and saw that it was Elizabeth who was sitting at the spinning wheel. Jane was reminded of her younger self and how her mother had told her that a similar instrument had replaced the earlier method of hand spinning with a spindle.

It was her father, though, who had described how the first stage in mechanising the process had been to mount the spindle horizontally so it could be rotated by a cord encircling a large, hand-driven wheel. She had been fascinated because before then he had seldom bothered explaining anything to her. His interest in her had been brief. After the sudden death of her older brother, who was to follow in his footsteps, her father had changed and it had been her mother who had shown her how the fibre was held in the left hand at a slight angle to the spindle to produce the necessary twist whilst the wheel was slowly turned using the right hand. The spun yarn was then wound on to the spindle.

As Jane watched Elizabeth, she thought how, despite her youth, she was more skilful at spinning than Margaret.

The back door opened and Willem entered. He winked at Jane, but she did not smile, her eyes darkening as she remembered the pain and shame she had suffered because of her weakness where he was involved.

'What are you doing back here?' she demanded. 'I have not given you permission to come and go as you please in my house.'

He looked pained. 'Don't take offence, Jane. I only came to see how Master Hurst is.'

She did not believe him, convinced he was out to cause trouble for her because she had turned him down. 'He is well enough,' she said. 'Now you can go.'

He did not move. 'Your stepdaughter has a definite skill when it comes to spinning. It is a pity she is so young,' he said. 'Although she's not going to win any prizes for her singing.'

Jane sprang to Elizabeth's defence. 'She sings well enough to please me. It is a sign that her spirits are recovering. These last few months have been difficult for her. What with her father's sudden death and us having to make the move here, I think she has done extremely well.' She paused, suddenly remembering the package that he had opened. 'Anyway, why are you back here so soon? Is it for the package you left on the table?' she asked with an air of innocence.

His eyes flickered over her face. 'What package?'

She had seen that expression of his before

and wondered what falsehood he would come up with.

He surprised her by saying abruptly, 'I was curious. I deem it belongs to Master Hurst.'

She nodded. 'Most likely. Is that why you're here? You want to ask him about the contents?'

'No, I would like to practise on your loom,' he said, placing a hand on its wood and stroking it. Then he immediately changed the subject. 'Do you think Master Hurst will stay in bed?'

'I am determined he will, at least for the next few days.'

Willem's expression was almost comical in its disbelief. 'Don't be a lackwit, woman. He'll be up and about within the day unless you tie him to the bed.'

She stiffened. 'You speak of him as if you're someone who knows him well.'

'He is famed for being an explorer. He hasn't achieved his success by a woman insisting that he stays put.'

She glared at him. 'He says that he has had enough of roaming and wishes to settle in England.'

'And you believe him?'

'I deem he is a man to be trusted,' she said, exasperated. 'Now I must see what the other children are doing before I repair Nicholas's shirt.'

Willem seized her by the shoulder as she would have passed him. 'Don't be angry with me, Jane. I'm pleased for you. I don't blame you for wanting to marry him, but I wish you would marry me instead.'

So was that why he had returned—to try to persuade her? 'My answer is still no,' she said firmly. 'Now let me go.'

She glanced at Elizabeth, but all of the girl's attention seemed to be on her work, so perhaps the noise of the spinning wheel meant she had not heard them. When he did not release her, she wrenched herself free and told him to leave. She did not wait to see what he did, but hurried outside where she found Margaret with Simon tied to her back with a length of cloth. The girl was cutting spring greens and as for James, he was chasing one of the chickens with an axe. She was horrified. 'What are you doing, James?' she called, hurrying after him.

'Are we not having a feast today, Mama?' he panted.

'I had not planned on it.'

'Master Godar said what Master Hurst needs to build up his strength is some good chicken broth,' called Margaret. 'And I remember Papa saying that it was excellent for sick people.'

'That is true, but I had planned to wait until Easter day before killing a chicken,' said Jane, exasperated.

The children's faces fell. 'But it would do Master Hurst so much good. Please, Mama, I am so tired of barley or pease broth or salted and smoked fish,' pleaded Margaret. 'Master Godar said that he'd enjoy tasting meat again, too.'

'I would like to wring Master Godar's neck,' said Jane savagely, snatching the axe from her son. 'Anyway, he is not invited and will be eating at the inn.'

She walked over to the woodpile and left the axe there. Perhaps some chicken broth would do them all good? It would certainly put strength into Nicholas, but she could have done without Willem Godar putting thoughts into the children's heads and making himself at home here. She *must* tell Nicholas the whole truth about what had once been between her and Willem. She would not put it past the weaver to do so himself. In the meantime she would deal with the hen herself and prepare a broth. Then she would visit the alewife and Anna whilst Nicholas rested.

As soon as Jane finished plucking and drawing the chicken, she prepared it for the pot and added vegetables and the last of the elderberry wine she had made the autumn before last. To her relief there had been no sign of Willem on entering the house.

She decided to take the children with her and went to Anna's first. She asked Anna's husband if he could get a message to the constable for Master Hurst, then spoke to Anna briefly of Willem's return and of his offer to be her weaver, but said that she would not be taking up his offer. She was relieved that Anna had never known how far hers and Willem's relationship had gone. Then, whilst Anna fed Simon and Matilda, Jane visited the alewife.

On her return, Anna brought up the subject of Willem, asking Jane did she know what his plans were in the light of her turning him down.

Jane hesitated. 'He would like to stay here in Witney. He is a widower now with four sons. Perhaps I should tell you that Master Hurst has asked me to marry him.'

'I thought he might,' said Anna smugly.

Jane frowned. 'I know what you are thinking. A marriage between us would be very convenient.' She sighed. 'I must go and see how he fares and I will see you later.'

She hurried home, leaving the girls and

James playing outside with some of the neighbouring children. She placed Simon in his cradle and tucked Matilda in alongside him. She stirred the chicken broth and then prepared a tray with some bread and cheese, an apple and a cup of freshly brewed ale. At the last moment, on impulse, she picked up a length of rope and placed it over her shoulder and then she went up to Nicholas.

To her dismay she found him standing by the window, gazing over the High Street. She slammed down the tray. 'What are you doing, Nicholas! Have you lost your wits? You should be in bed!' She hesitated before sliding the rope from her shoulder.

Nicholas whirled round and stared at Jane. 'Why do you have a rope?'

'Willem Godar said I wouldn't be able to keep you in bed without tying you down and he was obviously right,' she snapped.

His expression altered. 'He is mistaken, Jane, but I would happily be your prisoner.'

Her eyes glinted. 'You say that because you are convinced I will not tie you to the bed.' She twirled the rope that the girls sometimes used for a skipping game between her hands.

He frowned. 'This is a jest, of course, but I'm

willing to submit if you want to play games, but perhaps we should wait until we are wed. I still wait a definite answer from you.'

Chapter Six

~~~~~~~

She dropped the rope on the bed. 'No doubt you will expect me always to be a dutiful wife.'

'It would save us many an argument, don't you think? Although I am a reasonable man and would listen to your opinion on certain matters if it differs from mine. I cannot say fairer than that, do you agree?'

'I would not argue with you,' she said, smiling faintly. 'But allow me a little longer to come to a decision.'

He agreed and changed the subject. 'I noticed you returning. Did you get all you needed?'

'Aye. I also spoke to Anna's husband and asked him to get a message to the constable.'

'My thanks—if the constable is the same man I dealt with last autumn, then I deem him a man of sense. Neither of us was satisfied with the punishment meted out to Tomas Vives, who would have stabbed me in the back.'

'But isn't he under house arrest?'

'Supposedly, but he has friends in high places,' said Nicholas, returning to the bed and stretching out on the mattress. 'Whilst I was looking out of the window I thought I saw him, but I could be mistaken. The glass in the window here is of a poor quality.'

'I know it is too thick and contains bubbles,' said Jane, looking worried, none the less. She went over to the window and peered out. 'If it was him, do you think he had anything to do with this latest attack on you?'

Nicholas reached for the ale and took a mouthful. 'Possibly, although how would he know I was here? Unless word reached him that I had been seen in Cardinal Wolsey's house and had brought news of the Holy Roman Emperor, who is also the King of Spain. He could have sent a message to his uncle, who is a tutor at one of the colleges in Oxford and has the ear of Queen Katherine. He helped Princess Mary with her studies. Did you ever meet Vives, Jane?'

'Aye, when he visited Oxford last year with Rebecca's brother, both being members of the Princess's court. They had escorted Rebecca home after a visit to Ludlow where Mary was lodging at the time.'

Nicholas bit into a slice of bread and cheese. 'I must get a message to Pip and see what he can discover about Vives.'

'How?'

'Maybe Master Godar would be willing to do me a favour if I paid him enough?' Nicholas said casually, even as he stared at her intently.

Jane hesitated before responding, thinking the less the two men saw of each other the better. 'You cannot trust him. Besides, he is not in the house. You would be better sending for Matt.'

Nicholas stared at her from narrowed eyes. 'Why can't I trust him? Will you explain yourself? After all, if Sir Gawain trusted him enough to send him here, why shouldn't I use him? What do you know about him, Jane, that Sir Gawain doesn't?'

Her heart began to beat heavily in that uncomfortable fashion at the sheer thought of pouring out the truth to him and she felt sick. She could not do it, but she had to tell Nicholas something. Then she remembered what her stepdaughter had told her and clicked her tongue against her teeth. 'I have just remembered. Did you not leave a package downstairs?'

His eyes narrowed. 'Aye, why do you ask?'

'The seal has been broken and my step-daughter said that Willem was inspecting its contents.'

Nicholas's mouth tightened. 'I see. Would you bring the package to me now, Jane?'

'Certainly.' She hesitated. 'What of Vives? If it is he you saw, would you like me to see if I can find him?'

'No. Unless he calls here I'd rather he didn't know that we are aware of his presence.'

She chewed on her lip. 'This package of yours…?'

His gaze locked with hers. 'You want to know what it contains?'

Jane flushed. 'You don't have to tell me.'

He smiled faintly. 'No, but I don't mind you knowing. It contains a legal document I had my lawyer draw up before I left London regarding Simon. There is also a plan of a ship which I have designed.'

'Oh.' She decided not to ask what was written on the legal document, hazarding a guess that Nicholas had made some kind of financial provision for Simon. His thoughtfulness touched and pleased her.

Nicholas's hazel eyes gleamed and he settled himself more comfortably on the bed. 'Would you like me to tell you about the ship?' He did not wait for her reply, but continued enthusiastically. 'It is a much improved version of the Portuguese galleon on which I sailed to the Americas. Did you know that the explorer John Cabot set out from Bristol in search of a passage to the east by going west? He did not succeed in his aim, neither did he reach the Americas. Even Christopher Columbus knew that other men had crossed the ocean, for the west, before he did.'

'Is it because so many other explorers have sailed from Bristol that you are intent on living there?' asked Jane, fascinated.

Nicholas shrugged. 'Columbus didn't sail from Bristol, but the port's merchants had heard of an island to the north-west where the waters teemed with fish. They were having strife with the Hanseatic League at the time about buying fish from the Icelanders without involving that organisation, so they wished to find a new source of fish for themselves.'

She stared down at him, frowning. 'I don't understand. Why should Willem Godar be interested in a plan of a ship? I must admit I did wonder if what the package contained had aught to do with Cardinal Wolsey, because Rebecca let slip something about you and Pip that I suppose should have remained secret. It made me wonder if whilst you are abroad you spy for him.'

'Spy!' He gave her a look of mock horror. 'That's not what I would call what Pip and I do for the Cardinal. The word smacks of slyness and dishonesty. All we do is keep our ears and eyes open where'er we travel and if it involves our king, country and their enemies...'

'Then you report back,' said Jane drily. 'You could still be carrying information that others would be interested in knowing about.'

'No, unless I have a document to deliver to the Cardinal, I keep what I know inside my head,' said Nicholas, reaching for more bread and cheese. 'I deem that Godar was just curious, perhaps hoping he would discover some information that he could sell for money. He must have been disappointed. Now the package, Jane, if you would be so kind.'

She nodded and went downstairs, pondering on all that Nicholas had said, not only about Vives and Willem, but of the ship he had designed. Did he have it in mind to build the vessel and possibly sail in it?

She picked up the package and carried it upstairs. As she handed it to Nicholas, there came a knocking at the front door. 'You'd best go and see who it is,' he said, inspecting the seal on the package.

She hesitated, wanting to see him reveal its contents, but it seemed he was waiting for her to leave, so she went to answer the door.

Standing on the doorstep was a serious-faced Anthony Mortimer. For a moment she could only stare at him. 'Aren't you going to invite me in, Jane?' he asked.

'What is it you want? I—I am busy.'

'I feel I should warn you,' he said.

She frowned. 'About what?'

'I noticed you at the bedchamber window with Nicholas Hurst. You must have been up there a long time alone with him. I consider that not at all seemly.'

She felt the colour rush to her cheeks and for a moment was too angry to speak. Then she squared her shoulders. 'If I had, indeed, been up there since before you left then it would seem a long time to you, but I have not! I have been up and down attending to various matters. It is a wonder you did not see me visiting the bakery. I had just carried up some food to him when you saw us. Not that I need to explain my actions, but I will tell you this,' she added impulsively, 'he has asked me to marry him and I am seriously considering doing so. Good day to you, Master Mortimer!' And on those words she closed the door.

Mortimer banged on the wood.

Jane would have ignored him except that she did not want him waking Simon or bringing Nicholas downstairs, so she whipped the door open. 'Please, go away, Anthony! I have nothing more to say.'

'You must listen to me, Jane,' he urged. 'I have only your well-being at heart. You are newly widowed and need a sensible man to advise you. I can understand the attraction that Nicholas Hurst's fame must have for you, but your connection with him could put your life in danger. This attack on him yesterday—I suspect the pair of you were not listening attentively when I told you I had callers yesterday at Draymore Manor. I did not make the connection between them and the attack on him until a short while ago, but now I have thought on the matter more deeply, I feel I must tell you of these travellers.'

Jane hesitated. 'I admit I was distracted, so it was a little difficult to give you my full attention.'

He nodded. 'I understand that, but I deem you will find what I have to say interesting. May I come in?'

She held the door wide and he stepped over the threshold. She showed him to a chair by the fire and sat down opposite him.

'Well?' she asked.

He settled himself comfortably. 'Two women came seeking shelter during the blizzard. I had not long arrived at the house when they came banging at the door. The younger of the women's faces was bruised and she was very agitated. Apparently she had fallen from her horse during an attack by two men.'

'Go on!' urged Jane, unable to take her eyes from his face. 'Who was this woman? Did she tell you her name?'

'She was Flemish.'

Jane started. 'Are you certain?'

'Of course! I speak the language.'

'What of the other woman?'

'She was also Flemish, much older and of a better class.'

'I presume you offered them shelter?'

'Naturally. I could scarcely turn them away when they were in obvious distress.'

'Where are they now?'

Anthony hugged his knees and sighed. 'When I rose this morning they were gone. I admit to being extremely annoyed by their rudeness, especially as I found the older woman very interesting. She told me that her family was involved in the tapestry-weaving business and I thought she could have been of use to you.'

'That is thoughtful of you,' said Jane hastily,

'but returning to what they said about an attack by two men—did they tell you more about what happened? The two men—did they mention their names?'

'No, instead they spoke of a child whom the older one said was some kind of princess.'

'A princess!' Jane was flabbergasted.

Anthony nodded. 'Apparently the younger woman was doubtful about this and their conversation became heated and a bit confused. I could not understand every word they said because they spoke so fast.' He paused. 'I have to say that they were speaking between themselves some of the time and I eavesdropped.'

'Did you catch what the child's name was?'

'Matilda!'

Involuntarily Jane glanced upwards to where the bedchamber was and wished Nicholas could hear this conversation. Then she went over to the cradle and gazed down at the sleeping Matilda before turning to Anthony. 'What are you saying? That this child is the one that woman refers to?'

He scrubbed at his face with his fist. 'Nicholas Hurst claims the child he brought here to be his daughter. What if that's not true and he abducted her? She could be a member of the European royalty.'

Jane gasped. 'I don't believe it!'

'Why not? I assure you, Jane, that there is much about Nicholas Hurst that you do not know. You know so little about the places beyond the area you inhabit here in England. There is much that goes on abroad that you are completely unaware of,' said Anthony earnestly.

'I do not believe him capable of abducting a baby,' said Jane firmly. 'The younger woman you mentioned must be the wet nurse he hired, but I have no idea of the identity of this other woman. What else can you tell me about her? Describe her to me. Master Hurst might recognise her from your words. Please do not delay; I have much to do this day.'

Nicholas rose from the bed and went over to the window and gazed out, wondering how long it would be before Jane came back upstairs. So far there had been no sign of Anthony Mortimer leaving the house and he wondered what he and Jane could be talking about. Should he go downstairs? He needed a message to be taken to Matt. Even as he debated about what to do, he heard the front door open and the murmur of voices.

He watched as Mortimer crossed the street and walked down the High Street before disappearing from sight. He was about to turn away from the window when his eyes were drawn to a woman emerging from an alley. He pressed his face against the glass because there appeared to be something familiar about her. He stared intently and then drew back, squeezing his eyes shut before opening them and gazing out once more. She had vanished. Surely that bump on the head was not causing him to see ghosts now?

At the sound of the bedchamber door opening, he turned.

Jane stared at him and shook her head. 'You just cannot be trusted, can you?' she said vexedly.

'Is that the way to speak to your future husband?' he said lightly.

'There is no guarantee of that.' She could not disguise the sharpness in her voice. 'The way you are behaving, your shoulder wound will never heal.'

'Forgive me, Jane. I was curious to see who was at the door and when I realised it was Mortimer, I was glad I went over to the window. I heard what you told him about seriously considering marrying me.' He touched her cheek with a gentle hand. 'You have lovely skin.'

'There is no need to flatter me.'

'I speak only the truth.' He lowered his hand.

'So what else did Mortimer have to say after you invited him inside?

'He told me that he gave shelter to two travellers yesterday.' She paused, toying with her fingers.

Nicholas's eyes narrowed. 'Go on?'

'He tried to tell us earlier in the day, but we weren't listening,' said Jane rapidly. 'They were two Flemish women. The younger woman had fallen from her horse and suffered bruises. The older woman said that they had been attacked by two men. What does that say to you?'

He sat down on the bed. 'One of the women was Berthe. Did he find out who the other one was?'

'Apparently neither woman gave their name.'

He frowned. 'Didn't he consider that odd?'

Jane pursed her lips. 'I didn't think of asking, but now you mention it I suppose the natural thing to do if you ask for shelter would be to identify yourself.'

'But they didn't and Mortimer didn't think of asking,' he said drily.

Jane shrugged. 'Maybe he did, but the moment passed and he was more concerned in providing them with warmth and food.'

'Surely they spoke to each other, addressing themselves by name?'

'Of course they conversed,' she replied.

'Otherwise he wouldn't have been able to tell me what he did.'

'And what was that?' asked Nicholas sharply.

Their gazes locked and Jane said slowly, 'Matilda! They mentioned a child called Matilda. The older woman seemed to believe she was some kind of princess.'

'What?' exclaimed Nicholas incredulously. 'It's all nonsense. Surely Mortimer didn't believe it?'

'He said the younger woman didn't seem to want to believe it.'

'Berthe shows sense.' Nicholas paused and there was something in Jane's expression that caused him to add, 'You're holding something back. What else did he have to say?'

Jane bit on her lower lip. 'That perhaps Matilda isn't your daughter, but a member of the European royalty and you abducted her.'

Nicholas's eyebrows shot up. 'Tell me you told him that he's been listening to too many travellers' tales, Jane.'

'I can't believe you'd abduct a baby,' she said.

'You're right—I wouldn't.' His eyes glinted with anger. 'Matilda is my daughter!'

'I believe you and I told him so,' said Jane hastily. 'But who is this woman?'

Nicholas shrugged. 'Did she tell him anything about herself?'

'That her family are tapestry weavers.' She hesitated. 'But perhaps she spoke falsely, having heard that Witney was a weaving town. I think she made an impression on him.'

Nicholas rolled his eyes. 'Did he describe her?'

'He told me that she must have once been beautiful, but now her skin was pockmarked.'

'I see.' He frowned in thought. 'So what happened to these women?'

'They'd gone when he got up this morning.'

'By all the saints, didn't he have the sense to keep a watch on them?' he exclaimed, exasperated. 'I wonder what happened to the two men? I presume he did not ask their names either.'

'I don't think so.'

'Perhaps the women thought they'd manage better without them?' mused Nicholas. 'I'd guarantee Mortimer wouldn't have allowed two strange men into his house.'

'You think they must have been hiding somewhere in the vicinity?'

'Or they've abandoned the women and their attempt to kill me and left for the coast.' Nicholas lay back and closed his eyes. 'So Mortimer is prepared to believe me to be an abductor of children?' he said beneath his breath. 'I think he's jealous and trying to blacken my name.'

'If he is, it didn't work,' said Jane softly.

'Thank you for that, Jane.' He held out a hand to her and then let it drop for she had turned away.

'I'll leave you to rest and mull over what I've told you,' she said, standing in the doorway. 'I wonder where the women are now?'

'I wonder. Will you send a message to Matt about my wishing to speak to him?' said Nicholas, yawning.

She nodded and went downstairs.

He waited until the sound of her footsteps faded before rising from the bed and going over to the window. He gazed out, but could see no sign of Mortimer or the ghostly figure he had thought he had seen earlier. If he did not ache all over, he would have chanced Jane's anger and left the house in search of old man Mortimer.

He returned to the bed and noticed the rope Jane had brought up earlier. He smiled and placed it beneath the pillow and lay down. For a while he lay there thinking of Jane and what she had told him and then fell asleep.

Outside in the garden, Jane was attempting to scrub the bloodstains from Nicholas's doublet. As she worked she imagined that she could still feel the touch of his lips on hers. She wanted him to make love to her, but not only were there were so many questions she'd like answers to before she could definitely agree to be his wife but she also needed to gather her courage and be completely honest with him about Willem. She sighed and put that aside and thought instead about what Anthony had told her. Why should the older woman believe Matilda to be a princess? Could she have got her mixed up with another baby? Who was the woman? Nicholas appeared to have no idea. If he did, he was concealing it well.

Jane decided it was pointless letting the thoughts go round and round in her head and concentrated on what she was doing, but came to the decision that she was fighting a losing battle trying to rid the doublet completely of bloodstains, so hung it outside to dry. As she did so it occurred to her that she needed to visit the priest and explain that there would have to be a delay in Nicholas fulfilling the proxy vows his brother had made on his behalf.

It was evening when Jane returned from the priest's house. She went round the back into the garden to bring in Nicholas's doublet. Fortunately there was no sign of Willem in the workroom when she entered the house. But on entering the other room, to her astonishment she saw Nicholas leaning over the cradle, attempting to lift out a crying Matilda. She dropped the doublet on a bench and hurried over to him.

'What do you think you're doing?' she demanded.

He glanced over his shoulder and showed her a harassed expression. 'As there was no one here to respond to Matt's knocking, I came downstairs. He's not long gone. I decided to wait down here to keep a watch on the babies until you came and then my daughter began to cry.'

She remembered the children were outside playing with their friends and felt guilty. 'I should have told Margaret to keep an eye on the babies. I've just had so much on my mind.'

He nodded. 'I understand. Anyway, I have rested enough and wanted to speak to you about making arrangements with the priest for our wedding.'

She gave him a baffled look. 'You must be patient. Anyway, I visited the priest earlier,' she said, nudging Nicholas out of the way with her hip and lifting Matilda out of the cradle with ease.

'Obviously not about our wedding,' he said tersely, raising an eyebrow.

She flushed and explained her visit, adding, 'Besides, we couldn't possibly get married until your wound has healed and the men who attacked you are apprehended and only the Almighty knows when that will be.'

'I see that I must visit the priest myself and discuss the need for a special licence for our marriage,' he said, tickling his daughter under the chin. 'Best to be prepared so we can marry at a moment's notice.'

'Why should you consider that necessary?' asked a startled Jane, watching his lean face relax as Matilda gurgled up at him. She wished Anthony could see Nicholas with his daughter now.

'You're a sensible woman, Jane, surely you can see the sense in being prepared as a family to move away from here at any sign of trouble? For the children's sake,' said Nicholas.

She hesitated before saying, 'Maybe an earlier wedding is perhaps just what the children need, but I could be wrong, even if the older three are already exceedingly fond of you.'

'And for that I am glad,' said Nicholas lightly.

There was a silence and both were busy with their thoughts. Jane was filled with indecision.

'Of course, you'll have to inform your brothers of your intentions,' said Jane. 'Surely they'll both want to attend your wedding if we decide to go ahead with it?'

'I'm not so sure about Christopher.'

She looked surprised. 'You cannot be serious? Not attend his own brother's wedding?'

Nicholas grimaced. 'Last time we saw each other we quarrelled. I can imagine the excuses he will make. He'll mention the state of the roads and pressure of work. A simple ceremony, Jane, is what I have in mind. Just the two of us and the children would suit me.'

'Well, it would not suit me,' said Jane honestly. 'A wedding should involve all one's family and friends and be a real celebration. I deem you do not appreciate your family enough. I would have so loved to have my brother returned to me, but as that is not possible I would have your family here.' Her voice cracked and for a moment there was silence. Then Matilda began to cry. 'Now see what you've done,' muttered Jane, rocking the child.

'Me?' exclaimed Nicholas with a comical expression. 'It was you doing most of the talking and loudly too.'

Jane took a deep breath. 'I might have raised my voice, but that is because I was upset. Perhaps after all we should not rush matters and wait until the period of mourning is over.'

He swore. 'You would drive me away, Jane, have me believe a marriage between us is not what you want after all.'

Instantly she changed her mind. 'I did not

say that. I do believe a match between us is the right way for us to go. What about waiting until May? The evenings will be long then and the roads fit to travel, as well as there being more food available.'

'But May is more than a month away,' protested Nicholas. 'Why is it that you women have to keep changing your minds?'

Her eyes widened. 'I would that you would not lump me with the whole female race. It is not surprising in our case that I cannot make up my mind what is right and best. I certainly do not wish the preparations for our wedding to be rushed. What will people think?' She almost said that her last wedding was rushed and folk must have gossiped. Fortunately she managed to bite on her tongue. 'Now if you don't mind I will take Matilda to Anna and when I return we will have supper,' she added hastily. 'We can discuss this another time.'

As she made for the door, the children entered. She paused to watch their reaction to Nicholas. As she expected, as soon as they saw him they hurried over to him.

'We thought you might die when you swooned and we didn't want you to die,' said Margaret, beaming at him. 'You gave us such a fright.'

'I swear I will not do so again,' said Nicholas gravely.

'And you will not be leaving for a long time?' asked Elizabeth, hopping from one foot to another.

'No, and when I do, I have no intention of going without your mother or you children,' said Nicholas, glancing over at Jane.

'You mean you will take us with you?' asked James, looking delighted and hugging his leg.

'Aye.'

'Are you going to marry Mama?' asked Margaret seriously.

'That is my plan.'

Elizabeth turned to Jane. 'Mama, you must say aye.'

'I have not said no,' she said, giving Nicholas a look of reproof. Why could he not be patient? 'But the date must wait. Do not forget we are still in a period of mourning for your father. Now you two younger ones warm yourselves by the fire. The evening has turned chilly again. Margaret, get Simon and come with me to Anna's house.'

She watched Elizabeth and James hurry over to the fire. They kept glancing at Nicholas as if they could still not quite believe they could be having a man living with them who would protect and provide for them in the future. Such a man that they could be proud of, no doubt. Hopefully he would not disappoint them by finding living within the confines of a family too mundane and want to go off on his travels again. Suddenly she was filled with excitement at the thought of changes ahead, even though the next moment she had more misgivings.

'I'm ready, Mama,' said Margaret, approaching with Simon in her arms. Jane opened the door and the two of them went out.

As soon as the door closed behind them, James and Elizabeth, who had been whispering together, hastened over to Nicholas where he was sitting in a chair. 'Is there aught I can get for you, Master Hurst?' she asked, resting a hand on the arm of the chair.

'No, Elizabeth. I am content to sit here and wait for your mother's return.'

James leaned again Nicholas's knee. 'Will we live here when you and Mama are married, Master Hurst?' he asked doubtfully. 'It's not a big house.'

Nicholas placed a hand on the boy's head. 'Would you like to move to a larger house, James?'

He nodded. 'If it does not cost too much.'

Nicholas smiled. 'I am glad your mother has taught you to consider such factors at such a young age. I tell you that I already have two houses and they are not such a great distance from each other that we cannot spend time in both.'

'You must be very rich,' said the boy, his eyes wide.

'Are they near Oxford, Master Hurst?' asked Elizabeth eagerly.

Nicholas hesitated. 'Perhaps you are thinking that you would like to live near your Aunt Becky and Uncle Pip? If so, I deem that you will have to give up such a dream and make do with visiting them just now and again.'

Elizabeth looked disappointed, but James said, 'Where will we live, Master Hurst?'

Nicholas lifted the boy onto his knee. 'One house is in Bristol, which is a port and approximately three days' journey away from here, depending on the state of the roads and the weather. The other is outside the town and nearer to the sea. Does that appeal to you?'

James crinkled his snub nose. 'I've never seen the sea, but I know it is dangerous because of what Aunt Becky read to us of your adventures. I am not sure I will like it.'

Nicholas had foreseen such a reaction and knew he must reassure the lad. 'All life can be dangerous, James, that is why one must take care and watch one's step and always keep looking and listening. I will take you to see the sea before too long and you will realise not only its power, but also its beauty.' He changed the subject. 'But now I can smell your mother's chicken broth. Are you hungry?'

Both children nodded and Nicholas rose from his chair. Within a short space of time the two children were seated at the table, eating their supper. Having decided he would await Jane's return before having his meal, Nicholas left them alone and sat by the fire, staring into the flames. His shoulder throbbed painfully, but his megrim had eased and he was able to think more clearly about the message he was to send with Matt to Pip. He decided he would mention his plan to marry Jane, as well as the attack on him and of the women who had visited Mortimer's manor and what the elder one had said about Matilda. He must not forget to ask whether his brother had heard aught about Tomas Vives. There was something else, too, he intended asking him, but at the moment he could not remember what it was.

Chapter Seven

By the time Jane and Margaret returned night had fallen. Elizabeth and James had settled on their pallets in front of the fire and were asleep. Nicholas thought Jane appeared distracted and, telling her that the children had been hungry so he had fed them, he asked if all was well with Anna and her family. Jane nodded, then she told him that Anna's husband had granted his permission for his wife to stay here overnight.

His brow puckered. 'You thought that necessary to protect your reputation?'

'I do not want us to be the object of unsavoury gossip,' she said hastily. 'I also remembered to remind Matt about the care of your horse, but he told me that you had already done so and that he was to borrow it to travel to Greenwich on the morrow.'

He nodded. 'I will need to exchange a gold coin.'

'I have already paid Anna's husband for her to stay here this night.'

Nicholas thanked her and handed most of his remaining small coinage to her. She placed it in a pot. 'Sooner or later, Nicholas, we will have to hire another wet nurse for Matilda and Simon.'

He nodded. 'I have already realised that. Do you know any women able to take on such a position living in the area?'

Jane nodded. 'There are several professional wet nurses used by the gentry in this shire, but I believe they are paid at least three pounds a year. The difficulty is not whether they are able to take on the role, but whether they would be willing to move.'

'Are these women married?'

'Aye, and I believe their husbands deem their role worthwhile—although it does mean them giving birth at least every other year in order for them to have a sufficient supply of milk.'

Nicholas ran a hand through his hair. 'I never considered any of this when I decided to take on the responsibility for Matilda.'

Jane said lightly, 'It is not usually the province of men to concern themselves with such matters. If only Berthe could have been trusted. Anyway, it is something we are going to have to give thought to before too long. If Ned could spare Tabitha, I would have her come to live with us whilst he is at court. She is still nursing Edward and so hopefully she would have sufficient milk.'

'I will mention it in my missive to Pip.'

She nodded, hoping that Ned would agree to being parted from his wife and son. There was something solid and reliable about Tabitha.

After that Nicholas told Jane about his having spoken to Elizabeth and James about moving to Bristol and their reaction. 'Elizabeth would have liked to have returned to Oxford and James is worried about the sea being a dangerous place. His mistrust apparently is due to what Rebecca has read to you of my adventures.' He pulled a face.

'That doesn't surprise me,' said Jane, stifling a yawn, thinking it was too late to say anything amiss about that now. *This day seemed to have gone on for ever.* 'I will not ask how you plan to reassure him,' she murmured.

Nicholas was glad about that because it needed some thought and besides, there was a question he must ask her. 'What about the constable? Has Anna's husband managed to get in touch with him?'

Jane groaned. 'I forgot to ask and he did not mention it. I will speak of it to Anna when she comes.'

After that, she suggested that they have supper. She had watched him eat and was glad he appeared to have a good appetite. He praised her cooking and she thought how swiftly life could change in such a short time. It seemed longer than yesterday since Nicholas had collapsed and she feared he might die. Sleep was the great healer, she remembered her mother saying when she was a girl.

They did not converse much at table, although Nicholas suggested to Jane that she and Margaret should take the bed whilst he slept downstairs on a pallet. Instantly Jane shook her head. 'That will not do, you are forgetting that Anna is to stay overnight and will be down here with the babies. Besides, you must not overtax your strength and it will be more comfortable for you in bed. Fortunately the weather is improving so it is not so cold upstairs as it has been during the winter.'

He would have argued with her, but he understood her reasoning and so fell in with her wishes. He bid her goodnight, kissing her lightly on the lips as he did so before going upstairs. She stared after him for a moment before taking out her account book and writing down the amount of money she had spent that day. Then she sat, considering what another house move would entail and the pitfalls that might be involved.

There came a knock at the door and she guessed it would be Anna. She welcomed her inside and they settled the babies in the cradle and then, over a tot of apple brandy, they talked in low voices as women do about matters close to their hearts. To Jane's surprise Anna returned some coin to her and told her that she could not stay the night after all as her husband had had an accident and cut two of his fingers.

'I'm sorry, Jane, but I am really needed at home. He cannot prepare the bread dough for the oven as the cuts are too painful. Our eldest son will do the bulk of the work, but he cannot do it all. If you are in agreement, I will take Master Hurst's daughter back with me and return at dawn for Simon,' she suggested. 'I will use the back door. No one is going to think the worse of you for Master Hurst staying under your roof, knowing that he is wounded and the pair of you will shortly be getting married.'

Jane had no option but to accept Anna's words, so she saw her out with Matilda. She decided it would be pointless to inform Nicholas of the change of plan at this late hour, so she unfolded her pallet and covered herself with a blanket. It was only as she was on the edge of sleep did she remember she had forgotten again to ask whether Anna's husband had heard from the constable.

It seemed hours later that Jane was disturbed by the sound of a door opening. She murmured Anna's name, but had difficulty opening her eyes. She thought her neighbour answered her and so drifted back into slumber.

She was roused for a second time by a hand on her shoulder and an urgent voice saying, 'Jane, where is Simon? I have come to collect him and he is not in his cradle.'

Instantly Jane was wide awake. The room was full of sunshine and she could hear the children stirring. 'What's happening?' asked Margaret sleepily.

Jane blinked up at Anna. 'I heard you come in earlier. Did you not take him then?'

'No! I was kept busy with the baking and then I fed Matilda, changed her and I have come straight here to collect Simon.'

Fear gripped Jane and she pushed back the blanket and stood up. She stumbled over to the cradle and stared down at where her son had lain last night. 'Who could have taken him?' she gasped.

'Perhaps he is with Master Hurst?' suggested Margaret. 'Maybe he heard him crying in the night and came downstairs?'

Jane thought it unlikely, convinced she had heard a woman's voice earlier. But remembering how Nicholas had tried to tend his daughter yesterday when she had been crying, she rushed upstairs despite knowing she was clutching at straws. She found him sitting on the bed, attempting to pull on a boot. There was no sign of her son. Her face crumbled and she sank onto the bed.

Nicholas stared at her with concern. 'What's wrong?'

'Simon has disappeared!' she croaked, her voice raw with emotion.

Nicholas dropped the boot and slid an arm about her waist. 'What about Anna? Isn't he with her?'

'There was a change of plan. Her husband cut his fingers so needed Anna's help.' Her voice shook. 'She decided to keep Matilda with her and to bring her back in time for Simon's morning feed. It was Anna who woke me and told me he wasn't in his cradle!' A sob burst in her throat. 'I—I thought I heard a noise earlier and presumed it was Anna, but I was so tired. It was such a long day yesterday that I just went to sleep again. If only I had woken up properly, I would have seen who has taken him. What am I to do?' she cried, clutching Nicholas's shirt front.

'Hush now,' he said, kissing her forehead and covering her shaking hand with his own. 'Let me think.'

'What is the use of thinking? I should have made sure both doors were bolted. A woman got into the house and stole him away!'

His fingers tightened on her hand, almost crushing it. 'Aye, but if she was who I'm thinking she was, then she made a mistake and took the wrong baby.'

'You mean she thought Simon was your daughter?' said Jane in a trembling voice, catching on quickly.

'Aye! Was it still dark when you thought you heard Anna?'

She tried to think, but her head was in a whirl.

'Well?' he asked.

'I can't think straight,' she wailed.

'Breathe slowly and try not to panic.' He held her tightly against him, not wanting to believe what was happening. She dropped her head on his shoulder and attempted to do what he suggested and suddenly her head cleared. 'It *was* still dark.'

'And I presume she was able to get into the house because you left the door unlocked for Anna to enter?'

Jane nodded. 'It was her suggestion that I did so.'

'I wonder which one took him,' said Nicholas slowly.

Jane drew away from him, remembering what Anthony had told her yesterday. 'You mean whether it was Berthe or the older woman?'

His expression was grim. 'Aye. I would prefer it to be Berthe. For all she appeared to have betrayed me, she was fond of Matilda and, having lost her own child, my daughter filled a place in her heart.'

'And the other woman?'

His shoulders slumped. 'I don't know. A strange occurrence happened yesterday whilst I was standing at the window. I thought I saw a woman whose figure and gait seemed familiar, but I could not see her clearly so as to distinguish her features.'

Jane started at him in disbelief. 'What is this you're saying? You think you saw the woman who was involved in the attack on you?'

Nicholas said, exasperated, 'No. I did not see

her clearly enough during the attack to recognise her. And yesterday I received just a vague impression of someone I knew to be dead.'

For several moments Jane could only stare at him and then she said, 'You mean this woman was a ghost?'

Nicholas grimaced. 'I know. It's madness. I decided the bang on the head could have made me hallucinate.'

'Who was this *ghost*? Why did you not mention her to me at the time?'

'You distracted me with other matters when you came into the room, so she went out of my mind.'

'So I am to blame for what's happened!' cried Jane, clapping a hand to her head.

'You're putting words into my mouth. Now be quiet and let me think.' His lean weatherbeaten features were tight with concentration. 'It couldn't have been Louise who took Simon, so I deem it was probably Berthe who took him by mistake. We just have to find her.'

'What do you mean *it couldn't have been Louise*?'

'I thought I saw Louise, but I was obviously hallucinating.'

Jane hated that he was imagining he saw Louise, but all that mattered right now was getting Simon back and that meant finding Berthe.

'Berthe could have seen *you* standing at this window, but to take such a chance and enter the house knowing it was occupied?' exclaimed Jane, starting to her feet.

'She had set her mind on it. She must be in the pay of the other woman.'

'No doubt they are miles away by now,' said Jane, staring at him from wild eyes. 'I did not take what Anthony Mortimer told me seriously enough. Matilda is a princess and the other woman was set on getting her back. This is all your fault!'

Nicholas seized Jane by the shoulder. 'Perhaps you are right to lay the blame on me, but Matilda is my daughter and no princess. You are still not thinking straight.'

'And what about you *hallucinating* about Matilda's mother?'

He scowled. 'Forget Louise. She has nothing to do with this. I could say that if I'd stayed downstairs as I suggested and remained awake I could have prevented Simon from being abducted, but I didn't. We must stop blaming each other.' He released Jane and ran a hand through his untidy thatch of reddish-gold brown hair and winced. 'Stay calm and let me think.'

'I cannot remain calm. I only know for certain that my son is missing and I must find him,' said Jane, her voice cracking.

'And we will.' He forced her to sit down on the bed and sat beside her.

'How?' She stared at him.

'Let me first reassure you, Jane, that if Berthe does have Simon, then you do not need to fear for his life.'

'I want to believe you,' she said in a tight voice.

'Then trust me,' he urged. 'I will find him for you.'

'You?' She shook her head and got to her feet again. 'You are forgetting your wounded shoulder. I will go after her myself. It could be that they will head for the nearest port. Despite your attempt to reassure me that Berthe will not harm my son, I will not rest until I find him.'

'I understand how you feel.' Nicholas stood up and would have brought Jane against him, but she resisted and he experienced an unpleasant sinking sensation and released her immediately. 'You cannot go looking for him on your own. Besides, it's possible that if Berthe took him, as soon as she realises that she has the wrong baby, she will return him. You must be patient and wait here.'

'You really think so?' Jane looked at him with hope in her eyes and then slowly her expression changed. 'I cannot believe it. She knows that you will be furious with her and likely hand her over to the constable. Besides, stealing into this house will not be so easy again. As well as that she has lost a baby and wants another, so it is more likely that she will keep Simon. If Berthe has a horse, then she will head for Dover and return to Flanders and I will never see him again.' Her bottom lip quivered and her chin wobbled.

'You're letting your imagination run away with you. Berthe is fond of Matilda. It is my daughter she wants, not Simon.' His mouth set in a straight line. 'You can forget about going in search of her unaccompanied. Besides, you have no mount—and what of the girls and James? I couldn't keep them in order the way you do, not with an injured shoulder.' He smiled faintly.

A muscle in Jane's throat tightened and it was a moment or two before she could speak and when she did her voice was husky. 'I am sure you will manage and Anna will help you if you get into difficulties. I will ask Anthony Mortimer for his assistance. He has seen Berthe and the other woman so will recognise them.'

Nicholas flinched. 'You might as well say that you don't trust me and turn to Godar for help, as well.'

Jane took a deep breath. 'I can assure you that I would never do that.'

'Why, what wrong has he done you?' he asked harshly.

Jane was silent.

'Perhaps I can hazard a guess? You fell in love and he was married and he did not tell you and you were deeply hurt when he returned to his wife.'

If only that was all! She dropped her gaze and gripped her hands together. 'Aye, that was the way of it. It was not the best time of my life, but let's not speak of it further now. We have more important matters to discuss. I will find Simon even if I have to search all the highways and byways of England,' she said, a tremor in her voice.

'You must be patient,' insisted Nicholas, reaching for his boot again. 'I will find out from Anna whether her husband has sent a message to the constable and enlist his help if Simon is not returned to us by this evening. Right now I will visit the inn and see if Mortimer is staying there.'

Her eyes flew wide. 'Why should he be?'

'It's just a thought. He just might have met that woman again and decided to put up at the inn.' Nicholas managed to get on his second boot.

'What of Berthe and Simon?'

'I don't know, but I'm determined to find

out. Do as I ask and all will be well, my dear.'
He opened the door and headed downstairs.

Jane did not immediately follow him but
went over to a corner of the room and lifted
with ease a short length of planking that formed
part of the floor. From beneath it she lifted out
a box and unlocked it, taking out several coins
that she kept there for a rainy day. She just
might have to hire a horse. She replaced the
box and the short plank and went over to the
window. She could see no sign of Nicholas so
presumed he was still speaking to Anna below.

Hurrying downstairs, Jane plucked her coat
from its hook and donned it. Nicholas had already taken his, but had not left. She overheard
Anna telling him that a message had been
taken that morning to the constable by one of
her sons. What else he might have said to the
wet nurse in Jane's absence, she had no idea.
She heard him thank Anna and then he left the
house without appearing to have noticed Jane.

She walked over to Anna. 'Could you take
the girls and James with you when you go
home, whilst I go after Master Hurst? I will
make it worth your while,' she said.

Anna hesitated. 'For what purpose, Jane?
I understand your worry, but aren't you best
leaving this to Master Hurst? He seems to think
Simon will be returned to you.'

'I hope he is right, but he has never been a mother, so cannot possibly understand the way I feel,' said Jane in a tight voice. 'I cannot just sit twiddling my thumbs.'

'Hush now, have some faith in the man you are to marry.'

Marry Nicholas Hurst? There was definitely some doubt about that right now, thought Jane, her heart in her mouth.

Nicholas came to the Blue Boar Inn and enquired of a woman there to whether Master Mortimer of Draymore Manor was within.

'He was, but left last evening after dining here with a woman and another man.'

Nicholas's mood lifted and he asked if the woman was pockmarked and a foreigner.

'That's her,' she said, nodding her head vigorously. 'She wasn't English and neither was the man, although he spoke in a different language again by the sound of it. She spoke Flemish. I've heard that tongue from weavers when they've visited the fair.'

'She didn't have another woman with her, did she?'

'Aye, some kind of maid. I don't know what happened to her except she didn't go with the woman and Master Mortimer.'

'What about the other man?'

'He had his arm in a sling and his face was bruised. He left separately.'

'Did you happen to hear where they were going after they left here?'

'It could be that the woman and Master Mortimer were returning to Draymore Manor.'

Nicholas thanked her and handed her a penny.

'You're welcome, Master Hurst,' she said.

'You know my name?' He could not conceal his surprise.

She smirked. 'Stranger to the town and an injury to the head and carries himself as if he's got a stiff shoulder—who else can you be but Master Hurst, the renowned explorer? Master Godar told me if you came seeking him, then you were to be shown up to his bedchamber.'

Before Nicholas could comment, she bellowed to someone to come and take Master Hurst up to see Master Godar.

'Hold on,' said Nicholas. 'I made no request to see Master Godar.'

'Even so, go with the lad. He thought you might like to speak to him,' said the woman. 'He was eating his supper at the same time as those you showed interest in, so he might have heard something that I missed.'

A lad appeared, wiping his hands on a sack-ing apron, and gaped at Nicholas. 'You still be alive, then?'

'So it seems,' drawled Nicholas, the corner of his mouth twitching. 'Don't waste time, lad. Lead me to Master Godar.'

The youth did as he was told and soon Nicholas was standing outside an ill-fitting door on the first floor. The lad thumped on the door and called, 'Master Hurst to see you, Master Godar.'

The door opened and Willem stood there. 'Come in, Master Hurst. Is it about the lease?'

'The lease? No,' said Nicholas, baffled. 'Why should I wish to discuss a lease with you? Now I'm in a hurry, so let's not waste time.'

Willem looked disappointed, but waved him inside.

Nicholas pulled up a three-legged stool to the table where the weaver had obviously been partaking of a meal of salted fish, bread and ale. Nicholas stared at the food and wished he'd managed to exchange one of his gold coins so he could have ordered breakfast. Still, he should not be thinking of food because he had no time to waste.

'I told Jane she wouldn't be able to keep you indoors without tying you to the bed,' said Willem, sitting down.

'I'd like to punch you on the nose, Godar,' said Nicholas frankly.

Willem cocked an eye at him. 'What's Jane told you? If she said I seduced her, then she was lying. We were in love. She might not be what one would call a beauty but she had a certain innocence, generosity of spirit and grace that I found extremely appealing at the time.'

Nicholas was aware that Willem was choosing his words carefully, but even so they caused him pain. 'She said as little about you as possible, only stressing that period in her life was bad,' he said harshly, still tempted to punch Willem on the nose, despite being aware that in his present condition the other man could floor him in no time.

Willem looked injured. 'Naturally she has regrets and I don't blame her for being upset. I wasn't honest with her about my wife and women set store by honesty in a man.'

'Aye,' said Nicholas, feeling slightly uncomfortable about the secret he was keeping from Jane and forgetting for a moment about Mortimer. 'Setting that aside, I want to know what you were thinking of, prying into my private papers?'

Willem pulled a face. 'She told you, did she? No harm done, Master Hurst. I didn't see anything that was of any worth to me.'

'I'm glad to hear it.'

'Although having said that, it wouldn't surprise me if the man who was in company with Master Mortimer and the women would have found that ship's design interesting.' He paused to chew. 'Master mariner if I'm not mistaken. They spoke in a mixture of Flemish and Spanish, which I understand reasonably well.'

Godar now had all Nicholas's attention. 'Go on.'

'Mortimer was discussing your writings with them. She seemed very interested, even more so when he told her that he had bought your latest one fresh off the presses. The mariner was showing a lot of interest, too, despite looking green about the gills and he had his arm in a sling. Afterwards he excused himself and went out. The younger woman stayed behind, but not with Mortimer and the pockmarked one.'

'So what happened next?'

'She left with Mortimer and I suspect they could have been going to Draymore Manor. I can only guess what was going on there,' said Willem, grinning as he reached for his tankard. 'So what are your plans now? I wager Jane isn't pleased about you leaving the house.'

'No, but needs must when the devil drives,'

said Nicholas, adding succinctly, 'Jane's baby son, Simon, has been abducted.'

Willem gave a low whistle. 'Why should anyone abduct him?'

Nicholas proceeded to tell him what he suspected, finishing with the words, 'If it was Berthe who took him, I deem it was in error.'

'The woman must be crazed! Surely abduction is a hanging offence?' said Willem, shaking his tawny head.

'Aye,' muttered Nicholas, getting to his feet.

'Jane must be half out of her head worrying about her son.'

'She is but I have every intention of recovering him.'

'Of course you do. You want to win her favour.' Willem hesitated. 'I'd thought of going along to the house and using the loom. Have you any objections?'

Nicholas frowned. 'That's up to Jane, but if you upset her, you'll have me to answer to. Good day to you, Godar, and thank you for the information.'

Jane had decided to force some breakfast down her before leaving the house and was just about to do so when the front door opened and Nicholas entered. Her eyes met his across the room. She thought she saw something in his expression that gave her hope and she hurried over to him. 'What is it? You have information that might lead to Simon?'

'I came to tell you that I'm going to Draymore Manor,' he said.

Jane gripped his sleeve. 'You believe Simon is there?'

'I consider it a possibility,' said Nicholas, covering her hand with his. 'Although I cannot swear to it, I suspect the older woman returned there with Mortimer.'

Jane paled. 'Are you saying that Anthony Mortimer *is* involved with Simon's abduction? I can't believe it.'

Nicholas hesitated. 'He was seen at the Blue Boar in company with a wounded man, whom I'm informed is a master mariner. I suspect he's one of those who attacked me.' He could not help wondering what had happened to the other man.

'I see,' she said in a low voice. 'Rebecca will be shocked, although perhaps I should not judge her father yet.'

Nicholas nodded. 'If I am honest, I cannot seriously believe that Anthony Mortimer had a hand in Simon's abduction or the attack on me the other day. It's obvious he's interested in the woman, but we don't know what either had said to the other that caused them to leave together. Anyway, I mustn't linger. I only came to tell you of my plans.'

Jane forced a smile. 'I thank you for that, but you're right, we mustn't linger.'

Nicholas caught that *we* and immediately guessed what was coming next. 'I have a feeling you're going to suggest accompanying me,' he said, smoothing back one of her light-brown curls that had escaped the confines of her cap.

'Aye, I deem you need someone to keep their eye on you,' she said. 'And besides, I know the way and I suspect that you don't.'

He wasted no time arguing with her and they left the house. Only later did he remember that he had forgotten to mention that Willem Godar had expressed a wish to use the loom.

Soon they had left the town behind and were heading through the countryside.

'Have you ever been inside Draymore Manor, Jane?'

'No, despite that my husband was involved in the plans for its rebuilding.'

'Did you see the plans?'

She nodded.

Nicholas smiled. 'Good. Describe them to me?'

She hesitated. 'There is a hall and several

chambers downstairs. There is a still room…'
She paused.

He stopped in mid-stride. 'You're not giving me a clear picture, Jane. You've forgotten what you saw.'

'I had no need to remember,' she said fiercely, carrying on walking. 'I don't know why you're getting so angry with me.'

'I'm not getting angry with you.'

She continued as if she had not heard him. 'I know it would have helped to know the layout of the building if we do have to break in to search for Simon, but—'

'I don't intend to break in,' said Nicholas, frowning.

She stared at him. 'I don't understand. I thought this kind of derring-do would be nothing to you. According to the tales Rebecca read to us from your first book it would come easy.'

He blinked at her. 'Are you saying you believe I made them up?'

'I'm not saying anything of the sort, but I would have thought if you were attempting a rescue, then you would not hesitate to break in to rescue Simon.'

He frowned. 'I would break in if I believed it necessary to rescue my godson, but in truth I am still convinced Berthe will return Simon to us.'

Jane stared at him in bewilderment. 'Then why did you insist on making this journey to Draymore House?' She came to a halt.

He reached out and took her hand. 'Because I want to be sure and you were hell-bent on searching for him. Besides, I would like to see for myself this woman who says my daughter is a princess and is determined to get her hands on her. I have a suspicion who she is.'

'Who?'

Nicholas squeezed her hand. 'I'd rather not say yet.'

'Why not?'

'I want to be sure. Anyway, I'm glad to have this time alone with you, but if you feel differently and would rather go back now, I'm sure I can find the rest of the way myself.'

Jane shook her head. 'No, we haven't much further to go. Why are you glad to have this time alone with me if you aren't prepared to speak to me of your suspicions?'

He grimaced. 'It would involve even more explanation and I deem this is not the right time.'

Jane thought, *Explanation about what?* But perhaps it was better if she remained silent. After all, there were matters she was keeping from him.

They continued on their journey in silence

with Jane leading the way through trees which opened on to a clearing. It had a grassy area and a path that led up to a yellowish-stone building with a large metal-studded door and a window on either side. Both of them listened, but could hear only the sound of an occasional bird in the trees and a stealthy movement in the undergrowth.

Nicholas murmured, 'It seems deserted.'

The words were barely out of his mouth when there came a thud and then the sound of men's voices. Instantly Nicholas threw himself down on the ground, dragging Jane with him. The violence of the action caused him to stifle a groan as he landed on his wounded shoulder.

'I can see you,' said a voice. 'You might as well get up and show yourself.'

Jane recognised that voice and pulled on Nicholas's arm. 'He is one of the masons who used to work with my husband.'

Gritting his teeth against the pain in his shoulder, Nicholas struggled to his feet.

Jane smiled at the mason. 'Good day to you,' she said.

'Mistress Caldwell,' said the larger of the men, returning her smile. 'If you are seeking Master Mortimer, he left early this morning for Oxford.'

'Was he alone?' asked Jane.

'No, he had a woman with him.'

'Was the woman Flemish?' asked Nicholas.

'She wasn't English,' said the mason, giving him a curious glance.

Jane burst out, 'Was there another woman with her who had a baby?'

The man glanced at his two companions. 'Did either of you see another woman with a baby?'

The men shook their heads.

Jane and Nicholas exchanged glances. 'May we look inside?' he asked.

The man shrugged. 'If you wish, but you won't find anyone. Only ghosts. There was murder done here, you know.'

Jane paled and she reached out a hand to Nicholas. 'Don't be worrying,' he said, taking her hand. 'We'll have a quick search of the place and then we'll go.'

Chapter Eight

Willem yawned, stretched and rose from the loom. He walked across the room to the door that led into the main room of the house. He wondered where the children were and how long it would be before Nicholas Hurst and Jane returned and what news they would bring.

He went over to the hearth and noticed that the fire was almost out, so placed wood on it, thinking of his own children whom he had left in the care of his mother-in-law, who was really too old to cope with the boys. He found the loaf that Anna had brought and cut himself a couple of slices and placed cheese between them. He sat down and ate, conscious of the crackling of the wood in the silence and wishing he had a way of persuading Jane to hand the lease of the house over to him without delay.

It was as he poured himself a drink of ale that he heard the sound of the back door opening and then the soft pad of feet crossing the floor of the other room, accompanied by rapid breathing. There was something about that sound that told him it wasn't one of the girls. A young woman of medium height appeared in the doorway. Her face was partially hidden by her headdress and she appeared to have something concealed beneath her coat.

Willem sprang to his feet and seized her by the arm and twirled her round. She started back and said in a foreign tongue, 'Who—who are you?'

Willem did not immediately reply because the bruised, plump face was tear-stained and the pale blue eyes were wide with fright. Then he pulled himself together and shook her. 'Who I am, wench, is none of your business. Who are you? Or perhaps I can guess,' he said in Flemish.

She started and responded in the same language, 'Where is Master Hurst? Is he still abed?'

Willem scowled. 'Never mind Master Hurst. I asked you a question and am waiting for an answer.'

'Which I do not wish to give you,' she said
in a dignified manner, again in her own tongue.
'I would speak to Master Hurst.'

'What if I tell you that he is not here, but
gone in search of a stolen baby that belongs to
the mistress of this house?'

The young woman paled and struggled to
free herself. 'I have the baby here. Release me
and I will return him to his cradle.'

Keeping a firm hold on her, Willem pushed
her in the direction of the cradle. Only then did
he release her, watching as she took the child
from beneath her coat. She placed him carefully in the cot and covered him with a blanket.
No sooner had she done so than she went over
to a chair and sat down and stared at Willem.

He had expected her to try to escape. 'What
are you up to, wench? You think you can take
me off guard by behaving in this way?' She
pressed her lips firmly together and stared at
him defiantly. 'Well, are you going to answer
me or do I hand you over to the constable when
he arrives?' he snapped. 'Master Hurst has sent
for him. Abduction is a serious felony and he
suspected you immediately of being the guilty
party.'

Her chin quivered and for several moments
she appeared to be struggling to control her
emotions, then she said, 'I have righted a

wrong. Master Hurst will forgive me when he knows I have information for him. All I ask of you is that you tell me if Master Hurst's daughter still lives?'

'Aye, she does.'

She looked relieved. 'I must see Matilda. You will take me to her?'

'Don't be a lackwit, girl! You're in no position to make demands. I know who you are: Berthe, the wet nurse Master Hurst hired. He is furious with you and so is Mistress Caldwell.'

Berthe reared up in the chair. 'I did not believe they would try to kill Master Hurst. I thought they only wished to question him about the plan of a ship he had designed. *She* had said that she had a right to Matilda and that I could continue to care for her.'

Willem frowned. 'If that's true, then you're best telling me all you know about them—and you'd better be right when you say that Mistress Caldwell's baby is unharmed. How would you feel if you thought your baby had gone for ever?'

To Willem's dismay, Berthe's eyes filled with tears and she dropped her head into her hands and began to sob. He swore beneath his breath, moved by her obvious grief despite himself. 'Hush, girl,' he muttered. 'Do not think your tears will soften my heart so that I free you.'

'I do not wish to be freed,' she cried. 'I will stay here until Master Hurst and the mistress of the house return and will explain to them my actions.'

At that moment there was the sound of footsteps outside and the front door opened. Jane and Nicholas entered in a rush, only to freeze as their eyes were drawn to the young woman sitting in the chair.

'Berthe!' exclaimed Nicholas.

She sprang to her feet and babbled in her own tongue, 'Master Hurst, I have returned the child to its cradle. It was a mistake and I beg yours and Mistress Caldwell's forgiveness!' She fell on her knees in front of him, placing her hands together in entreaty.

'What did she say?' asked Jane.

Nicholas translated Berthe's words.

Jane wasted no time, hurrying over to the cradle. She bent and lifted out her son and hugged him to her breast, whispering soothing words.

As for Willem, he left the room, having decided he'd had enough of women's tears.

Nicholas stared at Berthe sternly. 'Get up. You've got some explaining to do, my girl,' he said in Flemish. 'You were in league with the woman who wanted Matilda—and what of the men who tried to kill me? Were you aware they wanted me dead?'

Berthe rose to her feet in one swift fluid movement. 'No, I did not know those men wanted you dead when she approached me in Bruges. Otherwise I would not have listened to her when she told me you were in need of a wet nurse.'

Nicholas's eyes narrowed. 'I presume you are talking about the woman who was there during the attack?'

'Aye, your dead wife's sister, Madame Dupon!'

So he had guessed aright, thought Nicholas, shooting a glance at Jane. Fortunately she was engrossed in Simon and hopefully she understood little Flemish. He thought how he had never met Eugenie, Louise's older half-sister, who had lived in Bordeaux.

He gave his attention once more to Berthe. 'Why should Madame Dupon get involved with those who wished me dead?' he asked.

'She holds you responsible for the death of her sister.'

Nicholas was stunned. 'She told you this?'

'Not immediately. She spoke to me only of your need for a wet nurse at first. She knew how deep was my grief after the death of my husband and son. She is a widow, but has never had children. Instead, she has spent her time in good works. She said that having another child to care for would help me deal with my sorrow.' A tear rolled down Berthe's cheek and then another.

Nicholas said carefully, 'Do you know the names of the men who tried to kill me?'

'I heard her address one of them as Señor Carlos Vives. He is half-Spanish and sailed on one of the ships that crossed the great sea to the Americas. I overheard him say that you had killed his kinsman.'

I don't want to believe this, thought Nicholas, resting both hands on the back of a chair. *How many kinsmen did Louise's betrothed have? He must have been the man he saw from the window, although his arm had not been in a sling then as far as he had noticed.*

'What is it, Nicholas?' asked Jane, coming over to him. 'You look pained.' She scowled at Berthe. 'What else has she to say for herself? Has she provided you with the name of the other woman involved?'

He glanced at Jane still nursing her baby. The tears had dried on her cheeks and she looked a changed woman from that of earlier. 'Her name is Madame Eugenie Dupon and apparently one of the men who attacked me is a kinsman of Tomas Vives.'

Jane's mouth fell open and then she snapped it shut and took a deep breath. 'I am beginning to think that there will be no end to these attacks on you from those who would avenge the death of *that woman*'s betrothed. Why can't they accept that she deceived you as much as she did him? It is not as if you killed him. He died of his wounds!' She stared at Berthe, her expression hardening. 'Did she tell you why Madame Dupon believes that Matilda is a princess? And who is the other man? Is he also related to Vives?'

Nicholas lifted his head and spoke to Berthe in Flemish.

'I have heard the name Tomas Vives,' she said cautiously. 'He is in London, I think. Madame Dupon and Señor Carlos Vives had planned to travel to the coast once she had Matilda in her possession, but she changed her mind. I was to meet her at Draymore Manor, but I was distraught because I had taken the wrong child, so I did not go to the meeting place and hid instead.'

'You're telling me they decided not to make another attempt on my life?' said Nicholas.

'I think so.'

'What about the other man?'

'I don't know where he went. I think he hoped you would die from your wound.' She gazed up at him. 'What are you going to do with me?'

Nicholas glanced at Jane. 'That depends on what Mistress Caldwell has to say.'

Jane now asked Nicholas to translate for her. He hesitated and carefully edited what he told her.

When he had finished, Jane realised that if Berthe had not taken the wrong baby then Matilda could have been lost to Nicholas. At least she had returned Simon, so she should be grateful for these two things. It was obvious that Berthe had acted under duress and was suffering, but her behaviour was still reprehensible.

Jane kissed her baby's downy head before saying, 'On the morrow I will decide, although surely you will also have a say in this matter, Nicholas? You must also come to a decision about what to say to the constable.'

It was at that moment the workroom door opened and Willem entered. He had meant to say that he was returning to the inn, but at the mention of the constable he lingered to listen to the conversation.

'Of course, although what Berthe had told me makes it even more imperative that I get a message to Pip,' replied Nicholas. 'With all that has happened I have yet to write my missive to him and give it to Matt.'

'I agree.' Jane frowned. 'But do not be so concerned with catching the men involved that you let Berthe go unpunished. She betrayed you and if you had not reacted so swiftly you could have been killed.'

Berthe's eyes flashed as she looked at Jane. 'What is Mistress Caldwell saying about me?' she asked of Nicholas.

He told her.

She gasped. 'It was not my intention to betray you. I might have spoken to Madam Dupon of the route we would take, but I say again I did not know an attack on your life was planned. I just wanted Matilda.' Berthe paused. 'It did occur to me that Mistress Caldwell might not wish to accept the burden of another woman's child if you should die from your injury—' she pressed her hands to her breast '—whereas I already loved Matilda. She has filled a place in my heart that was bleeding and bare after the loss of my son.'

'What is she saying?' asked Jane suspiciously.

Nicholas hesitated.

'I will think the worst if you don't tell me,' said Jane, having no notion of what that might be, so he told her almost word for word what Berthe had said.

Jane was torn by conflicting emotions. She felt a wave of sympathy for the younger woman in her loss, but was also annoyed by her judgement of Jane's charitable nature. Of course she would have taken care of Matilda if Nicholas had died, although she would rather not think of him dying.

'I don't know what to make of her,' muttered Jane. 'I certainly don't trust her and I don't trust myself to make a fair judgement where she is concerned. I do know I want her out of this house.'

'What is she saying?' demanded Berthe, turning to Nicholas again.

He hesitated, thinking that if the house had been bigger he would have suggested locking Berthe in another room, so they could all have some peace and quiet, but in the circumstances that was out of the question.

Unexpectedly Willem spoke, taking Nicholas and the two women by surprise. 'Has the wench mentioned one of the men being interested in that ship you designed?'

'Aye,' said Nicholas, staring at Berthe. 'Is there more?'

She shrugged. 'Señor Carlos thought you planned to sail in it to the Americas. This did not please Madame Dupon—she considered it wrong that you should have the care of Matilda, due to you being an adventurer.'

'She is mistaken,' said Nicholas harshly.

Berthe nodded. 'I know. I have seen the way you care for your daughter. Señor Carlos was not really interested in the child, only the knowledge you have gained of ocean-going vessels during your travels.'

'You heard him say this?' asked Nicholas.

'Aye, he deemed that you planned to build vessels of a design much improved on that of the Portuguese, so as to compete with them and the Spanish for possession of the Americas.'

Nicholas smiled. 'You have big ears, Berthe. Tell me what else you know and I will be inclined to be more lenient with you.'

She hesitated. 'They are aware that King Henry's main interest is in ships for his navy to fight the French, but they have heard that you have royal blood and could set up a kingdom of your own across the sea, if you had a mind to do so.'

Alarmed, Nicholas sat upright, wincing as he did so and putting a hand to his injured shoulder. 'Who told you this?'

'Matilda's mother believed it to be true! She was convinced that the child she carried could one day rule that far country.'

Nicholas groaned inwardly, wishing that he had never told Louise that his Flemish grandmother had been Edward IV's mistress. Their liaison had taken place when the Yorkist king had taken refuge in Flanders in the last century and it should have remained a secret. Obviously Louise must have written to her sister whilst she was with child and told her.

'It's nonsense,' he said firmly.

Berthe said, 'Madame Dupon believes it.'

'She is deceiving herself.'

'Then you do not have royal blood?' Berthe sounded disappointed.

'No,' he lied. 'It is true that I have designed a galleon that can compete with the Portuguese and Spanish ships, only my interest lies solely in building ships for commerce, not sailing them,' he added firmly.

Jane was wearying of the endless conversations in Flemish. 'Are you going to translate?' she asked. 'I wish she could speak English.'

'Our conversation is mainly about shipbuilding,' said Nicholas.

Jane was not convinced because she had caught the name *Madame Dupon,* but she was not going to force the matter now. 'So what are you going to do with Berthe this evening?' she asked.

Nicholas was undecided and told Berthe to sit down and await their decision.

'But what of Matilda? Can I not see her?' she pleaded.

'Is she asking to see Matilda?' said Jane, catching the child's name and hazarding a guess.

Nicholas agreed that was so.

'Does she really think that you would allow her to go near your daughter after what she's done?' asked Jane in amazement.

'What is she saying?' asked Berthe hesitantly.

Willem told her and Nicholas glanced at him, frowning.

Berthe said, 'I cared for her well. I do not see why I should not continue to do so.'

Without understanding a word, Jane said, 'She has far too much to say for herself. When the constable comes have him take her and lock her in a dungeon and throw away the key.'

Again Willem translated for Berthe, whose eyes flared in alarm. 'Master Hurst, you will not allow it, I beg you. I was good for Matilda and I have told you all I know.'

Nicholas agreed that was so, but he knew he had to satisfy Jane's need for justice to be seen to be done, although he was reluctant to hand Berthe over to the constable.

'Why don't you leave her to me?' suggested Willem, taking Nicholas and Jane by surprise. 'She's a fool of a woman. What she needs is a strong hand on her bridle. Hand her over to me. I will give her some work to do and that will keep her out of mischief.'

Jane was unsure whether that would serve and darted a look at Nicholas to see what he thought, not knowing he was wondering just how much of his conversation with Berthe the weaver had understood. Fortunately Godar had been out of the room when she had mentioned his wife and Madame Dupon being sisters.

'What have you in mind, Godar?' he asked.

Willem turned to Berthe. 'Have you ever spun, wench?'

She stared at him from limpid eyes before letting her gaze slide over Jane and Nicholas and then returning to Willem. 'Aye, back in my own country before my parents died and I had to leave my own town to live with my brother. This was before I met my poor dead husband.'

'Then come,' he said, beckoning with a crooked finger.

'Wait,' said Nicholas, not quite trusting the weaver's motives, whatever they were. 'I am not so sure that this is a good idea, Godar.'

To his surprise Jane intervened, 'Why not?

I will be glad to have her out of my sight for a while.'

Willem looked at Nicholas and raised an eyebrow. 'Well, Master Hurst? Are you going to go against Mistress Caldwell's wishes?'

Nicholas hesitated and then beckoned to Berthe and whispered to her in Flemish. She nodded and so reluctantly he gave his permission. He waited until the workroom door closed behind Willem and Berthe before sinking into a chair and closing his eyes.

Instantly Jane banished all thought of the other two from her mind, placed Simon in his cradle and fetched the brandy. She poured some into a goblet and said, 'Here, drink this!'

Nicholas forced his eyelids open and took the goblet from her. She hovered over him until he had drained it, determined to have a look at his shoulder and redress it. She went over to one of the chests and removed what she needed before returning to where Nicholas was slumped in the chair. She guessed he was not going to suffer her ministrations gladly.

His eyelids lifted and he watched her place the bindings, pot of salve and a bowl on a stool. 'Is this necessary right now, Jane?'

She hesitated. 'I could delay if you agreed to go upstairs and rest whilst I prepare a meal and then I will tend your wound.'

'That sounds a much more sensible notion,' he murmured, placing his hands on the arms of the chair and pushing himself upright.

At that moment the door opened and Anna entered, followed by the children. 'So here you are,' she said, looking relieved. 'What of Simon?'

'He has been returned to us,' said Jane, a smile breaking out over her face.

'He's unharmed?' asked Anna, hurrying over to the cradle.

'Aye!' replied Jane, joining her.

There was a babble of noise from the girls and James as they trailed in Anna's wake.

Nicholas stood, a hand on the back of the chair, watching the two women and children. *Will it always be like this when we marry? Being interrupted by children or women, seldom having any time to ourselves?* At least their arrival meant that he could slip away upstairs and not be drawn into conversation with Jane concerning Berthe. He wasted no time making a move to the staircase.

Instantly Jane was aware of his actions and glanced his way. She saw the strain in his face and excused herself and hurried after him. She made to place an arm round him, but he said, 'I can manage. You can tell Anna and the children what's happened.'

Jane gazed up at him. 'Don't be foolish! You're obviously suffering because you've done too much. My tale can wait.' Without further ado she slipped an arm around him.

In silence they climbed the stairs. Once inside the bedchamber she helped him off with his coat. He sank onto the bed and did not protest when she knelt in front of him and removed his boots. That he should not tell her to desist said much about the extent of his exhaustion, she thought anxiously as she helped him stretch himself out on the bed. There came a moment when he held on to her as she would have pulled away.

'What is it?' she asked, gazing down at him.

His eyes searched her face. 'I will tell you another time, Jane,' he said, loosening his grip and closing his eyes.

She stepped back, hoping he intended telling her those parts of his conversation with Berthe that he had skipped over. Especially that hurried whispered exchange before the wet nurse had departed with Willem. Leaving the bedchamber, she went downstairs.

Anna looked up from feeding Simon. 'I thought I might as well feed him here. How is Master Hurst?'

'He has overtaxed himself as I knew he would,' said Jane, going over to the cooking pot and hooking it over the fire. 'Is there any news of the constable yet?'

'He's away over in the next shire.'

Jane pulled a face and fetched onions and began to peel them. 'Have you any idea of when he will be back?'

'Hopefully within a sennight.'

Jane frowned, but made no further comment, praying that by then Nicholas's condition would be much improved. If only she could make him behave sensibly, but she had little hope of his doing so. No doubt as soon as he felt a little stronger he would be out of the bed again and visiting Oxford in the hope of finding Anthony Mortimer and Madame Dupon. Who was she that she should take such an interest in Nicholas's daughter? And what was she to make of Anthony Mortimer being prepared to accompany her to Oxford? She thought of Willem intervening and taking charge of Berthe. She had not thought of asking him at the time what he was doing here in her house earlier. She wondered what the two had said to each other before she and Nicholas had arrived on the scene.

She sighed, thinking of Nicholas and hoping he had not set his healing back. Perhaps she really would need to tie him to the bed whilst he slept! A faint smile curved her lips at the thought of his reaction. Then she forced herself to concentrate on her preparations for supper, emptying the chopped onion into the cooking pot, as well as spring greens, to add to the leftover chicken. She poured in more wine and added dried sage, rosemary and thyme, as well as a little salt and a grinding of nutmeg.

Margaret came over and asked if she could stir the contents of the pot. Jane nodded and left her to join Anna. She had only managed to tell her briefly how the Flemish wet nurse had returned her son and been surprised by Master Godar.

'Is that him working the loom now?' asked Anna.

'Aye. He has volunteered to take charge of Berthe until the constable arrives.' Suddenly she realised that Margaret was listening and told her to leave off stirring the pot and see to the hens. 'You can also tell Master Godar I would prefer it if he and Berthe had supper at the inn.'

Margaret nodded. 'I would like to see what this Berthe looks like,' she said, her eyes alight. 'I am curious as to why Master Godar should be prepared to put up with her company if she is so wicked.'

'Indeed,' muttered Jane, 'but that need not concern you. Now go.'

Margaret said no more, but skipped across

to the door that opened into the workroom and went out. Jane heard Willem order her to close the door after her. If Jane had been alone, she might have crept over and put her ear to the wood in the hope of hearing what her step-daughter said to him.

'I must go now,' said Anna a short while later after returning Simon to the cradle. 'I was thinking—is there any need for me to return for Master Hurst's daughter if that wet nurse is here? I have less time to spare since my man cut his finger.'

Jane hesitated. 'The thought of her feeding either baby displeases me. If I have my way, then she will certainly not get her wish to resume her role as Matilda's wet nurse, however fond she is of the child. For now that will be a just punishment for her, I suppose. I would rather you fed her.'

Anna shrugged. 'If that is what you wish.'

A short while later Margaret reappeared with the news that Master Godar would be eating at the inn. 'And to save you further distress, Mama, he said that he would take the baby stealer with him.'

Aware that the loom had stopped clacking, Jane hurried over to the workshop and looked through the open doorway, but the room was deserted. She turned to Margaret. 'Did he say that he would return her to us later this evening?'

Margaret shook her head.

Slowly, Jane walked over to the fire and stirred the broth. She could not help wondering why Willem had volunteered to keep his eye on Berthe. Had it been to please her? She thought how he had told her he was recently widowed. Perhaps he was weak where women were concerned and missing sleeping with his wife and would bed Berthe? She thought of her own liaison with him when she had been much younger than the wet nurse. Had he ever really loved her or just wanted sexual release? If she had known the truth earlier about his marriage, would she have remained strong and resisted the attraction he had held for her? She hoped so. Yet he had been so persistent and made her feel as if she was the only girl he had ever loved. What if he had not been married and they had wed, would he have been faithful to her? As for Nicholas, could she really trust him to be true to her?

'Do you think the baby stealer is a witch and has cast a spell on Master Godar?' asked Margaret, startling Jane so much that she dropped the ladle into the broth.

Jane was about to scold her when she realised the girl was not to blame. She should have been concentrating on what she was doing instead of letting her mind wander. She fished out the ladle and removed the cooking pot from the heat and placed it on the hearth.

'Prepare the table, we'll have supper,' she said with a sigh.

'What about Master Hurst?'

'I will take his food up to him later,' said Jane. 'Let him rest for now.'

It was an hour or so later and Nicholas was in the grip of a nightmare. He was struggling to reach the surface of the water, but the tide kept pushing and dragging him down, down, down, and his fear threatened to spiral out of control.

'Nicholas, what are you doing?' The woman's voice seemed to be coming from a long way off; recognising it, he could make no sense of her being there. Yet he was glad that she was near.

'Nicholas.' The voice was louder this time and he felt his shoulder being seized and suddenly he was being drawn up to the light. 'Nicholas, wake up!'

The nightmare subsided and he gazed up into Jane's face. He felt a rush of warmth towards her and wanted nothing more than to have her lie beside him. She was carrying a tray on which there was food and drink. A candle on the chest sent shadows flickering around the bedchamber.

'You're real,' he said with satisfaction.

She looked at him in surprise and then noticed the sheen of perspiration on his face. Worried, she placed down the tray and sat on the bed and felt his forehead. She sighed with relief. 'I was worried you might be getting a fever.'

'A bad dream,' he explained succinctly.

'What was it about?'

'Something that happened a long time ago.' He yawned.

'Was it something that took place on your travels?'

'No.' Wincing, he managed to raise himself into a sitting position.

'So it won't be in your books?'

'It happened when I was a lad.' He changed the subject. 'How is Simon?'

'He's sleeping.'

'And Matilda?'

'Anna has taken her. I thought it would be safer if she kept her for the night feed.'

'Is that because you don't trust Berthe?'

'I have every reason not to trust Berthe,' said Jane, her eyes glinting in the candlelight.

She stood up and went over to the window and gazed out for several moments before closing the curtains. Then she took the tray from the chest and placed it on the bed. 'Even knowing that Willem was going to take Berthe to the inn with him, most likely I would have still asked Anna to have her.'

'You were thinking of Matilda's safety?'

'Aye.'

Nicholas nodded, appreciating her decision, even as he wondered whether she minded deep down inside Godar going off with Berthe. He had not forgotten the weaver's words about his not having seduced Jane, but her being a willing partner in their lovemaking. Had he lied? And how far had their lovemaking gone?

'I thought it best if Godar and Berthe ate at the inn,' said Jane, sitting on the bed. 'Although he apparently told Margaret he wished to save me further distress by not leaving her here.'

Nicholas ran a hand over his stubbly chin. 'I don't trust him.'

'Me neither, and I'm glad to have them both out of the house. I'm sure if it was needful, you'd make every effort to protect us if anyone attempted to break in. This despite your injuries and your tiredness, but I deem we are safe behind locked door from our enemies.'

'Our enemies?' said Nicholas.

She shrugged. 'Your enemies then, although I now regard them as mine as well.'

Nicholas was glad she was so firmly on his side. 'Berthe reckoned *our* enemies are miles away by now.'

He reached for the tankard of ale and gave her a smile of such charm, Jane's heart seemed to turn over in her breast. 'I am not taking any chances.' She paused. 'Margaret suggested Berthe might be using witchcraft where Willem is concerned and that is why he is keen on her company.'

Nicholas shook his head. 'If she was practised in such arts she would have used them to keep Matilda. It could be that he thinks she has valuable information he could sell or simply that he thought Berthe would be a willing bedmate if she thought he'd help her to escape.'

'You think he will?' murmured Jane, prepared not to put anything past Willem, even breaking the law.

He picked up a spoon. 'Maybe. Berthe is a desperate woman.'

They were silent for a moment and then Jane said, 'You mentioned earlier that you had something to tell me.'

'Did I?' Nicholas was caught off guard, but in a heartbeat he remembered what he had intended telling her. However, whilst there appeared to be such accord between them, he was wary of telling her the truth about his wedding Louise. 'I have forgotten,' he said, tapping the side of his head and grimacing. Then he lowered his eyes and began to eat.

She watched him, gratified that he appeared to appreciate her cooking, but why did she have this feeling he was not being honest with her? She wished she understood Flemish.

As if aware of her gaze on him, he looked up. 'If Berthe were to persuade Godar to leave Witney with her, I'd be glad.'

She frowned. 'Because that would mean you wouldn't have to hand her over to the constable?'

'That's one reason. She has suffered a double loss and still mourns the loss of her husband and baby. But also I don't trust him around you.'

'Don't trust him or don't trust me?' she blurted out, her heart beginning to race.

He glanced at her. 'Is there any reason why I shouldn't trust you?'

Her nerve failed her and she shook her head. 'Of course not. I don't know what made me say that. All I felt for him is in the past.'

Nicholas wanted to believe her. 'I meant Godar, of course. He told me that he had been in love with you and he came here with the intention of staying. I've just remembered that he mentioned something about a lease to me at the inn. At the time I brushed it off, but now I'm wondering if he meant the lease on this house.'

'He did. He was convinced that if you and I married we would not stay here and he was of a mind to move from Kent. I told him that I would think about it.'

'I wonder if he is still of that mind now you have rejected him?'

She shrugged. 'Who is to say? I have no idea what goes on in his head. I doubt if I ever did. After all, I never suspected he had a wife despite his maturity and assured manner around women. I was such an innocent.'

'He told me that was a trait he found attractive in you, that and a certain goodness in your nature. I must admit that I envy him for having met you then.'

Her eyebrows shot up. 'You would prefer the maiden to the woman I am now? I was a fool! It didn't do me any good wearing my heart on my sleeve and falling for his banter. If it is a virgin you want for a wife, then you should not have proposed to me.' She rose from the bed and headed for the door.

Chapter Nine

'Stop. You misunderstand me, Jane,' he called, pushing the tray aside and making to get off the bed.

She whirled round. 'In what way do I misread your words? You seemed to regard me as some kind of perfect mother. It is true that I feel I must put the children first, so I understand that as a father you obviously want me to be a mother to Matilda, yet as a man you yearn for an innocent virgin. That I am not! I am just a plain, ordinary widow with a love of children and who has seen the worst in men and occasionally the best. I care for you, but the sooner you accept the person I am, there will be fewer misunderstandings between us.'

Her words hit him hard because there was

some truth in some of what she said. He would have liked to have been the first man to have broken through her maidenhead and carried her to the heights. He believed that Godar and her husband had never considered her feelings because they had never looked beneath the front she presented to the world.

'I would argue that you are plain or ordinary,' he said, 'or you would not have caught my attention. A galleon in full sail presents a very different picture than a rowing boat.'

'What!' Startled by the comparison, she turned and faced him, leaning her back against the closed door because otherwise her legs might have given way.

He said ruefully, 'I doubt you have ever seen a galleon in full sail, Jane. It is well worth it. I likened you to such in my thoughts when I first set eyes on you, storming to James's rescue.'

She blinked. 'A ship! You compared me to a ship?'

'Not just any ship. A galleon.'

She thought about his words and remembered that, although it was true she had never seen a galleon in full sail, he had written about such and Rebecca had read a description to her. She also recalled that he was a shipbuilder and slowly her anger evaporated and her lips twitched. 'I don't know what to say. A galleon.'

'Say you understand that there are all kinds of crafts, but some are finer than others.' He grinned.

'You have a silver tongue just like your brother,' said Jane.

'And you are a galleon full of treasure, my dear,' he said cheerfully.

She shook her head at him. 'You're doing it again. You cannot know what lies deep inside me. Now shall we change the subject?'

He sighed. 'If that is what you want.' There was still much he would have liked to have said to her, but after a silence he simply asked, 'Is there is any news of the constable, by the way?'

She sat on the bed. 'Apparently he is in the next shire and it could be a sennight before he returns.'

'Then that settles it. It would be best if Berthe ran away with Godar. I cannot wait around for the constable to come here and sort matters and mete out justice. Especially as the trail will have definitely gone cold where my attackers are concerned.' Nicholas reached out for the bread and bit into it and chewed before dipping it into the juices remaining in the bowl.

'But you can't go charging off, trying to find them on your own,' Jane protested. 'You must realise by now that even the journey to Draymore Manor and back was too much for you.

You were exhausted and in pain when we arrived here.'

'That's because I fell on my shoulder. I'll make sure I don't do something as foolish next time and I won't be walking either,' he said firmly. 'Horseback and boat will be my means of travel.'

She rose from the bed. 'I can't believe you would be such a fool.'

Nicholas's brow knit. 'Don't worry, I'm not planning on leaving for at least a week. I haven't forgotten I must reaffirm the vows Pip took in my place.'

Jane sat down again. 'So you are going to be sensible?'

He nodded. 'But it's even more imperative that I speak to Matt about getting a message to Pip since hearing what Berthe told me.'

'What did she tell you that you didn't tell me?' asked Jane. 'Be honest with me.'

Nicholas hesitated. 'I have not lied to you. I am just considering what I must tell Pip. Hopefully when he receives my message, he'll be able to find me some answers.' He paused. 'You can provide me with writing implements in the morning?'

'Of course,' said Jane in a long-suffering tone, removing the tray. 'And now I must look at your shoulder.'

Nicholas's lips twisted. 'Can't it wait until morning? After a night's rest I will be a better patient. Right now I'm not sure my well-being would be improved. What would make me feel better, Jane, is if you rest with me for a while and we discuss my plans for our future, in comfort.'

'Rest with you!' said Jane, taken aback, placing the tray on the chest. 'I will do no such thing, Nicholas Hurst—that is, unless you tell me what Berthe told you,' she said crossly. 'I'd like to know more about Madame Dupon or I will begin to suspect she might be another mistress of yours.'

His hazel eyes widened with shock. 'God's blood, Jane, of course she's not my mistress. Never has been.'

Jane could not deny that his reaction appeared utterly genuine. 'I believe you,' she said quickly.

'Good, because I'm telling the truth. You have no competition for my affections.' He stretched out and seized a handful of her skirt and tugged. She allowed herself to be pulled closer and sat down once more on the bed. His lips feather-brushed the curve of her eyebrow and then her cheek and the corner of her mouth. 'Does that reassure you?'

She did not reply, but it was extremely pleasant being held so close and having his lips gently nuzzling her skin after the worrying day she had suffered. It had seemed to go on for ever and was still not over. She could not resist cradling his jaw and bringing his mouth against hers.

Their lips met in a kiss that was deep and sensual and when that kiss trailed off, they took a breath before melting into another kiss. She felt as if she was floating and, reaching out for his hand, she drew his arm further around her. His strong fingers cupped her left breast, caressing its peak through the fabric of her gown. She felt a thrill ripple through her and she pressed even closer to him and instantly became aware of his arousal. She found it gratifying that he found her so desirable and did not consider her wooden as the galleon he had likened her to. It would be so easy to surrender herself to him, but hardly sensible in the circumstances. Especially when a voice in her head was telling her that she was still no wiser about Madame Dupon.

She broke away from him and gasped, 'But why should Madame Dupon care about Matilda? Why should she believe that she is a princess?'

He did not immediately reply, but looked

dazed. 'How can you talk of such matters now?' he asked.

'Because I need to be sure I can trust you,' she said unsteadily. 'What is your daughter to her?'

Nicholas groaned inwardly. *How was it that minds seemed able to behave separately from their bodies at the most inconvenient moments?* Yet he knew that he could not put off the truth any longer—to avoid answering the question would only make Jane more suspicious. It might not bode well for further kisses and a wedding, still…

He sighed and ran a hand through his hair and grimaced as the edge of his fingernail caught the cut. 'She is Matilda's aunt,' he said.

His reply was definitely not what Jane had expected. 'You mean that—that…she is Louise's sister?'

'Aye! Although I have never met her.'

'Then—then she could have taken charge of Matilda?' said Jane slowly.

'Aye, but it was not my wish and Louise wanted me to bring Matilda to England and rear her as my daughter, so I took the necessary steps to ensure that I was legally able to do so.'

'How?' she croaked.

'I married Louise.'

Jane felt as if her heart was about to leap out

of her chest and she could neither speak nor take her eyes from his face. 'You—you married Louise despite her having deceived you?'

His expression was suddenly angry. 'What would you expect me to do in the circumstances? She wanted to be absolved of her sin, so I sent for a priest and we were married. At least my daughter is no bastard child! Surely you can understand why I did it? There really is no reason why it should make any difference to us.'

Jane could only stare at Nicholas and wonder how he could think that. He had cared enough for the tempestuous and beautiful Louise to fall in with her wishes. This despite his having met Jane since parting from his mistress last summer. At the back of her mind had been the thought that their meeting that day had been what caused him to alter his decision to enter the church. Obviously she had been mistaken and only when Louise had died and he had a child on his hands had he begun to consider that a marriage between himself and Jane would be extremely convenient.

'I know what you are thinking,' said Nicholas, reaching out a hand to Jane and caressing her shoulder.

She trembled beneath his touch, wishing that he had kept his secret. Perhaps he would have done if she had not insisted on answers. 'Tell me then, what am I thinking?' she asked harshly.

'You want to know what I would have done if Louise had not died.'

'You're mistaken,' she said, ducking away from his hand and getting up from the bed. 'I know what you would have done. You'd have kept your vows—and no doubt next time I saw you it would have been under very different circumstances.'

He shook his head. 'Her death was imminent, Jane, otherwise I would not have agreed to her request. She really did die not long after giving birth. There might have been a time when I desired Louise with an intensity that was painful, but I was cured of such feelings when I met you and the children. However, I did pity her. Most of all I was determined to take responsibility for my actions and care for the child Louise had given her life for. This despite knowing taking Matilda was going to complicate my life. Especially when I truly was already considering asking you to marry me. I had already agreed to be Simon's godfather so that was one step nearer to being closer to you. Yet I could not be absolutely certain that you would agree to be my wife. Not only because of what you knew about Louise—for

I was aware that you were a woman of high moral standards—but also because, despite all I could offer you of a material nature, you might have begun to consider it too dangerous to be married to me.' He paused briefly. 'As the last few days have proved, there is some truth in the latter. According to Berthe, Louise's sister blames me for her death and so the number of my enemies has increased. I would understand if you no longer wish to marry me, as being my wife could be even more dangerous.'

'I realise that now,' said Jane slowly. She knew that she had to give all that he had just said a lot of consideration for the sake of the children, not only herself.

'It is not a decision I would rush you into making, Jane, if I didn't believe it the right path to take,' he said, gazing at her intently. 'What has happened today has changed matters. I would not want you and the children hurt, but I would add that there are safe places in the world to which we could go if you were still prepared to accept my proposal of marriage.'

She nodded. 'Perhaps we should not discuss this any further now,' she said wearily.

'Aye, let us see what the next few days bring. May God grant you a good night's sleep, my dear,' he said quietly.

'I'll leave you to rest,' she said, opening the door before picking up the tray.

'Thank you, Jane, for your care and your cooking. I will see you in the morning?'

'In the morning,' she whispered, closing the door behind her.

Neither spent a good night, having much on their minds. Nicholas realised just how much he wanted to marry Jane after having held her in his arms and shared kisses with her. He toyed with the idea that he might even be falling in love with her. It was not a word that he used lightly after his experience with Louise—even Berthe had betrayed him in a fashion despite her denial. He believed he could trust Jane. He spent a large part of the night considering ways that she and the children could be kept safe, if she did marry him, that did not involve risky sea voyages.

As for Jane, she could not forget his speaking of her as a ship and a marvellous ship full of treasure at that. He wouldn't have done so if he knew she had committed adultery, even if she had not known Willem was married at the time. Not only that, but she had not been honest with Simon when she had accepted his proposal of marriage.

She gnawed on her lip until it bled, her

thoughts going round and round in her head
as she lay on her pallet. Could she tell Nicholas
the whole truth? Admit that she had been with
child when she had married Simon Caldwell?
If she did, what right had he to be angry with
her? After all, Nicholas had not immediately
told her that he had married Louise—and he
might not have done so if she had not been
so insistent about Madame Dupon. She had to
admit, though, that he could have lied to her
about the Flemish woman being Matilda's aunt
and Jane would have been none the wiser. But
he had not done so, which meant his behaviour
could not in any way compare with hers. She
had to confess that the thought of telling him
the truth still filled her with dread.

It was just after dawn when Jane rose, having been shaken awake by Margaret who had
told her that not only was someone knocking
at the door, but that Simon was crying. She
went and looked out of the window and saw
that it was Anna and so unbolted the door and
invited her inside. She had brought a freshly
baked loaf for the household and after Jane had
paid Anna what was due to her, the two women
talked and exchanged babies. Jane remembered
to ask for Matt to call that morning so Nicholas
could give him the message he wanted deliv-

ered to his elder brother's shipyard in Greenwich. Shortly after, Anna left with Simon.

James and Elizabeth were awake by then and so Jane had breakfast with the children before preparing a tray for Nicholas. At the back of her mind was still the thought of what he had told her about Louise and her own failing. It came as no surprise to discover him awake. He had already divested himself not only of his shirt, but somehow had managed to remove the dressing on his shoulder. She thought he looked drawn and guessed that he was also in pain.

'That wasn't very wise of you,' she said, frowning as she placed the tray across his lap and inspected his shoulder wound closely. To her relief it appeared to be healing. Nevertheless, she wasted no time cleaning the wound and smoothing on salve and binding it up with a fresh dressing.

'So, how long before you deem it has healed enough for me to be able to ride?' he asked. 'Two weeks?'

'Surely from your previous experiences of such wounds you should be able to answer that yourself.' Jane gathered up the soiled dressing and the rag she had used and placed them in a bowl.

He shrugged. 'I have forgotten. Did you remember to ask Anna to speak to Matt?'

She nodded. 'I will bring writing implements to you within the hour.'

He stroked his jaw. 'I could do with a shave, but perhaps I should grow a beard. Would you like me with a beard?'

'I suppose it could act as a disguise if our enemy was to come looking for you.'

'That is not what I asked, but I take your meaning,' he said with a wry smile.

Their eyes locked and there was a silence. She wondered if he was waiting for her to say that she was prepared to take the risk and marry him, despite the possible danger to her and the children. Yet she could not bring herself to say it right now.

She hurried out and went downstairs, telling herself that she was all kinds of a coward.

Jane returned a short while later with the writing implements that Nicholas had requested and removed his eating utensils, but left him the tray which she dusted before placing two precious sheets of paper on it.

'Is there aught else you need?' she asked.

'Only a kiss from you, Jane,' he said, reaching out and seizing her hand and drawing her close. She found herself melting towards him and pressed her lips against his. 'Perhaps I will marry you, but not for a while,' she blurted out before she could stop herself and hurried from the bedchamber.

He called her back, but she continued down the stairs. Why had she agreed and then put off the wedding when she knew she wanted to be his wife? Why couldn't she just be honest with him and then she would know where she was with him? She must visit the priest, confess her sin and ask his advice. Most likely he would tell her what to do, but she knew what she should do, so what was the point of confessing? She needed more time to think. In the meantime Nicholas would wish to see his daughter, so she had Margaret carry Matilda upstairs. Later she would go up herself and see if he had finished writing the missive for Matt to take to Philip in Greenwich.

Nicholas had obviously been pleased to see his daughter and thanked Jane for her thoughtfulness. 'I also am grateful for your trust in me by agreeing to be my wife. I wish it could be sooner, but I understand your reasoning. I promise you, though, that I will not fail you,' he said with obvious sincerity.

Emotion had her by the throat and she could only nod, aware of the guilt that weighed heavy on her conscience. 'I would like to see where we are to live first,' she murmured, lifting his daughter into her arms.

'That can be arranged,' he said.

She thanked him. 'I presume we'll take the children with us. I have to say that Matilda is such a pretty baby and I am glad she has your eyes.'

'Thank you, Jane.' He paused. 'Is there any sign of Willem and Berthe yet?'

'No. I wonder...'

'So do I.'

At that moment there came a call from downstairs and she excused herself.

Matt had arrived and Jane took him upstairs and left him with Nicholas. No sooner had he left than Anna came with Simon, bursting with the news that Master Godar and that baby snatcher had been seen riding out of town. Jane wasted no time, climbing the stairs to tell Nicholas the news.

'What are we going to do?' she demanded.

'Wait,' he said succinctly.

'For what?' She sat on the bed and stared at him.

'To discover what game Godar is playing and also to see what results from the message Matt is taking to Pip.' Nicholas rose from the bed. 'In the meantime I will speak to the priest, if you will give me directions to his house.'

'What for? Besides, he could visit you up here. There is no need for you to get up,' insisted Jane.

'I have no intention of remaining abed any longer. It's time you and the children stopped sleeping on pallets downstairs and had your privacy once again,' he said firmly. 'I will make do on a pallet whilst you all sleep up here. In the meantime, I will do as you ask and see the priest here if you will let him know that.'

Jane agreed, knowing it would obviously be a waste of time insisting he stayed in bed. Once downstairs, she left him talking to James whilst she went to visit the priest and to buy fish for their midday meal. She returned to the house with the news that the priest would call later that afternoon.

Jane soon realised that the cleric was more than a little in awe of Nicholas and she admired him for the way in which he put the man at ease whilst answering several questions on the sacred sites that he had visited during his travels. Then Nicholas asked her to leave them alone and she had no choice but to do so. Even so, she could not help wishing she could have listened in on their conversation.

After the priest left, Nicholas told her that the cleric had suggested that this coming Sunday he should attend church with Jane and the children if he felt well enough to reaffirm the vows his brother had made in his place. With that settled, Nicholas discussed with Jane the journey to Bristol so that she could inspect the two houses he had inherited. 'I would like to go after Easter,' he said.

'It is not that long off,' said Jane. 'We will need another wet nurse as Anna cannot come with us.'

'I have mentioned our need for a wet nurse in my letter to Pip. Hopefully Tabitha is able to fill that role. If not, then we will have to look elsewhere,' said Nicholas.

Jane could only agree.

Sunday dawned and Nicholas affirmed the proxy vows. It was a solemn but happy occasion, although Nicholas found it unexpectedly alarming to officially be responsible for the well-being of Simon's soul.

On the following Wednesday morning, Nicholas told Jane that he was considering travelling to Oxford to visit a friend, Magnus, who was a tutor at one of the colleges. Jane's heart sank, convinced that he was feeling restless due to his staying in one place too long. She was not in favour of his going to Oxford alone and told him so, reminding him that he had sent a message to the constable and if he was to arrive whilst Nicholas was absent, the constable would not be pleased.

'I deem it a waste of time his coming,' said Nicholas, scowling. 'The trail has gone cold and we do not have Berthe as a witness to the attack on me.'

Although Jane agreed with him, she suggested that he wait until after Palm Sunday. It would give his wound further time to heal and surely he would enjoy the celebration that took place then. Reluctantly Nicholas agreed.

As she snipped a thin leafy branch, Jane thought of the girl she had spoken to yesterday. Having decided not to wait until Matt's return to see whether Tabitha was able to help with Matilda, she had taken steps to hire another wet nurse. Dorothea was young and inexperienced, being the younger sister of a woman who was in the employ of one of the richer families in the shire. The girl was also unmarried and willing to leave Oxfordshire and travel to Bristol.

A sigh escaped Jane, as she thought of Dorothea telling her that she had deliberately got herself with child so she could be a wet nurse. It had not seemed to have occurred to her that she could die in childbirth—as it was her baby had not survived the birth. Still she appeared to have an abundance of breast milk, apparently just like her professional wet-nurse sister, and as she had no parents, her sister was positively encouraging her to take the situation with Jane, having brought disgrace on the family by lying with a travelling tinker. Jane was uncertain how much truth there was in that tale, but she had gone ahead and hired the girl once she had Nicholas's approval. It wasn't a perfect arrangement, but would have to do for now.

She thought of Nicholas back at the house, writing letters to the manager of the wine business in Bristol and the couple who looked after his house in the country, whilst keeping his eye on the babies as well. Dorothea was dealing with the washing, leaving Jane and the other children to gather greenery for the procession on Palm Sunday that signalled the beginning of Holy Week.

'I deem we have enough now!' called Jane, placing her shears with the greenery in the wicker basket.

She and the children began to walk back to the village. Later they would weave some of what they had gathered into crosses for the next day. To her surprise and delight as they strolled along the High Street in the sunshine, she caught sight of riders outside the house.

Instantly she began to run, having recognised Rebecca, Matt, Ned and Tabitha.

Jane told Margaret to hurry into the house and tell Nicholas that they had visitors. Her stepdaughter wasted no time in doing so. Jane watched Matt dismount from the horse on which Rebecca was seated on a pillion seat.

'It is so good to see you, Rebecca!' Jane called up, shielding her eyes from the sun. 'Are you well?'

Rebecca beamed down at her. 'Aye, I am very well now that the sickness is passing.'

'The sickness!' Jane stared at her and then a slow smile lit up her face. 'You are with child?'

'Aye, I kept it secret for a while as I feared miscarrying, but I've prayed to Our Lady constantly and I trust now that all will go well.'

'That is marvellous!' said Jane. 'But you will be weary from the journey so make haste inside out of the sun and rest.'

Rebecca admitted to being tired and accepted Matt's hand to help her from the pillion seat. She thanked him and smoothed down her skirts before kissing Jane on the cheek. 'I see you have been gathering greenery.'

'Aye, it is a fine day for it,' said Jane. 'Hard to believe that we had snow not so long ago.'

Rebecca smiled down at her niece and nephew and held out her arms. 'Elizabeth!

James! Come and give your aunt a big hug and a kiss!'

James flung himself at her. 'Will you be staying long, Aunt Becky?'

'Just for one night, if there is room for me, and then Tabitha will take my place. This night she and Ned will put up at the inn with their little boy.' She kissed the top of her nephew's head and reached out an arm to Elizabeth and brought her niece against her. 'And you, my dear, how are you?'

'Better for seeing you, Aunt Rebecca,' said the girl, hugging her.

'How is Pip?' asked Jane, watching them both fondly. 'Nicholas hopes you have news from him.'

Rebecca's eyes clouded. 'I have news, but not that which he will be glad of.'

Jane's face fell. 'What is it? Pip, he isn't— oh, he couldn't be sick, otherwise you would look miserable.'

'Oh, Pip is in excellent health,' said Rebecca hastily. 'Unfortunately, when he called in at the shipyard shortly after Nicholas's message was delivered to the palace, he found it was pandemonium there. They'd had intruders. Christopher was injured and one of the ships on the blocks was damaged. Apparently it had been commissioned by the king and as you can imagine Christopher is in a state of shock.' She took a breath. 'So Nicholas's presence is required. Pip has said that he will spend as much time as he is able at the shipyard until Nicholas can come and replace him.'

Jane could not conceal her dismay. 'But his shoulder is not completely healed. He cannot possibly work in the shipyard.'

Before she could say more, a smiling Nicholas appeared in the doorway. 'Rebecca, what news do you bring? How are my brothers?'

She gazed at him with concern and, reaching up, kissed his cheek. 'It is good to see you, Nicholas, although Jane tells me that your shoulder is still not healed.'

Nicholas shrugged. 'It is much improved, so there is no need for you to worry. Tell me, have you a message for me from Pip?'

'He would speak to you, himself, of the matters you wrote about. He has sent me to tell you that Christopher has need of you at the shipyard. Even if you cannot work on reconstructing the ship that has been damaged, your presence will bring some comfort to the family and you can oversee the labourers. I know you and Christopher have quarreled, but he has good reason for sending for you now. You have an authority and knowledge that cannot but soothe his and Mary's anxiety and the labourers' ruffled feathers.'

Nicholas raised his eyebrows. 'I find it difficult to believe these are Christopher's words. This damaged ship—was it the work of his labourers? Did they rebel because of his bad temper? He expects far too much of everyone.'

Rebecca sighed. 'No, it is not that. Christopher is confined to bed with a broken leg and he has what the physician thinks are cracked ribs after his fight with the intruders. Mary is worried that he will have an apoplexy if he doesn't calm down. Forget your quarrel and—'

'Intruders! What intruders?' interrupted Nicholas, frowning.

Rebecca wasted no time, telling him what had happened.

'Did he see their faces?' asked Nicholas, deeply disturbed by this latest development.

'No, they were masked.'

'Did he hear them speak at all?'

'That I don't know.'

His frown deepened. 'I see that I must go.'

Jane opened her mouth to protest, but a look from him silenced her.

Rebecca's relief was obvious. 'Thank you, Nicholas. Pip's presence is needed more than usual at court during the next month—and when he is not there, I will need him at home.

The building work at Oxford is at a critical stage and my father will insist on interfering when Pip is not around.' She paused. 'Not that I have seen him since my return. I can only presume he is staying at Draymore Manor.'

'I would not be so sure of that,' said Nicholas.

She stared at him. 'What do you mean? Is there something I should know?'

Obviously his brother had not discussed with his wife what he had written about Anthony Mortimer, thought Nicholas, swiftly debating with himself how to answer her. 'Your father was in Witney a short while ago, but he did not linger. We were told that he had gone to Oxford, but if he is not there, then perhaps he is visiting your brother at the court of Princess Mary, Rebecca?'

'No, I doubt that very much. The princess is expected at Greenwich. I received a message from Davy and he made no mention of my father.'

'I see.' Nicholas hesitated to mention Louise's sister and instead changed the subject, reaching for Jane's hand. 'Did Pip tell you that Jane and I were considering getting married? I can tell you now that we have decided definitely to do so.'

Rebecca clapped her hands and looked delighted. 'So you have made up your minds. We've thought since we married that the pair of you could make a love match of it one day. Tell me, when is the wedding to be? Soon, I hope.'

Chapter Ten

There was a long silence and then Nicholas said, 'I see Pip had set his mind on winning our last wager.'

Rebecca chuckled and then lowered her voice because of the children. 'We could do with a pot of gold right now, but it was obvious to me from the moment you and Jane set eyes on each other that you were meant to be together. Otherwise why would you have agreed to be Simon's godfather? Of course, you scooting off to Flanders was a bit of a setback, but as it is you're here now and everything's working out just as I prayed it would. So when is the wedding to be?'

'Not for some time,' said Jane, glancing at

Nicholas. 'There is so much to do and it is not so long since Simon died.'

Rebecca frowned. 'Jane, you don't want to be kicking your heels. One never knows what's just round the corner. When one thinks of the latest attack on Nick, he's fortunate to be alive.'

'You're saying we should make it soon,' said Jane, a tremor in her voice.

'Let's not discuss it here on the doorstep,' interrupted Nicholas. 'It's time we went inside.'

Despite his words, the three of them made no immediate move to go indoors. At that moment Tabitha called a greeting to Jane and she turned to speak to her. The other woman had remained on the pillion seat behind her husband. The two women exchanged pleasantries for a few moments and Nicholas spoke to Ned and Matt. Then the latter led away the horse and Ned and Tabitha rode after him towards the inn.

Once they had gone, Jane turned to Nicholas. 'When must you leave?'

'On the morrow if matters are as serious as Rebecca says,' he murmured, frowning. 'I wish I didn't have to go. I would have liked to see you and the children to Bristol before doing so, but I fear there is not enough time.'

'What's this about Bristol?' asked Rebecca, her face alive with curiosity.

Jane turned to her. 'We'll be leaving Witney once we are married to make our home there.'

'Of course, Nicholas has a fondness for the place!' exclaimed Rebecca, slipping her hand through Jane's arm. 'I had almost forgotten.'

'I didn't know of his connection with Bristol, so it came as a great surprise to me,' said Jane, glancing up at him. 'But let's not dawdle out here any longer.' She ushered her sister-in-law into the house. 'I am so pleased that Ned has agreed for Tabitha to spend some time with me and the children. She will be an asset to the household despite my having hired another wet nurse—although Dorothea has yet to prove herself completely satisfactory.'

'What about some refreshment?' suggested Nicholas, who along with the children had followed the two women inside.

Jane nodded and went to see to it, wishing that he did not have to go to Greenwich. She was concerned about his brother's shipyard being broken in to and could not help but wonder whether it was in any way connected with those who had attacked him in the past. Rebecca was right when she had said that one never knew what was round the corner.

Nicholas was thinking very much the same as Jane, but had no intention of voicing his thoughts and had begun to make plans. He caught her eye as she looked up from pouring elderflower wine into goblets and smiled.

Her heart fluttered and her pulse began to race. She wished she had the courage to say *Let's get married now!* What had he made of Rebecca and Philip believing they could make a love match of it? Perhaps the other couple were seeing what they wanted to see. She swallowed a sigh and resumed her task, handing a goblet to Rebecca, who stood with one hand resting on the back of a chair, whilst fingering with the other the greenery in the wicker basket that Jane had placed on the table.

'Shouldn't you sit down, Rebecca?' suggested Nicholas abruptly.

'I'll stand for a while if you don't mind.' She grimaced, rubbing her posterior. 'At least I was able to travel by boat most of the way to Oxford from Greenwich instead of horseback.' She sipped her wine. 'Thinking of ships, I'm reminded of what Jane said about your moving to Bristol and that you mentioned the port in your recent journals.'

'What did he say about it?' asked Jane, showing interest.

Rebecca looked thoughtful. 'That it is situated on two rivers, one of which is the Avon. The very first English expedition to the Americas departed from there. Pip remembers the town well, having visited it in those early days when he left the family shipyard to join the strolling players,' said Rebecca. 'You described the house where you stayed and where it was situated.'

'Is that the house we are going to make our main home, Nicholas?' asked Jane.

He nodded absently.

'You also mention another house and went into some detail about the view of the ships and talked about the tides and the tidal bore in your journal. You described a terrifying incident when you were a lad. Pip deemed it so exciting that he put it in your new book.'

Jane stared at Nicholas. 'I would like to hear that tale and the description of the houses.'

'I have two copies of the latest book with me. Pip considered it doubtful that you would have seen the finished book yet, Nicholas.'

'He is mistaken,' said Nicholas, looking pleased, none the less. 'I have two copies from when I visited the shop in Oxford on my way here. I put them in one of my saddlebags and then—with all that happened—I completely forgot about them.'

Rebecca shrugged. 'No matter. You now have four copies.'

The books were recovered and soon Nicholas held one of them in his hand and was stroking the vellum cover. He looked at Jane and smiled. 'Perhaps you would like a copy for your very own, my dear?'

Jane's face lit up, but she hesitated before taking the book from him and turning it over between her hands. In an awed voice, she said, 'This is the first book I have ever possessed. Those Simon left were for the boys.'

'It is indeed a rare gift,' said Rebecca, smiling.

'And one to be cherished,' said Jane softly, gazing up at Nicholas with such warmth in her eyes that he could not doubt that he had indeed given her something precious. 'You have such a fine voice, I would love to hear you read to me and the children before you leave for Greenwich,' she murmured.

'If that is what you wish and I have the time,' he said easily, picking up the other book. 'I have some business I must see to before I leave. If I could do that first…'

'Whatever you wish,' replied Jane, flushing beneath his appraisal and hoping he had not guessed that she was a poor reader. She made a vow to improve before he returned from his visit to his brother's shipyard.

Nicholas turned to Rebecca. 'If you would excuse me, I will see you later.'

'Of course,' she said. 'You'll have arrangements to make before leaving in the morning.'

After he had gone, both women turned to the other. 'I wonder what this business is?' said Rebecca.

'I have no idea, but I noticed that he took one of the books with him,' said Jane.

'Perhaps he wishes to show it to someone,' mused Rebecca.

Jane agreed, thinking that the only person he knew who could read well was the priest. Perhaps he had gone to ask for his blessing on his journey. She was anxious and felt depressed at the thought of being parted from him.

In an attempt to shrug off her mood she said to Rebecca, 'You must come and see how Simon has grown and no doubt you will wish to see Nicholas's daughter, Matilda, then you must lie down upstairs to recuperate from your journey.'

Rebecca agreed and wasted no time in going over to the cradle and cooing over Simon. Then she turned her attention to Matilda.

When she did not immediately comment on the little girl's appearance, Jane blurted out, 'What do you think of her?'

'She is an extremely pretty baby,' murmured Rebecca. 'It must be difficult for you having her here.'

'Mmm!' Jane changed the subject. 'Did Pip tell you that Nicholas's attackers planned to abduct her and that her wet nurse, Berthe, came here later and took Simon by mistake?'

'No, really!' said Rebecca, her eyes widening. 'How did you get him back? Tell me all.'

Jane wasted no time doing so, but decided to omit the part about Rebecca's father having Louise's sister staying at his house and his going off with her. Instead she spoke of Berthe and the possibility of her mind being slightly unhinged after the loss of her husband and baby.

After commenting on how worried Jane must have been at the time, but glad that all had ended well, Rebecca excused herself, saying that she would go upstairs and rest now. It was on the tip of Jane's tongue to tell her about Nicholas having married Louise on her deathbed, but decided that she had given her guest enough to think about for now.

It was a couple of hours later, whilst the supper was simmering, that Rebecca came downstairs and joined Jane and the girls at the table. They chattered about that holiest of weeks in the Christian calendar as they twisted leaves and stems into the shape of crosses.

'I wish you could stay longer, Rebecca,' said Jane with a sigh.

Rebecca's fingers faltered and instead of weaving the length of greenery into a cross she brushed it across her cheek and said, 'So do I, but if I don't go to Oxford on the morrow I won't have Nicholas and Ned's company on the road.' She paused. 'Although I admit that I am tempted to visit Draymore Manor to see if my father is there. If he is, then he can keep me company when I return to Oxford. What do you say?'

Jane found herself hesitating, thinking of Madame Dupon. If Nicholas had been there she might have sought his advice, for she did not find it easy not being completely honest with her sister-in-law. Surely she had a right to know of her father's actions?

'What is it, Jane?' asked Rebecca, her eyes narrowing. 'You appear to be trying to make up your mind about something.'

Jane took a deep breath. 'It is about your father. I must be honest with you.'

Rebecca gasped. 'He has had an accident and you didn't like to tell me? Is that it?'

'No!' cried Jane. 'He is in good health as far as I know, so you must not worry about that.'

'Then what is it?' Rebecca stared at her with an anxious expression on her slender face. 'Tell me, Jane. It must be important if you have hesitated to mention it before but now decide to do so.'

So Jane told her the little she knew about Louise's sister and Anthony Mortimer's interest in her, saying that she had no idea what Nicholas had told Pip in his missive about her.

'Pip has spoken little to me of what was contained in the message. Most likely because he wishes to protect me from upset at the moment,' said Rebecca, fiddling with a fastening on her gown. 'It must have come as a surprise to you that Louise had a sister.' She frowned. 'I wonder what my father was thinking of when he took her to Draymore Manor? Is she as pretty as Louise was, I wonder?'

'She is pockmarked, so I am told. I wish I could meet her and then I would know how to judge her actions better,' said Jane, relieved that Rebecca had taken the news fairly calmly. She placed the crosses into the basket along with the remaining greenery and, getting to her feet, said, 'And now I will see how our supper fares.'

Rebecca accompanied her over to the fire and asked if there was aught she could do to help. 'No, but you could tell me some of the court gossip and pour us some ale,' said Jane.

Rebecca did as bade. 'What I tell you now is part of the reason why Pip has to remain at the court for the near future. Princess Mary is to be betrothed to Henry, Duke of Orleans, the son of the King of France. No doubt Nicholas knows of this?'

'If he does he has made no mention of it to me,' said Jane, taking a container of preserved sliced apples in honey and opening it. 'He's had much on his mind these last weeks.'

'It will soon be a secret no longer as envoys and noblemen and their wives are expected at court for the celebrations. Pip says that it's doubtful whether Queen Katherine and her nephew, the Holy Roman Emperor, will welcome the news of a peace treaty between France and England. Apparently Henry is still annoyed with him for breaking off his engagement to the Princess Mary and marrying a Portuguese princess without informing him.'

Rebecca paused to drink some of her ale and then added, 'Henry has been funding the Emperor in the war against France but there has been little in the way of a victory that would benefit England. No doubt Nicholas will know of this from his sojourner on the continent. And while we are discussing Nicholas and the royal family I must say that it could be a mistake, his growing a beard, due to that vague likeness of his to the King. At the moment Henry is growing a beard. Nicholas is bound to meet

His Grace at the shipyard and one never knows how he would react if he were to suspect the Hurst brothers have a blood tie to the throne of England,' she said seriously. 'Of course their father built ships for the old King, so maybe Henry already knows of the connection.'

Jane's grip on the spoon she clutched tightened. 'What are you saying? Nicholas denied any kinship to the King.'

'He would, because the brothers do not want it known. No doubt now the pair of you are to wed he will inform you of it.'

Jane dropped the spoon and took a pace away from Rebecca. 'But what if the King does know already and begins to believe the brothers are no longer loyal to the throne?'

Rebecca twirled a loose strand of hair around her little finger. 'I see I should not have spoken of this, but I'm certain you are worrying unnecessarily. Henry admires Nicholas and has read of his adventures.' She paused. 'Now, let's change the subject. I have other gossip that you might find interesting and I doubt Nicholas knows of it.' She did not wait for Jane to comment but continued, 'It is to do with the King's sister, Queen Margaret.'

'The one who married the last King of Scotland?'

'Aye. He was killed in a battle up north. Henry is vexed with her.'

'Why?' asked Jane, all ears.

'Apparently her second marriage to the Earl of Angus has been annulled on the grounds that when it took place he was pre-contracted to another lady.'

Jane gasped. 'What about their daughter? Has she been declared illegitimate?'

Rebecca shook her head. 'No, and that is what infuriates the King. Apparently because Queen Margaret entered the marriage in good faith the Pope has declared her daughter legitimate. You might ask why the King should be so against the Pope's decision.' She paused again to drink. 'I know what Pip thinks.'

'What?' asked Jane with bated breath.

Rebecca hesitated. 'You mustn't repeat it. At least only to Nicholas. Although no doubt the two brothers will discuss it when they meet.'

'Naturally, but tell me what Pip thinks?' asked Jane impatiently.

'The King is envious of her. He wants two things: one is a legitimate male heir, and he believes it highly unlikely that the Queen will provide him with one now. She is nine years older than him. The other is Anne Boleyn, with whom he is deeply infatuated.'

'It is very sad for the Queen,' said Jane.

'Aye, especially as Anne Boleyn is refusing to be his mistress. If the King could bed her Pip says he would rid himself of that itch. He believes she is holding out to be queen.'

Jane gasped. 'Really?'

Rebecca nodded. 'No doubt if Henry could find a legal way to annul his marriage, so that his daughter Mary remains legitimate, then he would do so in order to marry Anne.' She paused and frowned. 'Henry is a religious man and is struggling with his conscience. He needs the Pope's agreement and for that he has to make certain His Holiness does not fall into the hands of the Queen's nephew. Emperor Charles is fond of the Queen and would never permit the King to annul the marriage.'

'Is there any likelihood of the Holy Roman Emperor having the Pope in his power?' asked Jane, fascinated.

'Pip says Nicholas is the person who knows. He gained information about the Holy Roman Emperor's army whilst abroad. Henry doesn't really want a French king sitting on England's throne. Which might happen if the Emperor was able to get his way.'

Jane said slowly, 'A French king on England's throne would certainly not prove popular.'

Rebecca agreed. 'It is certainly not the future for the dynasty Henry imagined when he became king.' She yawned and stretched. 'Anyway, Mary is only ten years old, so even if the marriage takes place it is unlikely to be consummated for several years.'

Jane agreed, and found herself thinking of Nicholas's deathbed wedding. She felt a spurt of anger. Had he been completely honest with her about it? Should she mention it to Rebecca? She really would like to have another woman's opinion on the matter.

She glanced in her stepdaughters' direction. They were now darning hose a few yards away and she decided it was unlikely they would hear her from that distance. 'He married her, you know,' she said in a low voice.

Rebecca looked startled. 'Who married who?'

'When Louise knew she was dying she asked Nicholas to marry her. He agreed and sent for a priest. She wanted her sins absolved and for Nicholas to rear Matilda here in England.'

For several moments it was obvious to Jane that Rebecca was lost for words. Then she said slowly, 'I can see why Nicholas would do that, because of course it means that Matilda does not have the taint of illegitimacy attached to her name. She is legally his daughter in the eyes of the world.'

'That is what he said, but what if Louise had not died but recovered?' whispered Jane. 'That is a thought that comes back to me, despite him telling me that she wouldn't have recovered. Maybe deep down Nicholas hoped that she would survive; he was very much in love with her, you know.'

Rebecca shook her head. 'You should not allow such thoughts to get a hold on you, Jane. She is dead and you are alive. Would you have cared that such a wedding took place if it had been Simon standing in Nicholas's place? Answer me honestly.'

'No, but I did not love...' Jane's voice tailed off and she could only stare at Rebecca. At last she had to admit that she loved Nicholas, and probably had done so almost since she first set eyes on him—when despite his broken arm he had defended James from that savage dog.

Rebecca placed a hand on her shoulder. 'I believe he has long stopped loving Louise and that it was noble of him to do what he did by marrying her,' she said softly.

Noble! Jane supposed Rebecca could view Nicholas's actions in such a way, because there had been a time when she had hero-worshipped him. 'I feel that I will never match up to her beauty,' she whispered.

Rebecca shook her slightly. 'I am surprised

at you, Jane. You always used to say that inner beauty was more important than outer appearance. The trouble with you is that you don't yet feel secure enough in Nicholas's love. These are early days for you both. It was different for me and Pip; we had known each other from childhood.'

'You could be right, but Nicholas has never said he loves me,' murmured Jane with a hint of sadness. 'I've certainly never told him that I love him.'

'But he's asked you to marry him and you've agreed.'

'He wants a mother for his daughter.' Jane sighed. 'Simon was the same.'

Rebecca's eyes widened. 'You must be blind if you think it's solely for that reason Nicholas has asked you to marry him. Few men would be prepared to support a penniless widow and four children who aren't his without having strong feelings for her. Don't be a fool, Jane! Put Louise out of your mind, accept what Nicholas has to offer you and be joyful that you are to marry the man you love.'

Jane felt her heart lighten. 'You always were able to lift my spirits.'

'Then do what I say,' said Rebecca, giving her a hug. 'I'm only sorry I brought news that means him being taken away from you. Hopefully it won't be too long before his return.'

At that moment Simon began to cry, and the two women separated and Jane went to tend her son.

She was still thinking about what Rebecca had said a while later, when the door opened and Nicholas entered. Rebecca went over to him and slipped a hand through his arm. 'I have been admiring your daughter. She is beautiful.'

He smiled. 'So you were able to tell her and Simon apart?'

She darted him a reproachful look. 'As if I wouldn't recognise my handsome nephew now I have a beautiful niece.'

'I had not thought of her being your niece. I pray that her beauty will not be a fault in her,' said Nicholas quietly.

'It would be wrong of you to judge your daughter by her mother's deeds. Besides, I cannot believe any woman you fell in love with wouldn't have some saving grace,' said Rebecca.

A flush darkened Nicholas's cheekbones and he glanced at Jane before murmuring to Rebecca, 'You are saying that my judgement was not lacking after all? Jane would not agree with you.'

She nodded. 'It is true that Louise was not

honest with you about being betrothed to another, but perhaps that was because she saw all that was good and exciting in you. So she behaved rashly by living for the moment and no doubt hoping that her betrothed would not return.'

A muscle tightened in Nicholas's jaw. 'I appreciate your defence of her. She gave her life for Matilda and not one word of reproach did she speak to me on her deathbed. It is her sister who lays the blame for Louise's passing at my door.'

'That must have been difficult for you.'

He nodded. 'When Louise gave birth I could not help comparing the experience I had with Jane.' A faint smile lifted the corners of his mouth. 'She didn't care an iota about her appearance at the time, and when the birth was over and she held Simon in her arms I thought she looked beautiful—like a Madonna.'

'Jane considers herself lacking in beauty and that you're marrying her simply because you need a mother for Matilda,' said Rebecca.

He frowned. 'I have told her otherwise but I can see I must keep on telling her. She has the most beautiful eyes and the gentlest of touches.'

'Tell her that, too,' said Rebecca, smiling.

There came a knock on the door. 'If you will excuse me?' said Nicholas.

She nodded and exchanged a glance with Jane as he went to open the door. A priest stood there. 'I've come as you requested, Master Hurst,' he said.

Jane's astonished gaze flew to Nicholas's face, but before she could speak he asked the priest to excuse him and hurried over to her. 'You will understand my being away so long when I explain what I've been about, Jane,' he said. 'I'd appreciate it if you obeyed my wishes without question.'

With Rebecca's earlier words about Nicholas's reasons for marrying her playing in her head, Jane nodded. 'Tell me what they are and I will obey.'

His eyes softened. 'Will you, Jane? I am honoured that you are prepared to trust me so blindly.'

'I am certain you have my well-being and that of the children at heart.'

For a moment their eyes met and she felt an unexpected moment of pure happiness.

'The priest has agreed to marry us here in the house before I leave,' he said, taking her hand.

Her breath caught in her throat and she heard Rebecca gasp. Out of the corner of her eye she saw her stepdaughters' heads turn. How had he managed this? Why was he doing it? Could it be that he thought he might be killed? For a moment she was gripped by fear, and then she told herself to calm down. If a wedding was what he wished, then she would marry him.

'May I tidy my hair and change my gown first?' she asked, surprised at how calm her voice sounded.

He looked relieved, and she realised that he had not been as confident of her willingness as he appeared. 'Of course,' he said.

'I'll come with you,' said Rebecca hastily.

Jane nodded and hurried upstairs. She was followed not only by Rebecca but her step-daughters, too.

'Are you really going to marry Master Nicholas now?' asked Elizabeth, panting up the stairs.

'It is his wish, and a woman must obey her future husband,' said Jane brightly, opening the door of the bedchamber.

'But I thought the wedding would not take place for some time,' said Margaret, 'and that we would have new gowns.' She looked disappointed.

'You will have your new gowns, but not yet,' said Jane, flinging open the lid of the chest beneath the window and beginning to root amongst the garments there.

'But why now?' asked Margaret.

'Because Master Nicholas's brother has been hurt and he has to go to his shipyard at Greenwich and help him,' said Jane.

'Can't we go with him?' asked Margaret.

Jane shook her head. 'He must go soon, and there is no time to make arrangements for us now—'

Rebecca interrupted. 'You will wear a gown that is bright and gay?' She nudged her hip against Jane's so that she could also peer into the chest.

'You mean as is fitting for the occasion,' said Jane, dragging out a gown she had made from cloth bought at the autumn fair in Oxford eighteen months ago. She had scarcely worn it, because first she had become with child and then her husband had died. On the heels of that thought came the memory of her wedding to Simon Caldwell. All the strength seemed to drain from her and she fell back and put her face in her hands.

'What is it, Jane?' asked Rebecca, putting an arm around her.

Jane smothered a sob.

Rebecca looked at her nieces. 'Go and fetch a bowl of warm water, soap and a drying towel, girls. Your mother will need to wash.'

Elizabeth made to speak, but Rebecca said, 'At once!'

The girls left.

'Well, Jane, they've gone,' said Rebecca softly, stroking her back. 'There's just me and you here. Tell me, what's wrong?'

Jane lifted her gaze to Rebecca. 'I can't marry him!' she cried.

'You are not still thinking of Louise, are you?'

'No, but I am not the woman he believes me to be. I have not been honest with him in the way he has been with me. I carry the shame of something I did and I will be a disappointment to him. He believes I have such high standards that he will find it difficult to accept that I have not always behaved as I should.'

'I can't accept that you've done anything so bad that it wouldn't merit Nicholas's forgiveness,' said Rebecca firmly.

'You can't really know that,' said Jane, wiping away a tear with the back of her hand. 'I must speak to him before it is too late for him to change his mind.'

'You want me to fetch him?'

Jane nodded and, getting to her feet, went and sat on the bed.

Rebecca hesitated, as if waiting for her to reconsider.

'Go!' said Jane, her expression fixed.

Rebecca went.

No sooner had she gone than Jane rose to her feet and paced the floor, playing over in her head the words she would say to Nicholas. She did not have long to practise them, because it seemed only a few moments before he rapped his knuckles on the door before entering the room.

Jane stared at him and saw the tension in his face. She wished that she could rewrite the past. She ached with longing for him and wanted to be to him all that he believed her to be.

'What is it, Jane?' he asked quietly. 'Have you changed your mind and decided that it would be too dangerous being married to me after all?'

Instantly she realised that she did not have to speak of her shame, could agree with what he had just said, but a voice in her head told her that would only be compounding her shame.

She cleared her throat. 'No, I am prepared to take that risk.'

He looked relieved and surprised. 'Then what is it?'

She felt as if she could scarcely breathe and dropped her gaze. How could she speak of it and look him in the eye? 'There is something I must confess.'

Chapter Eleven

He hesitated. 'Is it to do with Willem Godar?'

She hung her head. 'Aye.'

'I thought we had already discussed your relationship with him?'

'There is more!' She added rapidly, 'He got me with child, but I never told him because by then he had returned to his wife.'

For a moment Nicholas could only stare at her, so stupefied that for a moment he could not think or speak.

'Say something,' she croaked. 'Say you understand why I had to do what I did next.'

He found his voice. 'You mean you married Simon Caldwell to conceal your shame?'

She nodded wordlessly, struggling to find the words to explain what had followed after she had told her brother Giles of her condition, but they stuck in her throat because Nicholas's expression was set in stone and appeared just as unyielding.

There was a silence that seemed to go on for ever. Nicholas's emotions were in turmoil. His uppermost feelings were of anger and painful disappointment. How could the Jane he so admired and in whom he had such faith have behaved so dishonestly? Why had she not told him of this much earlier? She could have done so when she had spoken of having had a girlish infatuation with Godar. Instead she had remained silent. *Why?* He told himself that he would have understood how such a thing could happen, because hadn't he got himself into an emotional mess where Louise was concerned? Maybe it was because she knew how he would feel about her having made a cuckold of Simon Caldwell by tricking him into marriage? He did not want to believe that she was as much of a deceiver as other women, but how could he not when she had just confessed to it? He really had convinced himself that Jane was different from other women, but it seemed that when she had spoken of being far from perfect she had meant it. He had just not been hearing what she was saying. She knew how hurt he had been when he had discovered Louise had been deceiving him—surely she must have thought about how he would react on learning that she, herself, was not above a bit of deception? He hated the thought, and it filled him with rage—because he had started to believe that he might have found real love with Jane. He had been so looking forward to sharing a new life with her, different from anything that he had experienced in the past. Suddenly he felt such a sense of loss.

Jane coughed, drawing his attention. 'I had no choice,' she said unsteadily. 'A man can have no idea what it is like for a woman to find herself in such a position.'

Nicholas saw the misery in her lovely brown eyes and despite the emotions that gripped him found himself picturing that young girl who had loved unwisely, just as he had done in the past. Finding herself with child, and unable to turn to its father for help, she had taken the only way she'd thought open to her. Still, she had lost her virginity to Godar. He tried to convince himself that she had been a victim of Godar's lust, whatever the weaver might have said to the contrary. Yet an insidious voice in his head was saying that she had been willing and as much as a fool for love as he had been himself.

Her voice broke into his thoughts again. 'My brother insisted that I marry Simon and he made all the arrangements,' said Jane. 'I did not want to marry him—not as I want to marry you.' Tears trickled down her cheeks. 'I used to dream of you holding me in your arms when Rebecca read of your adventures. I believed you to be different from other men I had met.'

'Stop it. I don't want to hear you saying such things.' Nicholas's voice was raw. 'Besides, there is no need to lie. I will still marry you.'

Jane was stunned. 'No!'

For a moment he was taken aback by her refusal. 'You can't mean that?'

'I certainly do. How can I marry a man who does not believe me when I speak the truth?'

His eyes glinted. 'You will do as I say. You must marry, and both those men who would have taken you for wife are no longer in the reckoning.'

She flinched. 'I will manage somehow to support myself and the children.'

'How? Besides, they will be disappointed if we do not marry. You have just confessed it is what you want, and I do believe you when you say that.'

Jane stared at him, nonplussed. 'I see what it is and I do not want your pity!' she cried.

'It is not pity I am feeling. I will not have you making a fool of me, Jane.' His voice hardened. 'It is too late to back out now. All is arranged and the wedding will go ahead. I will send Rebecca back to you and expect you downstairs within the hour.'

Jane could only stare at him blankly from tear-filled eyes. She saw some unfathomable emotion flash across his face. Then he was gone. She sank onto the bed, scarcely able to believe that what she had dreaded had been dealt with. But the anguish that had tormented her was not over. She had proved a deep disappointment to him, and he was only marrying her because he didn't want to look a fool.

There came a sound at the door and she turned her head and saw Rebecca standing there with a bowl and a pitcher of steaming water. Over her arm hung a drying cloth.

'Do you want me to help you undress?' she asked.

Jane realised she was going to have to play the part of happy bride-to-be. She could not cope with trying to explain to Rebecca what had passed between her and Nicholas and so she forced a smile. 'If you would.'

'You are feeling better now you've rid yourself of whatever was on your conscience?' asked Rebecca, smiling.

Briefly a shadow darkened Jane's eyes. 'Aye, but if you don't mind I do not wish to talk about it now.' *If ever*, she added to herself.

'If that is what you want,' said Rebecca, placing the bowl on the chest and removing the soap and cloth before pouring in the warm water. 'Besides, your future husband is waiting.' She turned away. 'Now, where is the gown you chose?'

Jane indicated the one she had placed on the bed. The gown was of Lincoln green and made of fine linen, the bodice embroidered with yellow thread in a pattern of flowers and leaves.

As Rebecca helped Jane off with the grey gown she was wearing she murmured, 'He is making sure of you by marrying you now. It is just a pity that you must part so soon.'

'I know,' said Jane with a sigh, thinking that no doubt he was relieved to be parting from her on the morrow.

She made her toilette, forcing herself to hum a country air cheerfully. When that was done, with Rebecca's help she dragged the skirts of the other gown over her hips, smoothing them down as best she could for they were a mite crumpled.

'I understand now why you insisted on travelling with Pip wherever he went. Parting from Nicholas is going to be painful. I don't know how I will bear being separated from him,' she said, playing her part.

'I could have the children stay with me for

a while in Oxford, so that you and Nicholas can spend a sennight or more getting to know each other better without them around,' said Rebecca. 'I will have Tabitha and Dorothea to help with the babies, so it is not impossible.'

Jane's heart sank. She believed it was the last thing that Nicholas would want. Then she remembered that Rebecca had spoken of visiting Draymore Manor and knew that she could not leave her to go there without her. 'Maybe in a few days' time we could do that?' she suggested. 'It would be too much of a rush to arrange everything so soon.' She shoved back a hank of soft brown hair that had come loose from its pins. 'Now, if you'll help me tidy my hair?'

Rebecca did so. It was only as they were about to leave the bedchamber that Jane thought to remove her wedding ring. She placed it on the chest and went downstairs, where they found the priest and Nicholas, apparently discussing his latest book.

The two men broke off their conversation and Nicholas strode over to Jane. 'You look… different.' He thought how he had only ever seen her heavily with child, giving birth, or in mourning garb. He felt a flood of emotion that he did not want to put a name to in the light of what had taken place earlier.

'Fine feathers make fine birds,' she said nervously.

'Quite,' he said, hesitating before offering her his arm.

She placed her hand on his sleeve. She would have liked to say how well he looked, but the words would not come. He led her to the table over by the window, where the setting sun flooded in. It was the place that he and the priest had decided on for them to exchange their marriage vows. The girls and Rebecca came and stood nearby and James, who appeared only just to have noticed what was happening, scrambled up from the floor, where he had been playing with a simple wooden toy boat that Nicholas had brought him, and rushed across to them.

He tugged on Margaret's skirt. 'What is happening?'

'Mama and Master Nicholas are getting married,' she whispered. 'Now, hush!'

As Jane repeated her wedding vows she felt as if it was someone else saying them on the old Jane's behalf. No doubt it was foolish to think such thoughts, because she was the same person she had always been, and yet she did feel different as Nicholas placed a shiny new ring on her finger in the name of the Father, the Son and the Holy Ghost. She was amazed at how much he had managed to achieve during the time he had been absent from the house earlier.

But there was to be more, for when the ceremony was over he surprised her further with his forethought by producing two short documents that had apparently been drawn up scarcely three hours ago. For a moment she thought he might suggest that she read them and her heart sank, for although she had been taught her alphabet, and to be able to read what was necessary to organise a household and cook, she was certain that reading such documents would be beyond her. Fortunately Nicholas explained that one of the documents was a marriage agreement in which he had settled a sum of money on her and the other was his will, which stated that he had left half of what he owned to Jane, her sons and stepdaughters and the other half to Matilda.

It was more than she had expected. She wanted to tell him that she did not want his money, that she loved him, but she knew that he would find her words an embarrassment in the circumstances and no doubt would not believe her. It did prove to her, though, that he considered his life was still at risk by his rushing into taking such steps. As she watched the priest and Rebecca witness his signature Jane thought how she would exchange all that he was prepared to give her to keep him alive. He handed the documents to the priest for safe-keeping and surprised Jane afresh by telling her that he had reserved a bedchamber for them at the inn that night.

'That is if you are willing to take responsibility for the children, Rebecca?' he said, cocking an eyebrow in her direction.

She smiled. 'How can I refuse?'

Nicholas thanked her, and then he saw the priest out, after expressing his gratitude and having him paid for his services.

After that they ate the meal Jane had prepared, although her appetite seemed to have quite deserted her. She felt like an athlete, waiting for the signal to run the race and win through to the finishing line, and drank a little more than she would have done normally.

When Nicholas murmured in her ear, 'It's time for us to go, Jane,' she almost jumped out of her skin.

'I—I'll just get my coat,' she stammered.

Rebecca followed Jane, lifting the garment from its hook and helping her on with it. 'Now, you are not to worry about the children. Enjoy your wedding night, love,' she said, giving her a hug.

Jane nodded, aware that the fluttering beneath her ribs had increased. 'Nicholas took a lot for granted by reserving a room at the inn, don't you think?' she said in a low voice.

'No doubt if you had turned him down he would have slept there alone,' said Rebecca, 'but it would obviously not have been what he wanted. If you still prefer to believe he wants you purely as a mother for his daughter I consider you mistaken. Take it as a compliment if that *is* part of his reason for wanting you as his wife. Not all women make good mothers.'

Jane took a shaky breath. 'That is not the same as saying that he loves me. Still, I should be grateful, for I do believe he is that which you have said—an honourable man.'

Rebecca smiled. 'Pip is going to be vexed when he discovers he has missed your wedding, but he will be delighted, none the less, that you and Nicholas are husband and wife.'

'I also regret that he could not be at our wedding,' said Jane gravely, 'but I am determined that if all goes well then we will have a feast to celebrate later in the year.'

At that moment Nicholas approached, and Jane repeated that she would like them to mark their wedding with a feast in the summer.

He gave a barely perceptible nod. 'If that is what you wish, but I consider it unnecessary. Now, we must go. We wish you a good night, Rebecca.'

Only when they were outside did Jane glance over her shoulder and say, 'I didn't say goodnight to the children!'

She would have rectified her forgetfulness if Nicholas had not prevented her.

'Let's not worry about them now,' he said firmly. 'This is one occasion when they cannot join us.'

Jane glanced up at him and thought, *How stern he looks!* As they walked along the High Street to the inn, she said, 'I did not expect our wedding night to be like this.'

'Nor I,' said Nicholas, increasing his pace so that she had to run to keep up with him. 'I would have preferred to be heading for Bristol.'

'I would have liked that, too,' said Jane, slightly breathlessly. 'Just the two of us.'

His eyes blazed as he gazed down at her and came to a halt. 'Would you, Jane?'

'Of course! Do you ever wish…?'

'What?'

'That one could rewrite the past? I have so many regrets, and yet I am more fortunate this day than the bride I was when I married Simon Caldwell. I wish that you and I had met earlier. I remember you saying that not so long ago.'

'Aye, but what is the use of regrets? We can't alter what has happened and so we must make the best of what there is,' he said harshly, beginning to walk again, slower this time.

They reached the inn and he opened the door and ushered her inside. A maid lit the way as she showed them up to their bedchamber, and left the candlestand with them.

Jane removed her coat and gazed around at the plainly furnished room, with its whitewashed walls on which candlelight cast dancing shadows, thinking of the times she had walked past this building. She had never spent a night within its walls. She glanced at the bed and suddenly was filled with trepidation. What if she proved to be a further disappointment to him between the sheets?

Nicholas's eyes followed Jane's and he determined to block out all that she had told him earlier. He removed his coat and tossed it on a stool, and then turned to her. She seemed unaware of his regard as she gazed at the bed. He wondered if she was thinking of Willem Godar or the wedding night she had spent with her first husband. It suddenly hit him like a blow that Godar might have brought her here to seduce her—after all they had fallen in love at the Witney Fair.

'Do you know, Nicholas, I have never been in this inn before,' she said in a low voice.

He barely caught the words but they were

enough to send relief washing through him. 'Have you not?' he said.

'No.' She smiled at him, sensing his mood had lightened. 'No doubt you have slept in many an inn on your travels?'

'I've spent more nights aboard ship,' he answered with a wry smile. 'Admittedly they were not the most relaxing.'

'You should put decent sleeping quarters into your ship's plan,' she said boldly. 'After all I might wish to sail in your galleon with you.'

'You surprise me. I had received the impression that the sea frightened you.'

'Aren't most people frightened of the unknown?' said Jane, turning her back on him. 'Except a brave explorer like yourself. I never did doubt the adventures you described actually happened, you know. I believe in you.'

He was touched despite the doubts that plagued him.

'Jane!'

He spoke her name softly and instantly she turned and looked at him. Even in the candlelight he could make out every contour of her body and the blush on her cheeks. Yet he reminded himself that she was no virginal maiden, even if in that moment she appeared so. He imagined how she must have looked to Godar, and of their own volition his hands curled into fists. Then she took a step towards him and he reached out to her.

Whilst Nicholas's fingers busied themselves undoing the ties on her gown he lowered his head and kissed her. The garment's design told him that she had cast aside her widowhood and mourning and taken on the role of wife. *His wife!* The gown slid to the floor and he lifted his mouth from hers. His lips grazed the smooth white skin of her neck and descended in a wavering line to the curve of her breast. He felt her tremble as he tugged the bow of ribbon that was threaded through the neck of her chemise. His hand stilled, but she reached up and pulled on the other end of the ribbon so that it unravelled. He remembered what she had said about dreaming of being in his arms. The garment slunk downwards to form a puddle about her bare ankles. He gazed at her nakedness and desire flared inside him.

Instinctively Jane crossed her arms across her breasts and then, realising she was exposing her sex, she dropped an arm to cover that part of her. Only when she had done so did she realise how foolish she was being.

'Surely you're not shy of me, Jane?' he said, his voice deepening with emotion. 'Isn't this what you wanted?'

Of *course* she was not shy or scared of him!

She tilted her chin and placed her hands on her hips provocatively. 'Aye, to be scared or shy of you would be foolish, but to be honest I have never been completely bare with a man before.'

'Never? God's blood!' Her words pleased him and he slid his hands down over her shoulders to the rosy peaks of her breasts. He caressed first one and then the other with his tongue and his lips.

She gasped, for the sensations aroused such pleasure within her, sending a tingling heat to the core of her being. She felt as if she had come alive in ways that she had never experienced before, and was dismayed when he suddenly stopped.

'Are you certain this is what you want, Jane?' he asked, lifting his head.

'Aye,' she breathed. 'It's just that I've never experienced such pleasure before.'

'Never?'

'No, never.'

Was she being honest with him? Nicholas did not say aloud what he was thinking, but when next a shiver went through her somehow he managed to swing her up into his arms. He wanted to believe her because he wanted to pleasure her.

'What are you doing?' she cried.

'Carrying you!'

'You shouldn't,' she protested.

He ignored her, so she placed her arms about his neck to take some of the weight from his wounded shoulder. She marvelled at the profile that was only an inch or so from hers. She surrendered to the temptation to press kiss after kiss on the side of his face as he carried her over to the bed. She wanted to tell him that she loved him—only he dropped her when they reached the bed and fell on top of her. She could not help laughing, despite having the breath knocked out of her.

'I don't know why you're laughing,' he said ruefully, managing to get up from her. He eased his shoulder. 'I'd rather not be further handicapped this night.'

The hint of humour in his voice caused her to be honest with him. 'It's not what I want either. Can I help you? After all it wouldn't be the first time I've half undressed you.'

He remembered how she had tended his wounds and the gentleness of her touch. 'I'm glad you asked—except this time I expect you to complete your task,' he drawled.

The breath caught in her throat and for a moment she made no move to do what he asked, feeling all of a tremble. Then she took a deep breath, knelt on the bed and began to remove his shirt, keeping her eyes firmly fixed on his chest. What was it about that spread of skin, muscle and bone that was so attractive to her? She wanted to touch the sweep of hair that tempted her eyes lower and lower to that which lurked beneath his hose.

So what is stopping you? asked a voice in her head. *This man is now your husband and there is nothing to prevent the pair of you from making abandoned, passionate love. You must not hold back, nor be apprehensive of his taking you in a rush and hurting you.*

She felt him tremble as slowly she palmed down his hose until his strong lean hips were exposed and then his manhood. She had never seen aught quite like it, and her hand wavered before touching it lightly.

Almost instantly he covered her hand with his and said, 'Much as that pleasures me, best not.' He removed her hand and drew her down on the bed beside him, gazing into her shadowy features as he wrapped a strand of silken brown hair that had come loose around his hand.

Then he proceeded to remove the pins from her hair as he planted kisses on her face, gently at first, before his lips brushed hers in a sensual foretaste of passion.

She responded eagerly with a deepening, greedy hunger, taking her lead from him when the tip of his tongue weaved a crazy dance with hers, rousing within her an exciting spiral of pleasure that was taking her up and up. Their bodies brushed tantalisingly; the movement grew faster and faster, creating even more heat inside her and a growing urgency.

He removed his mouth from hers and took to kissing parts of her that might have caused her embarrassment if he had not chosen this moment when she was on a cusp of delicious delight. Then it was as if they were riding a tempest which resulted in an explosion of sensation that was wonderful beyond her belief. She clung to him, never wanting to let him go, but he tore himself away from her and lay panting beside her. She descended from the heights to the depths, aware of the lack inside her, knowing he had not spent his seed there. Could it be that he did not want her to be mother to any child he would father?

She reached out a hand to him, only to have him roll away from her and get up from the bed. She longed to ask him to forgive whatever fault he saw in her, but somehow she could not find the words. It was true they had made love with a passion that she had only ever dreamt about, but she was also aware that during that time neither of them had spoken one word of affection. So he could not love her—but despite that lack her body felt utterly relaxed. Every part of her appeared to have been wondrously touched by his possession of her.

She waited for him to return to bed, and he did so after blowing out the candle. If he had made a move towards her then she would have turned and melted in his arms. As it was he turned his back on her, and soon she could hear his steady breathing. She freed a sigh, thinking that perhaps he was not so different in that way from her first husband. So she buried her disappointment, composed herself, and gradually drifted into sleep.

She was disturbed by the sound of someone moving about the room. Instantly awake, she could see light penetrating the gap between the shutters. There was no need for her to reach out and touch the pillow next to hers to check that Nicholas was up and about. It could only be her husband getting dressed, ready to return to the house in preparation for the journey to his brother's shipyard. She felt miserable as she slid from beneath the bedcovers and searched for her chemise in the dim light. It was cold in the bedchamber that early April morning.

'Weren't you going to wake me?' she asked, placing her hand on the garment and dragging it on.

Nicholas turned to face her. 'I would not

have departed without taking my leave of you, Jane.'

'I wish you didn't have to go, or that I could go with you,' she said.

'Do you?' he asked, his voice hoarse.

'Haven't I just said so?' She took his hand and lifted it to her mouth, kissed each finger. 'Rebecca suggested in a few days' time I could take the children to her in Oxford and she would look after them with Tabitha's and Dorothea's help. It would mean I could spend a sennight or so with you at Greenwich.'

'Did she, indeed?' He withdrew his hand. 'I am not certain that is a good idea.'

'Why?' She wished she could see his expression clearly. 'Would I be in the way?'

'I would be occupied in the shipyard and have little time to give you.'

'Of course!' She could understand his reasoning, but persisted. 'I thought it would give me an opportunity to see the working of a shipyard at close quarters.'

'A shipyard is a dangerous place for the unwary,' he said, thinking also of his enemies and the shipyard having been broken in to. He did not want to be distracted when he needed to be on his guard. After last night he knew without doubt she would prove a distraction.

'No more dangerous than a building site,'

she retorted, reaching up and brushing her lips against his before resting her head against his chest. 'One cannot escape danger. A person can tumble downstairs at home. We can only do the best we can to guard against it. I have wondered about the safety of the children when we move to Bristol.'

'I suppose you are thinking of your sons and James in particular,' he said, moving away from her and going over to the window. It had suddenly struck him like a blow that James must be Godar's son.

She frowned. 'You sound as if I am wrong to do so. I do know that boys are adventuresome, but they can be taught to watch their step and avoid taking risks. You and your brothers grew up in a shipyard environment, so you are aware of that.'

'I'm sure you think James will find the shipyard interesting and could enjoy working there,' said Nicholas, forcing the words out.

Jane thought his voice sounded odd and remembered how his father had wanted James to follow in his footsteps and be a stonemason.

'What would your brother Christopher and his wife think if I were to arrive with the children in tow?' she asked lightly.

Nicholas, who had sat on the bed to pull on

his boots, slanted her a startled look. 'They're safer here.'

'You really believe that?'

'Aye!' he exclaimed emphatically. 'How is it that you now seem set on having the children with you? Earlier you appeared to want us to spend time together, just the two of us. You do realise that even though I have become better acquainted with the children since my return to England it will take some time for me to adapt to a completely different way of life? I know you will be doing the same once we move to Bristol, but it is possible that you will find it easier than I.'

She appreciated his honesty but was worried afresh by his words. What if he could not cope with family life and remaining in one place for months on end? She realised that she had stopped worrying about his life being cut short and instead was more concerned about their having a future together despite his not loving her. She was frightened she would not be able to hold him, but she knew she must fight to do so—for all their sakes.

'I am sure that if we are both prepared to pull together then we will manage,' she said stoutly. 'I do not expect it to be easy for either of us. As long as when difficulties arise we are honest with each other and discuss what is bothering us.'

Nicholas nodded, knowing what she said made sense, but he was filled with a sense of foreboding. Would they ever find it easy to be completely honest with each other? He finished dressing and then, telling Jane he was going to fetch his horse from the stable and that she was not to wait for him but to return to the house, he left the room.

Jane would have liked to have spoken with Tabitha, but as there was no sign of her when she came downstairs, and neither was there anyone around to ask her whereabouts, she went home.

It was Margaret who opened the door to her, and no sooner had she stepped foot in the house than her stepdaughter asked, 'Are we to call Master Nicholas *Papa* now, Mama?'

'Of course,' she said without hesitation, hanging up her coat. 'He will be joining us soon.' She glanced about her. 'Where is your Aunt Rebecca?'

'Upstairs. She has decided to stay a bit longer. Elizabeth and James are with her, and so are Tabitha and Edward,' said the girl happily.

Jane smiled and went over to the cradle, and was surprised to see both Simon and Matilda there. They were sleeping contentedly. Jane kissed Simon's cheek lightly, knowing that if she had agreed to Rebecca's plan to join Nicholas at Greenwich she would have found it difficult leaving her baby.

She set about preparing breakfast, and was in the middle of doing so when Rebecca, Tabitha and the children came downstairs.

'Good morning, Jane. Is all well with you?' asked Rebecca, her eyes twinkling.

Jane could feel her colour rising and nodded. 'I am glad you and Tabitha are staying,' she said swiftly. 'We must decide what day to visit Draymore Manor. We could take the children and gather wild herbs on the way. Maybe we could also pack some food and eat in the fresh air. It will do us all good.'

Rebecca agreed. Jane poured ale for them all and they sat down. The three women discussed Rebecca's pregnancy and then Jane asked how the builders had progressed with the house and the theatre that was being erected in Oxford where Pip and his players hoped to put on new plays for the students of the colleges. Halfway through their conversation Nicholas and Ned entered.

Soon the travellers were gathering their baggage together and were being escorted from the house. Ned took his farewell of Tabitha and his son before mounting his horse, whilst Nicholas kissed Rebecca goodbye and listened to the messages she wanted him to give to Pip. Then he prepared to take his farewell of those who were his family now. He did so reluctantly, because there were questions he felt he should have asked Jane about her first marriage. But it was too late now. He kissed the girls and hated himself for hesitating before ruffling James's hair and kissing him. Would he ever feel the same about him whilst he kept thinking about his being Godar's son? He felt a spurt of anger towards the weaver and found himself wishing that Jane had kept her secret.

Standing on tiptoe, the boy hugged him tightly about the waist. 'I wish you weren't leaving,' he said in a muffled voice. 'I wish I could go with you and have adventures.'

'You will one day,' said Elizabeth, attempting to pull him away from Nicholas. 'When we go to Bristol. Isn't that so, Papa?'

Nicholas felt a tremor go through him. It was the first time one of the girls had addressed him as such. He found himself agreeing that one day he and James *would* have an adventure. Then he turned to Jane, who had taken Matilda and Simon from the cradle and held them in the crook of each arm. He kissed Simon on the forehead before taking his daughter in his embrace. He held Matilda close before kissing her soft cheek and handing her back to Jane with a lump in his throat.

Husband and wife gazed at each other, both wishing matters between them could be different. For who was to say this might not be the last time they saw each other? Jane reached up and kissed him. He returned her kiss and pressed some coins into her hand, and with a final word of farewell he climbed into the saddle and rode off in Ned's wake without looking back.

Chapter Twelve

The rest of Palm Sunday passed in a blur of activity. The whole household attended church for the special celebration marking Jesus's triumphant entry into Jerusalem, being welcomed by the crowds waving palms and hailing Him as King and Messiah. It seemed strange to Jane not having Nicholas there.

That evening Rebecca read to them from his new book the tale of his boyish adventure. It held the children breathless with excitement and fear. Thankfully all ended satisfactorily, and they went to bed talking about what had happened and ready to pass a peaceful night.

Unlike Jane, whose sleep was disturbed by a nightmare that resulted in her waking up, drenched in perspiration, as she relived the horror of a youthful Nicholas caught up in the bore wave that swept in from the Severn estuary during the high spring tide.

The terror eased, but she wondered if the dream meant she was to lose him. She told herself not to be so foolish and by morning was prepared to face the day ahead. She rose and washed her face and hands before dressing and going downstairs to prepare breakfast. The rain was falling steadily, so Rebecca decided that perhaps she would wait until the weather improved before making the journey to Draymore Manor.

It was to be Wednesday before the sun came out. As Jane prepared food and drink to take with them she thought how, within the short space of time since Nicholas's departure, her routine had changed completely. Oddly, despite there being three more women in the house and an extra child, there was a much more relaxed atmosphere to the place. Perhaps that was because Jane no longer had to wait on Anna's coming but could leave the complete care of the babies to Tabitha and Dorothea if she so wished. Neither did she have to chide Nicholas about overtaxing his strength, although she was deeply worried about him. Part of her wished that she could have gone with him to Greenwich. Somehow she felt that by being with him she could ensure that he didn't do anything reckless and put his life in further danger.

She also worried about his feelings for her, and over and over had relived their wedding night. Surely he must feel some kind of affection for her for the experience to be so wonderful, and yet he had looked so stony-faced when she had told him about being with child when she had wed Simon. Hopefully with time he would accept her for who she was and not the person he had imagined her to be. She longed for the day when they could go to Bristol and start their new life together, choosing to forget the concern she still felt about his being able to settle down to family life in one place.

'So, are we going to walk to Draymore Manor later this morning?' asked Rebecca briskly as she sat on the bench the other side of the table from Jane.

'I thought that was what we'd decided if the sun were to shine,' said Jane, smiling across at her. 'How are you feeling this morning? You look to be blooming.'

'In my person I am extremely well,' answered Rebecca, reaching for the loaf and a knife. 'In my heart I yearn for Pip. I just pray that he will not get into mischief in my absence. You know what these Hurst brothers are like.'

'Most likely we are foolish to worry,' said Jane, offering a slice of smoked fish.

'Even so I do, and no doubt they are worrying about us, too,' said Rebecca thoughtfully. 'I admit to feeling restless, and suggest that we do not wait too long before setting out for our walk but leave as soon as the daily tasks are done and the children are ready.'

Jane nodded. 'I know exactly how you feel.'

'Good,' said Rebecca, smiling. 'I also suggest that we leave the babies here with Dorothea and Tabitha. I am sure they will not mind missing out on a walk. We will reach Draymore Manor the quicker without them.'

So it was settled, and within the hour Jane, Rebecca and the three children set out to walk to Draymore Manor. Both women were wondering what they would find when they arrived there.

Whilst James ran on ahead, Jane tried to answer Elizabeth's questions about what it might be like living near the sea. 'Do you think Papa Nicholas will want us to go aboard ship and sail along the coast?' she asked.

'Would you like to do that?' asked Jane, undecided as to whether she would enjoy the experience herself. This despite her having suggested doing so to her husband at the Blue Boar Inn. She had heard enough tales of Nicholas's adventures at sea to be in two minds about sailing on the sea.

'I would like it if I could be sure that the ship would not sink or that if I fell overboard he would come to my rescue,' said Elizabeth.

They had reached a stream by the side of which grew wild mint. The girls would have gathered some there and then if Jane had not told them to leave off doing so until their return.

'I will read to you again this evening,' said Rebecca, who had bent and picked a sprig of the wild mint and was squeezing one of its fragrant leaves between her fingers. 'I will read to you of his struggle with a monster.'

'What kind of a monster? You are a tease, Aunt Rebecca,' said Margaret.

'Indeed she is,' said Jane, smiling, and changed the subject. She began to talk instead about purchasing some fabric at the weekly market and making herself and her two stepdaughters new gowns.

'I wish Papa Nicholas had not had to go away,' Margaret sighed. 'After his being attacked on the way to visit us, I worry in case it happens again and he doesn't come back.'

'Of course he'll come back,' said Rebecca firmly. 'Of what use is it to imagine the worst? What colour gown would you like? You will not want to continue to wear drab colours. I'm sure if your father, Master Caldwell, were alive, he would understand you wanting to wear green or blue or even yellow.'

'I think you'd suit blue, Mama. I wish I could wear scarlet,' said Elizabeth, skipping through the grass. 'But only noble families can wear such a lovely colour. D'you think we can have new shoes as well?'

'Aye, why not?' said Jane, glancing about her for a sign of James.

'I do hope we'll be able to make new friends when we go to Bristol,' called Margaret, bending and picking up some dandelions. 'It makes me feel sad to think I will lose those I have made in Witney.'

'It is always good to have new playmates. Besides, you'll have Elizabeth. Now, where has James gone?' asked Jane anxiously.

'He'll be hiding,' said Elizabeth confidently, and ran on ahead.

Jane followed her but had not gone far when she heard a shriek. Her heart seemed to turn over and she began to run. A few moments later James came crashing through the undergrowth as if all the hounds of hell were after him. He threw himself at his mother.

Her arms went round him. 'What is it, son? Have you seen a boar?'

He shook his head vigorously. 'I was going to hide and jump out and frighten you but I found a shoe and there's a foot in it.'

'Just a shoe and a foot?' asked Elizabeth, crinkling her nose.

He shook his head. 'Don't be silly. There's a leg, too. But it isn't moving.'

'Show me,' said Rebecca, having come to an abrupt halt. She exchanged looks with Jane, who was stroking James's hair with a hand that shook.

'No!' exclaimed Jane. 'Not you. I will go. I suggest that you walk on with Elizabeth and Margaret to Draymore Manor. Even if your father is not there it is likely that the builders are still at work, renovating part of the house.'

Rebecca hesitated, then nodded, and held out both hands to her nieces. 'Come, girls, let's see how quickly we can get there.'

They did not argue but went with her.

James seized a handful of his mother's gown and pulled, but he was too close and she almost fell over him. She grabbed his wrist and ordered him to show her what he had found. He wasted no time in doing so, and as they went along the footpath Jane could not help worrying that the foot in the shoe might belong to Anthony Mortimer.

At last James came to a halt and pointed at

a scraped furrow that ran several yards along the ground. 'There!' he said.

Jane told him to stay back and walked forward until she could clearly see a shoe peeping out from beneath the undergrowth. It certainly seemed to be attached to a leg, and around the ankle was a curl of shooting bramble. She crouched down and tore at the brambles and nettles with her gloved hands.

The man was lying face-downwards. It appeared to her that he must have tripped over the bramble and fallen at first. She recognised that the garments he wore were in the Spanish style, so he was certainly not Rebecca's father, thank the Saints. She took a deep breath and pushed until he rolled over and she could see the face. She baulked.

'Is he dead?' asked James, touching her on the back.

Jane did not answer but whirled round and, seizing his hand, dragged him away. More than ever she wished that Nicholas had never left for Greenwich but was here by her side.

'So you've come,' said Christopher Hurst, who was fair-haired and blue-eyed and as unlike Nicholas in appearance as he was by nature. He shifted himself round on the daybed with a great deal of groaning and muttering until he could look him straight in the face.

'I thought that was what you wanted,' said Nicholas in clipped tones, pulling up a stool and sitting down.

'God's blood! Of course it's damned well what I wanted, but that's not to say I believed you would do what I asked after the disagreement we had. I even considered that maybe the news that masked men had forced their way into the yard and attacked me, as well as damaging one of the King's ships, might have strengthened your resolve to stay away from here for good. Especially as Pip told me that you were attacked on the way to visit that widow Jane Caldwell.'

Nicholas's mouth tightened. 'Are you suggesting that I might have been too scared to come back here?'

'It had occurred to me, and I'm not saying that I would have blamed you if you had felt like that,' said Christopher testily. 'You're lucky to be still alive and I hope you stay that way. Pip says you suspect the men who attacked you could have been Spanish. What's important is that the ones here haven't been back. It could be that they've been frightened off because the King is aware of their intrusion and has set a couple of guards to keep an eye on the shipyard.' He sighed gustily. 'My main concern now is that the damage to His Grace's ship is made good and the ship completed as soon as possible, so I'm grateful you've answered my summons. I presume you'll stay while I have need of you?'

Nicholas folded his arms across his broad chest. He had not been able to stop thinking about Jane, and it had occurred to him that he had been mistaken in wishing that she had kept her secret. He had realised it said much about her nature that was good that she would not marry him without being completely honest with him about her past.

'I'll stay as long as I can. I have a wife and children of my own to consider now.'

Christopher's mouth fell open and he appeared to be having some trouble speaking. Nicholas reached for the cup of ale on a small table at the side of the daybed and handed it to him. His brother gulped a few mouthfuls and then put the cup down. 'Am I to believe that you've married that widow and taken on those four children in her charge? You must have lost your wits. No doubt it's all those clouts on the head you've suffered over the years.'

Nicholas glowered at him. 'You surprise me, Chris. For the last few years, whenever we've seen each other, you've been on at me to find myself a wife. You should be glad that I've heeded your advice at last and done something about it.'

'A pretty young virgin with a decent dowry is what I had in mind after all the years you've spent travelling,' groaned Christopher. 'I don't doubt you could have had your pick of several well-born maidens at Henry's court with your reputation and fortune. Pip tells me you're greatly admired—even more so since your second book has gone into print. Which reminds me—he told me you expressed admiration for Bristol shipbuilders and mariners between its pages. I tell you, that didn't go down well with me.'

'I didn't write it to please you, and besides, it was up to Pip to decide what to put in and what to leave out,' said Nicholas, his eyebrows hooding his eyes. 'Anyway, you should know by now the King's court holds no attraction for me. If I'm able to then I will avoid it like the plague.'

Christopher swore. 'Why didn't you send for her and the brats when you were here if you had decided to wed her? You could have married in Greenwich and then the yard mightn't have been broken into and the King's ship damaged. I'm sure His Grace would have given you a handsome present. As he no doubt will do when you make his ship right and tight for the celebrations in honour of Princess Mary's betrothal. Now, that's what I call a celebration!'

Nicholas scowled. 'I hope to be away from here by then. How badly damaged is the ship?'

'If you help me up and lend me your shoulder then I'll show you,' said Christopher.

'The use of my shoulder is out of the question if you expect me to start work on the ship as soon as possible.'

Christopher pursed his lips. 'Then pass my crutch from under the bed and I'll show you the ship.'

'What of Pip? Isn't he supposed to be returning to Oxford now I'm here?' said Nicholas, complying with his brother's request.

'I doubt he'll be free to do so. The King has had a huge banqueting and disguising hall built in order to entertain the dignitaries who will be coming to Greenwich. It could be that you'll be here longer than you imagine.'

Nicholas forced down the irritation caused by his brother's words, but Christopher's stubbornness was making him even more determined to leave as soon as possible. Although he no longer carried a vision of Jane as a Madonna, spending time away from her meant that he had a clearer image of her in his mind and was able to appreciate even more all that she had done for him in the days after the attack on him. She had been so caring and warm-hearted, and despite how she felt about Louise had seen to Matilda's welfare in a manner that was exemplary. If only he could get out of his head the fact that she had deliberately set out to ensnare her first husband in marriage.

Yet even as that thought reoccurred he remembered what she had said about not wanting to marry Caldwell. So which one of them had been trapped in a marriage that had been purely for the convenience of both husband and wife?

He wondered what she was doing right now and whether she was missing him. Perhaps she might even be comparing him to Willem Godar after their wedding night? Where was the weaver now? Could he possibly have returned to Witney? What if Jane told him the truth about James being his son? He felt a chill go through him. Then it suddenly struck him where the weaver could be, and he wondered why he had not thought of it before. It would make sense his taking Berthe with him if Nicholas had guessed aright.

And what of Louise's sister? Was she still under the protection of Anthony Mortimer or had they parted? She could be in London, or here in Greenwich, having managed an assignation with Tomas Vives and his kinsman;

the latter had possibly broken into the ship-yard with other of his compatriots. At least if his enemies were responsible for the attack on his brother, Jane and the children were out of danger. Even so, he trusted that she would remain on her guard and not forget to bolt the doors at night.

Jane entered the hall of Draymore Manor, her breath coming unevenly. Holding James's hand, she came to a halt a few yards from where Rebecca and the girls sat on a settle and ushered her son over to sit with them. Only then did she turn to Anthony Mortimer and the woman who sat on a footstool, leaning against his knee. In her hand she held a silver dish of sweetmeats and crystallised fruit.

Was this Louise's sister? wondered Jane, staring at the woman who must have been perfectly lovely before the dreaded disease had left her pockmarked.

'Jane!' exclaimed Anthony, rising from the chair, dislodging the woman. 'Are you all right? Was it a dead body?'

She did not immediately answer but waited a moment to catch her breath before saying, 'It was a man whom, from his garments, I deem to be Spanish. It is my opinion that he must have been dead for a while.'

The woman who had bent to pick up some of the contents of the dish that had spilled shot a glance at her. Her expression was enough to cause Jane to say, 'You know who it is, don't you?'

'Her English is not good, Jane,' said Anthony swiftly, taking the woman's arm and helping her to straighten up.

'Then perhaps you can translate?' said Jane, her eyes hardening. 'Although I suspect she understood well enough my words if her expression is aught to go by. I suspect the dead man might have been one of those who attacked Nicholas and *she* was party to the act.'

'I only wanted him to stop Master Hurst from taking my niece with him,' said the woman in heavily accented English.

Jane glanced at Anthony. 'I don't believe her. According to Berthe, this woman connived with Nicholas's enemies to kill him.'

'What is she saying?' asked Eugenie, seizing his sleeve. 'She speaks too fast! I repeat that I only wanted the child of my sister.'

Anthony hushed her and drew her against his side.

'So you really are Madame Eugenie Dupon? Matilda's aunt?' said Jane, wondering how alike the sisters had been before this one had been ravaged by disease.

The woman nodded. 'And you are Mistress Caldwell.'

'Was,' said Jane. 'I am now Mistress Nicholas Hurst, and your niece is in the care of a wet nurse in our employment.'

The woman looked taken aback. 'But I thought Berthe had taken her!'

Jane glanced at Rebecca, who said, 'I didn't get that far in my explanation of why we are here.'

Jane nodded and turned back to Eugenie and Anthony. 'Berthe made the mistake of abducting the wrong baby and took my son instead.' Her voice quivered as she remembered the horror of that moment of discovery.

'Then why are you not searching for them?' asked Eugenie, looking bewildered.

'Because she returned him to me,' said Jane patiently. 'I, too, was furious with her, and wanted her punished despite her explanation. It is because of her that I know of your part in this whole affair. Since then Berthe has disappeared with a weaver—Willem Godar.'

Anthony let out an exclamation. 'We did not know that.'

Jane looked at him. 'Aye, they both left Witney the morning after she returned Simon. We have no idea where they have gone.'

'You have not considered that he might have returned to Kent?' said Anthony.

Jane stared at him for a long moment and then said in a relieved voice, 'Of course! I cannot understand why I did not think of it.' Even as she spoke she knew the reason. Her mind had been too taken up with Nicholas and her feelings for him, and all the talk of a wedding and moving to Bristol. She cleared her throat. 'What you have to say does not alter the fact that Madame Dupon was party to the attack on my husband. No doubt she would rather Berthe was not found because she can identify her and is a witness to what took place.'

Eugenie clutched Anthony's arm. 'Have I not admitted that I did what I did only because I wanted the child? She is all that I have left of my sister. I had never met Master Hurst—although I had heard of him, of course.'

'That child is a person named Matilda,' said Jane quietly. 'You keep calling her *the child*! My husband loves her and you must accept that you will never have her in your charge.'

Eugenie flinched but continued to stare at Jane. Then she looked up at Anthony and spoke to him in Flemish. He replied in the same language before pressing her into the chair he had vacated and turning to Jane and Rebecca. 'Eugenie is all alone in the world, so you must show compassion.'

Jane and Rebecca glanced at each other and Jane's mouth tightened. Rebecca said in an impassioned voice, 'I cannot understand, Father, why you continue to take Madame Dupon's side, knowing of her involvement in the attack on Nicholas's life.'

'I will explain.' Anthony sighed. 'You are only young and have not seen as much of the world and life as I have. I have come to know Eugenie reasonably well in the short time since we met and she has not had an easy life. She almost died several times, miscarried twice and was widowed. More recently she, too, was duped into behaving in a way that she now regrets. Two Spaniards approached her shortly after the death of her sister and suggested she might want revenge on the man responsible for her loss. In her grief she listened to them. They painted Nicholas Hurst as a womaniser and a murderer and offered to return her niece to her if she helped them to capture him. They said that he had stolen plans of a ship belonging to them and they wanted them back.'

'It's not true!' burst out Jane.

'Of course it's not true,' said Rebecca, getting to her feet and standing alongside her. 'Nicholas would never behave like that.'

'I believe what you say, because you are obviously women of integrity, but at the time I was grieving for my sister whom I had not seen for a long time!' cried Eugenie, stretching out an imploring hand. 'I was heartbroken and not thinking clearly!'

Jane was in a quandary. She knew only too well what it was like to lose a beloved sibling. 'Maybe you are telling the truth,' she said slowly, 'but I cannot approve of your behaviour—especially of your tricking Berthe into stealing Nicholas's daughter. I consider her more to be pitied because she lost a husband *and* her baby son.'

'But she took your child!' burst out Eugenie. 'How can you be so forgiving of her and not me?'

Jane stared at her and then faced Anthony. 'I've heard enough. I am not her judge, and in the circumstances I'm sure Nicholas would say the same thing. Let us return to why I am here. I have spoken to your master mason and one of his men and described to him the place where he will find the Spaniard's body. They have a wagon and will take the corpse to the parish church in Witney. My husband sent for the constable before he left for Greenwich and we are expecting him to arrive any day now.

When he does this whole affair will be handed over to him.'

'Then Eugenie and I will stay here and put ourselves at his disposal,' said Anthony.

Relieved, Jane said, 'I deem that would stand her in good stead. Now, what about the other Spaniard who was involved? I presume Madame Dupon knows who he is?'

Anthony nodded. 'He managed to escape but we will explain everything to the constable when we see him.'

Jane had to accept what he said, but she was thinking that Madame Dupon understood more English than he was admitting to, and that she must waste no time in getting as much information to her husband as she could after she had spoken to the constable.

Nicholas eased his shoulder, wincing as he did so, and decided to call it a day. He thought of Jane as he moved away from the table on which the design of the King's ship was displayed, remembering what she had said about wanting to familiarise herself with the workings of a shipyard. He thought of James and his first sighting of the lad, the feel of his small hand in his. A thought suddenly occurred to him and his heart lifted.

He was about to leave the workroom when

the door opened and his brother Philip entered. Nicholas's face lit up. 'So here you are at last, Pip! I thought I might have seen you over Easter, but Christopher told me that the King was keeping you busy.'

He clapped his younger brother on the shoulder and gazed into his handsome face with its lively vivid blue eyes, noticing traces of kohl about their lids and the odd smear of theatrical make-up. A lock of flaxen hair fell onto his brother's forehead beneath the russet velvet cap set at a jaunty angle.

'You're quite the peacock,' he added, running an eye over Philip's well set-up figure, which was clad in a doublet of dark green velvet over a cream-coloured silk shirt; his russet hose was of the finest wool and his codpiece was of soft leather. 'I presume you have the King's permission to wear velvet and silk?'

'Aye, one has to keep up appearances in my calling when in the King's employ,' said Philip, sweeping his brother a bow. 'It's good to see you—and looking better than I hoped. Could it be that marriage is going to suit you? My felicitations, brother. Christopher wasted no time in getting the news to me whilst you've been slaving away for him.'

Nicholas thanked him for his congratulations and extended his felicitations about Rebecca being with child. 'I must give you two gold coins. One you can keep for the baby, but the other is because you were right about me chasing after a wife—although I could have done without having to return here after just getting married. I did not like leaving Jane. But then we would not have wed so soon if Rebecca had not arrived when she did.'

'I know how you feel, but Christopher can't afford to lose the King's patronage and neither can I,' said Philip with a sigh. 'I thought I'd better warn you that Henry is here in the shipyard now,' he added in a low voice.

Nicholas swallowed a groan. 'Isn't he leaving it a bit late in the day to come and see how his ship progresses? I was about to leave.'

Philip perched on the edge of the table. 'It was a spur-of-the-moment decision on his part. Most likely due to my asking leave to return to Oxford for a few days after informing him of your arrival.'

'I presume he is aware that our brother sent for me?'

'Aye, and he knows of the attack on you a few weeks ago. Not that I was the first to inform him of it.'

Nicholas raised an eyebrow. 'Who did?'

'Sir Gawain!' Philip folded his arms across his chest. 'Twice he's visited court in the last month. He and Beth are in London at the moment. He told me that a weaver named Willem Godar informed him, and to tell you of this when I saw you.'

Nicholas swore softly. 'What else did he have to say?'

'Apparently the man has married a Flemish woman called Berthe.'

Nicholas stilled. 'That does come as a surprise. Did Sir Gawain tell you aught else about him?'

'Godar has decided not to buy the lease on Jane's house.'

Nicholas's eyebrows shot up. 'Does that mean he plans to remain in Tenderden?'

'Possibly,' said Philip cautiously. 'Although I wasn't always listening as attentively as I should have done. I presume you know this Flemish woman?'

'Of course I do! Didn't I tell you in my missive that she was my daughter's wet nurse? She disappeared with Godar from the Blue Boar Inn a few weeks ago. I wonder what Godar's game is? I can't see what he has to gain by marrying Berthe.'

'A mother for his children, apparently,' said Phillip, stifling a yawn. 'I remember that much because children are very much on my mind at the moment. I believe there was mention of four boys—one of them a babe in arms.'

Obviously Godar had decided that Nicholas and Jane were unlikely to bring a charge against Berthe for her abduction of Simon, thought Nicholas, so marrying her made sense. He frowned and changed the subject. 'Have you seen aught of Tomas Vives at court?'

'No, but that doesn't say the swine hasn't been freed from house arrest. I know the Princess has requested the King's permission for him to sing during the coming celebrations,' said Philip grimly. 'Another matter you need to know about right now is that the King wishes not only to discuss your book with you but would like your opinion on another secret matter. There's no doubt in my mind that he will invite you to attend him at court.'

Nicholas groaned and rubbed his forehead. 'I have no time to spend at court. I want to get finished here as soon as I can so I can move Jane and the children to Bristol.'

'So you really intend to settle there? How does she feel about that?'

'She is eager to see the house we will make our main home, so I'll make my recent marriage my excuse to the King. Besides, I'd rather not spend too much time in his company,' said Nicholas, stroking his bristly chin.

'Don't be a fool! You can't refuse the King. Just keep your head down so he doesn't get a good look at your face. I'd have a closer shave, too, if I were you. His Grace is growing a beard. Anyway, I must add that I want to show you the new disguising hall and have your opinion on my latest play.' There came the sound of voices and footsteps outside. 'Here comes His Grace now,' hissed Philip.

Nicholas stood and braced himself to receive his king. As Henry entered the workroom, followed by a couple of attendants, Nicholas swept off his cap, went down on one knee and kissed the huge ornate ring on the proffered royal hand. The King told him to rise. Nicholas did so, but remembered to keep his head down.

'I deem I am taller than you, Master Nicholas,' said Henry, sounding pleased.

Nicholas wondered why the difference in their heights was worthy of mention. Last time he had been this close to Henry, Nicholas had been a lot younger. He cleared his throat and glanced at the glittering bulk of Henry out of the corner of his eye. 'If I may speak, Your Grace?'

'Speak away, Master Nicholas.'

'May I add that your shoulders are also broader and you have a fine leg. I also doubt

I could ever match your strength in a tournament.'

'I swear you speak the truth,' said Henry, swaggering over to the table. 'I see you have the plan of my ship here. Rumour has reached me that you have it in mind to build a different ship altogether after you have finished mine, but not here in your brother's shipyard. Why is that?'

Nicholas did not immediately answer, wondering if it had been Christopher or Philip who had informed the King of his plans. He had thought his elder brother would keep quiet about it, hoping he would yet be able to persuade him to change his mind about setting up in the shipbuilding business for himself.

'Aye, Your Grace. I inherited property in the Bristol area from my godparents and—'

'Ha! Bristol! You mention that port in your book.' Henry lifted his eyes from his perusal of his ship's plans. 'So you really have decided to cease your wanderings and settle down now you are married?'

'Aye, Your Grace.'

'Hmm! I would not be too certain of that,' he said ominously. 'You will attend me at the palace. Your brother will bring you to me. We will have supper together and you can join me in worship on Sunday.'

Nicholas's heart sank, but he thanked the King and said he was overwhelmed by His Grace's generosity and would be delighted. The King gave him permission to don his cap and swept out of the room, calling over his shoulder that no doubt the brothers had plenty to say to each other and he would see them both late afternoon on the morrow.

Nicholas rammed his cap back on his head and blew out a breath. He resumed his seat. 'I cannot see how the King looks like me in any way,' he rasped. 'Even so, I wish I didn't have to attend him at court. I suspect that he has a fresh task in mind for me.'

'The likeness is there,' said Philip, drumming his fingers on the table. 'You just can't see it because you don't make a habit of gazing at your reflection in a looking glass—unlike Henry, who has numerous costly mirrors. Fortunately he didn't get a good look at you, but I reckon we need to alter your appearance slightly.'

Nicholas shot a glance at his brother. 'I was starting to believe that I really could settle down to family life, but now I fear that I was being too optimistic,' he said dourly.

'I've had plenty of time to study the King, and what he said about him being taller than you is his way of saying his stature is so much greater than yours.' Philip straightened up. 'It is possible he might already know of our tie to his maternal grandfather. At least you had the sense to flatter him.'

Nicholas said wryly, 'I haven't forgotten what you told me about his removing Buckingham's head from his shoulders due to his arrogance and closeness to the throne.' He changed the subject. 'Let's go and eat. On the way you can tell me about the new disguising hall at the palace.'

'I can do even better than that,' said Philip enthusiastically. 'You can watch us rehearse there and I will introduce you to the artist commissioned to paint a large painting on the wall of the disguising and banqueting halls, as well as two triumphant arches. His name is Hans Holbein and I deem that one day his name will be famous in all the courts of Europe.'

'I look forward to it,' said Nicholas, thinking that Jane would have enjoyed seeing the picture and watching Philip and his players perform. He should not have made so little of her suggestion that she join him here. Even so, she was probably safer where she was until the men who had broken into the shipyard were caught.

Chapter Thirteen

Jane held on to her hat as a gust of wind blew rain in her face. She was on her way with the constable of Oxfordshire and Berkshire to Christopher's house in Greenwich. The hem of her gown flapped against her ankles and the bag she carried bumped against her knee. If it were not for the thought of seeing Nicholas she might have wished herself back in Oxford with Rebecca and the children. They had gone there in company with Tabitha and Dorothea a couple of days after the constable had inspected the Spaniard's corpse and listened to all that Jane had to tell him. He had also spent some time in conversation with Louise's sister and Anthony Mortimer. Jane had no idea what they had told him, but he had made no arrest. Instead he had decided he must speak to Berthe. On the way to Kent he had decided he would visit Nicholas in Greenwich.

Even before the constable had spoken of his intention to Jane she had decided that she, too, must see her husband. Now she was feeling more than a little apprehensive.

They arrived at the house and the constable hammered on the front door. It was several moments before it opened, to reveal a woman of ample figure and homely features. She looked harassed and blurted out, 'What d'you want?'

Jane said, 'It's me, Mary. Nicholas's wife.'

Mary's eyes widened. 'By our Lady and St Joseph, what are you doing here? Is there something amiss with Rebecca?'

'Rebecca is well,' said Jane in a soothing voice. 'I have the constable of Oxfordshire and Berkshire here and he wishes to speak to Nicholas about the attack on him a few weeks ago.'

'Oh, my goodness,' said Mary, crossing herself. 'No doubt he is also interested in the attack on my husband and the break-in at the shipyard.' She bumbled aside to allow them to enter, looking askance at the burly figure in the sodden brown riding coat as the constable stepped over the threshold in Jane's wake.

He nodded. 'It could prove useful.'

'Is Nicholas within?' asked Jane, glancing up the ill-lit passage.

'He should be back from the shipyard soon, for he is late for supper,' said Mary, opening a door on the left. 'You'd best come into the parlour and warm yourselves. I will fetch refreshments as I am sure you are hungry and thirsty after your journey. My husband has retired to his bedchamber but I will inform him that you are here.'

The fact that Nicholas was late worried Jane, but she followed the constable into the parlour without comment. A few moments later a young maidservant scurried in and asked if she could take their coats and hats, adding that she would place them in front of the kitchen fire to dry.

That done, Jane and the constable settled themselves in front of the parlour fire. She was on pins, wishing Nicholas would come. Fortunately they had been there only a few moments when there came the sound of the front door opening and male voices. Instantly she recognised Nicholas's voice and relief and joy soared inside her. She hurried out into the passage and spoke his name in a voice husky with emotion.

He whirled round and stared at her wordlessly. Her heart sank. Was he so vexed with her for coming that he was lost for words? Then he strode forward with his hands outstretched.

'For a moment I thought I was imagining your voice, and due to the lack of light in here I could not see you clearly.'

Relieved, she grasped his hands. 'You are well?'

'Aye, and you? I pray you do not bring bad news. Matilda and the other children...?'

'They are well and staying in Oxford with Rebecca, Tabitha and Dorothea. We thought it safer, and it is more roomy and comfortable for Rebecca.'

He frowned. 'Why should you deem it safer, what with Vives's uncle lodging at one of the colleges?'

Before she could explain the constable spoke up, 'As much as I don't wish to interrupt, I need to speak to you, Master Hurst.'

Nicholas released one of Jane's hands and gazed at the man. 'Constable Treadwell, how good to see you! I presume you wish to discuss the attack of several weeks ago?'

'Aye—that and the recent discovery of a corpse not far from Draymore Manor.'

'What?' Nicholas shot a glance at Jane.

'James found it,' she said swiftly. 'You can imagine the shock it gave the poor boy. Fortunately it was concealed beneath a bramble bush, so he saw just the feet and came running to me.'

'Who was it? Surely not Mortimer?'

Before she could reply Constable Treadwell said, 'If you don't mind, Mistress Hurst? I'll take over now.'

Nicholas squeezed Jane's hand before releasing it. 'Let's go into the parlour and sit down.'

Philip came alongside Jane and whispered in her ear, 'Tell me it wasn't Rebecca's father?'

Jane whirled round and smiled. 'No, he is fine. Rebecca is also fit and well and sends her love.'

'Thank God.'

Nicholas caught the words and glanced over his shoulder at them, but no more was said until they were all seated in the parlour.

'So what happened?' asked Nicholas, sitting beside Jane on the settle. 'Has this discovery something to do with the latest attack on me? Although I don't see how there can be a connection.'

He felt Jane's hand slide into his left one and grip it tightly and knew then that the two were tied in some way and she was worried. He took a deep breath. 'How did this man die? Who was he?'

'A Spaniard named Vives. I thought you might be able to help me with the rest, Master

Hurst,' said the constable, his eyes intent on Nicholas's face.

Nicholas frowned. 'Are you saying that you think I killed him?'

'I know a man called Vives attempted to kill you last year, and this one is his kin. Apparently he attacked you and you retaliated.'

'Neither blow I inflicted on my attackers would have caused their deaths,' said Nicholas vehemently. 'I unsaddled one without wounding him and the other I hit across the forearm with my sword. How did this man die?'

'He was stabbed in the chest. Madame Dupon apparently believed you ran him through with your sword and he died later of his wounds on his way to meet his kinsman. I certainly wouldn't have blamed you, Master Hurst, if you were responsible for his death,' said the constable. 'You were, after all, fighting for your life.'

Nicholas's eyes glinted. 'I have just explained how I defended myself. Did you find any sign of a possible broken arm or a head injury? In my opinion Madame Dupon was not near enough to see what took place. The wet nurse, Berthe—now, *she* could have seen what happened.'

'There was some damage to the arm, according to the physician.'

Nicholas said, 'Did Madame Dupon swear that she saw me kill this man?'

The constable frowned. 'No, but she could see no other reason for his death. Although she seemed surprised about where the body was found. She had believed him to be miles away.'

Nicholas leaned forward. 'If you speak to Berthe then you should also speak to her husband, Willem Godar. He saw a Spaniard in company with Madame Dupon and Master Mortimer the evening after the attack on me.'

'I wonder why the other Spaniard wasn't with them?' said Jane.

Unexpectedly, Philip joined in the discussion. 'It could be that the two Spaniards quarrelled because their plans had gone awry. Maybe one of them wanted to try once more to kill my brother and the other disagreed. There was a fight and your man was killed and the other fled.'

The constable pursed his lips. 'It is a possibility. After I have talked with this Berthe and Master Godar I will speak to you again, Master Hurst.'

'You know where they are?' asked Nicholas.

'Tenderden in Kent,' said the constable, smiling suddenly. 'Your wife was able to inform me of that.'

Nicholas glanced at Jane. 'I, too, realised that

once I gave their disappearance more thought. Apparently he needed a mother for his children so has married Berthe. Hopefully, she will find fulfilment and contentment in that role,' he added lightly.

Before any more could be said on the subject, the door opened and Mary and two serving maids entered. One carried a pewter salver of drinking vessels and a steaming pitcher, whilst the mistress of the house and another maid bore trays of bowls of soup, bread, grilled perch and cheese. They set them down on two small tables and Mary bid her guests to help themselves.

Jane could only be relieved that she no longer needed to concern herself about Berthe and Willem. She poured out the mulled wine, listening to Mary informing the constable that Christopher would see him in his bedchamber after he had had some refreshment. Philip and Nicholas had their heads together and thanked Jane absently when she handed drinks to them.

She wondered what they were discussing. Obviously they did not wish to involve her and that hurt. So much had happened in the last week of an upsetting nature and she had keyed herself up to seeing Nicholas and providing him with her support, even if he might not welcome it. She felt weary and depressed, even thought it seemed that the constable no longer suspected her husband of being responsible for the Spaniard Vives's death. But who was? Could it be Tomas Vives?

Suddenly Nicholas turned to her. 'On the morrow, I have to accompany Pip to the palace. The king has requested my company.'

'Can you tell me why?'

'His Grace visited the shipyard earlier and there was no time to speak of what was on his mind then about what he thought of my latest book. No need for you to worry, Jane,' said Nicholas lightly. 'I suggest after you finish eating that you retire to my bedchamber. You've had an anxious few days and must be tired after the journey.'

'It is true, I am weary,' she responded, wondering if he wanted her out of the way because he did not trust her enough to listen in on what else he might have to say about the king and the death of the other Vives to Philip and the constable. At least he seemed to want her to share his bedchamber so surely that bode well for the future? Unless he was behaving how he deemed his brother would expect him to do as a new husband who had made a love match?

Within minutes she was alone in Nicholas's bedchamber washing the grime of the journey from her face and hands. She loosened her hair and began to comb it. Despite Nicholas's assurance that she was not to worry about his being summoned to court, she could not help doing so. She, too, had heard about Buckingham's execution and the reason behind it and could only hope that if the king was aware of the Hursts' link to the Tudors that he knew without a doubt that the family were as utterly loyal to him as they had been to his father when he had sat on the throne of England.

Nicholas entered the bedchamber, expecting his wife to be asleep. He stopped short when he saw her lying on top of the bed, still dressed. She had a book open before her and in the candlelight he could make out that her finger was following a line on the page and that her lips were moving as she read the words. It could only be the book he had given her and he was touched that she was making an effort to read it for herself. It was obvious to him from the speed with which her finger was moving that reading did not come easy to her. When he spoke, she jumped and swiftly closed the book. Bending over the side of the bed, she placed it on the stool there and then looked at him.

'You are finding the book absorbing?' he asked. 'So much so it seems that you haven't had time to undress. I'm flattered that you appear to be enjoying it so much.'

She slanted him a challenging look. 'There is no need to be. I wanted to discover for myself that a certain tale was exactly as Rebecca told it to us because—to be honest—how you were saved seemed like a miracle to me.'

Nicholas's smile faded and he picked up the book before sitting on the bed. 'I can't believe, Jane, that you still doubt that what I wrote about my travels actually happened. It is as if you are saying I deliberately set out to deceive my brother.'

'You misunderstand me,' she said swiftly, shifting over on the bed to give him more room. 'The part of the book I was reading is about when you were a boy and fell into the River Severn and were swept along by the great wave. You were terrified, but you still had the wits to seize the broken branch when it was swept along, climb on to it and paddle to the bank with your hands.'

Nicholas blinked. 'Is that what it says here?' He flicked over the pages until he came to where she had placed a marker and read what was printed there. He grimaced. 'Pip has made me out to be braver than I was. Little as I like to admit it, I didn't save myself alone. My godfather played his part. He ran like the wind along the bank, looking for a way to rescue me. He saw the broken branch on the grass and, seizing it, waded into the water and waited until I drew level with him. I managed to grab the end of the branch and he pulled me towards him. It took some strength on his part and mine to get me to shore.'

Jane smiled. 'So that was the way of it. Anyway, whatever the truth of the matter, your actions impressed James. He is proud of his new papa and said it didn't prevent you from having the courage to sail across the great ocean.'

'Foolhardy, that's what my father called me when I set off on what I called my first big venture,' said Nicholas wryly. 'And that was despite my godfather never having told him that I'd disobeyed his orders not to get too close to the edge of the river.' He closed the book.

'It was yours and your godfather's secret,' said Jane softly.

'Aye, I never told my father because he wouldn't have allowed me to visit my godfather again if he'd known. They were very different men. I admired and respected both men but there were times, like when my father took a strap to me, that I wished I could have changed them round.'

'So you believe that some matters are

best not discussed due to a fear of the consequences?' asked Jane.

Their eyes met and held. 'What are you trying to say?' asked Nicholas.

'I think you know, but perhaps now is not the time to discuss it,' said Jane abruptly. 'I'm weary and must be going.'

To his surprise, she rose from the bed and, before he could put out a hand to stop her, made for the door. Then to his further amazement, she appeared to change her mind and moved over to the window. 'What are you doing?' he asked.

She did not immediately reply, but waited for her eyes to adjust. She caught the gleam of the Thames beyond the garden. 'Thinking. It must feel strange to you coming back here and remembering those times you sailed away on your travels. Tell me honestly, will you miss doing so?'

He came over to her and placed his hands on her shoulders. 'Aye, but those days are over. I must tell you that Constable Treadwell believes there is no connection between the break-in at my brother's shipyard and the latest attack on me. Which means that I don't have to feel responsible for Christopher's injuries. Otherwise, I might have been tempted into staying here longer because of the guilt I felt.'

'So how long will you stay? How long before we can travel to Bristol? I—I suppose if I'd brought the children with us, then we—we could have sailed right round the southern coast and on up to Bristol?' she murmured.

'The view of the land is extremely attractive in places from the sea, but the Cornish coast in particular is rocky and it can be dangerous there. One needs an experienced master mariner and fair weather to navigate,' said Nicholas. 'But maybe it can be arranged.' He paused. 'Tell me, Jane, why have you not undressed and climbed into bed? I knew you were tired and thought to find you asleep, so I would have understood if you had not stayed awake, waiting for me to come. Why do you feel you must go? Go where? I order you to stay.'

A shiver went through her and she closed her eyes and leaned against him, thinking how much she would have enjoyed him making love to her. 'I have the curse on me. Perhaps I would not have if you had not withdrawn from me on our wedding night. Why did you? Is it that you believe I am not fit to be a mother to your children because of one mistake I made in the past?'

He was disappointed in more ways than one. 'How could you believe that of me, Jane?' His fingers tightened on her shoulders.

'Because I can think of no other reason why you should do so.'

'Well, there is one, but perhaps you would not believe that either?' he said, releasing her. 'I'll leave you to rest and will speak with you in the morning.'

Before she could prevent him, he strode from the bedchamber. She would have gone after him but there was that in his expression that stopped her in her tracks. She could only fall to her knees and pray that soon all would be well between them.

Chapter Fourteen

Nicholas spent the night in Philip's bedchamber and they talked far into the night. Amongst other things, he discussed with his brother the possibility of Jane accompanying them to the palace to view the new disguising hall and watch his brother's troupe of players rehearse.

'I don't see why not,' said Philip, shrugging. 'But it will mean us going to the palace earlier in the day.' He paused. 'Remember when we enter the palace to keep your head down and the brim of your hat well over your eyes—and adopt a seafaring gait. I will introduce you as my brother, an explorer of famed repute, but the fewer people who see your face full-on the better.'

Nicholas raised his eyebrows, but decided

that his brother knew what he was about. 'Has the king given you leave yet to go to Oxford?'

'Aye, but only for a few days.' Philip sighed.

'Then I would have you do a favour for me.' Nicholas wasted no time explaining exactly what he wanted his brother to do for him.

Nicholas was up very early the following morning, wanting to have a word with the constable before he left for Kent. After doing so he went up to the bedchamber where he found Jane gazing out of the window.

He felt a rush of love for her, but knew there was no time to discuss all those things that needed to be said between them now. 'Did you sleep well?' he asked politely.

She turned slowly. 'As well as could be expected, considering all that I had on my mind. You?'

'Pip and I were making plans.' His eyes washed over her face and he wanted to assuage her anxiety there and then, but time was now of the essence. He smiled. 'I have some good news for you. You are to accompany us to the palace. My brother wishes to show us the king's new disguising hall and we can watch him and the other players rehearse his latest play. We both thought you would enjoy such a treat.'

Jane's face lit up and there was no doubt in

his mind that the plan delighted her. 'When do we go?'

'Soon. Have you broken your fast?' She shook her head. 'Then go swiftly,' he said. 'I have to make some preparations and will meet you downstairs.' She thanked him and made for the door, only to hesitate. 'What is it, Jane?' he asked gently. 'We have little time to delay.'

'It can wait,' she said, opening the door and hurrying out.

Whilst she partook of breakfast, Nicholas had his head together with Christopher, who scowled but then shrugged and sent for his sons. Soon after Philip, Nicholas and Jane set out for Greenwich Palace. They had no difficulty in entering the royal residence. Philip was well known to the guards and they had been told to expect Nicholas's arrival. When it was explained to them that Jane was his new wife and that she had expressed a wish to see the king's new disguising hall, they congratulated the couple and waved them through.

Philip took them both straight to the quarters set aside for him and his players. There they found Ned and the other men in his troupe. Jane was about to give Ned her news from Tabitha when he told Nicholas that he had a message for him from the king's chancellor.

'Cardinal Wolsey arrived last evening and apparently as soon as he heard from the king that you would be coming to the palace today, he sent a servant here. He wishes you to visit him in his apartment as soon you arrive. There is no need for you to send word, just go there immediately.'

Nicholas frowned. 'Where is this apartment?'

'I'll show you,' said Philip.

'In the meantime, what do I do?' asked Jane, trying not to sound overly concerned. 'Shall I return to the house?'

'No, I would not have you leave the palace without an escort,' said Nicholas firmly. 'Maybe Ned could show you the disguising hall and we will join you there as soon as we can.'

Ned agreed and Nicholas and his brother wasted no time heading for Wolsey's apartments. They gained entry within moments and were shown into the Cardinal's presence.

His Eminence soon came to the point. 'I've had word since your return, Nicholas, concerning the defeat of the French army in Italy by the Emperor Charles's troops. The men have still not received their wages despite the time that has elapsed since their victory, so they are set on doing what you spoke about and forcing their commander, the Duke of Bourbon, to lead them to Rome. One way or other they are determined to be recompensed for their efforts.'

Nicholas and Philip drew in their breath. 'Have you any notion of the numbers of these mutineers?' asked Philip.

The Cardinal's expression was grim. 'Apart from several thousand Spaniards, there are thousands of German infantrymen, as well as Italian cavalry and, oddly, some Protestant followers of the heretic, Martin Luther. It is said that he looks upon the advance on Rome as a Holy War. The Pope, as we know, was on the side of France in the recent conflict, along with the states of Milan, Venice and Florence. So the Protestants are taking advantage of a revolt that has broken out in Florence against the Medici family to destroy the papacy.'

Nicholas was filled with a sense of foreboding. 'Why are you telling me this?'

'Because you must be prepared when you have your meeting with the king. He has it in mind to order you to Rome.'

'No!' shouted Philip. 'He could be sending my brother to his death.'

The cardinal turned on him. 'That is how I see it, too, even if your brother was going as himself,' he said ominously.

'What do you mean, as myself?' asked Nicholas harshly.

'If something is not done to change the rebels' minds, there could be an overwhelming catastrophe. The king has it in mind that he could avert such a disaster if he—or someone who looks very like him—could persuade the rebels that it would be to their advantage to turn back from the walls of Rome,' said the cardinal in a flat voice.

The brothers stared at each other, not needing to say aloud that the king knew of their blood tie to him, and so apparently did the cardinal. 'You're serious.' said Philip.

'The king certainly is,' said Wolsey. 'He does not want the rebels capturing the Pope and ransoming him to the Emperor. Henry would rather be seen as the Pope's deliverer and win his favour.'

'I presume Henry's idea is to persuade Pope Clement to annul his marriage whilst declaring the Princess Mary legitimate,' said Philip.

'I cannot see the rebels being persuaded by any argument Henry could offer them when all the wealth of Rome is before them,' said Nicholas vehemently. 'Besides, when information reaches them from England that King Henry never left his country, they will arrange for me to conveniently die as an enemy and imposter. Unless the king plans to hide himself away for a month or more?'

'There must be a way out of this dilemma,' said Philip.

'Your brother can hardly refuse the king. Nicholas does have a look of him, whereas you do not.' The cardinal paused, toying with the enormous ring on his hand. 'I doubt word has reached you that I had to release Tomas Vives recently.'

'How recently?' asked Nicholas, his eyes alert.

'Shortly after our last meeting. I had him followed as far as Oxford where he visited his uncle. After that my man grew slack, presuming he would stay in Oxford. He lost sight of him for a few days, then he suddenly turned up again and is here in the palace. He is to sing before the queen and the princess and their courtiers. Now there is a young Spaniard we know we cannot trust; no doubt if he were to hear of the king's plans for you, then he would do his utmost to get rid of you, not simply because he still would avenge his kinsman's death, but to foil Henry's plan and please his Emperor.' He sighed. 'Anyway, I have explained the situation to you. I have faith that a man of action such as yourself, Nicholas, can come up with a plan to save yourself.'

Nicholas gave a stiff bow and thanked him.

The cardinal blessed both brothers and dismissed them.

As they strode along the passage that led away from Wolsey's apartment, Philip said, 'If you go, it is most likely certain death.'

'I have no intention of going to Italy,' murmured Nicholas. 'One does wonder from his Eminence's words concerning Tomas Vives and the Emperor, whether it is Emperor Charles's plan to incite his soldiers and for Rome to be taken and the Pope captured.'

Philip shot him a glance. 'What are you going to do?'

'Put into place a delaying tactic that would fool the king.'

'You mean long enough for the rebels' army to reach the walls of Rome and for it to be much too late to put the king's plan into action?' said Philip rapidly.

'Aye, I have a cunning plan,' said Nicholas, his eyes alight. 'I will have need of your skills as a player, but my main concern is Jane. I gave her my word that my travelling days are over and I do not aim to break my promise to her. But, for my plan to work, she has to believe that I will soon be taking ship to Europe and I cannot see her being pleased about that.' He took a deep breath. 'But first we have to spread some rumours and make certain they reach Tomas

Vives's ears. I presume it has occurred to you that he could have killed his kinsman for reasons only known to himself. Now come close and listen to what I have to say.'

In the meantime Jane was doing her best to give all her attention to Master Holbein's painting, but she was distracted by the sight of the young man the other end of the hall. She was convinced that he was Tomas Vives, as not only was he dressed like a Spaniard, but he also sang beautifully. She had suggested such to Ned, who had agreed with her before excusing himself. She felt on edge, wishing that he would return, but at least she was not alone in the hall.

As the moments passed, she was aware of another man entering and hurrying to the far end of the hall. The singing faltered and then stopped before starting again. After that, every now and again, the singer turned his head and darted a look in her direction. Just as she had recognised him, surely Nicholas's enemy had recognised her and she felt a trickle of fear. How long before he approached her? It seemed an age since she had parted from Nicholas and Philip and she feared that perhaps Nicholas had already been put under guard or some such thing. Surely the king's chancellor must have finished speaking to him by now?

'So what are your thoughts on this painting, Jane?' asked a voice behind her.

Jane turned and gazed up at Nicholas with such relief in her eyes that he could not help but guess that she was really pleased to see him.

'You have been so long in coming,' she said weakly. 'I was getting worried. Besides, see that man the other end of the hall? I swear it is Tomas Vives.'

'You could be right,' he said in a low voice, then added loudly, 'I beg your forgiveness, Mistress Caldwell, for keeping you waiting, but the king had much to say to me.'

She felt a start of shock that he should address her so, but instead of reminding him that she had changed her name, she accepted his apology, believing he must have his reasons.

'I have much to tell you and you are not going to like it. I must leave this place and travel to Italy.'

'What? But—but you made me a promise!' cried Jane, further taken aback.

'When the king commands, this subject must obey,' said Nicholas, rather pompously. 'I will escort you to my brother's house and will arrange for a boat to ferry you to Oxford.'

He hustled her from the disguising hall and hurried her along a passage. 'I can't believe you are doing this,' she said. 'Unless—has the king threatened you?'

'His Grace has ordered me to Rome and I must leave immediately,' he bellowed.

She could not understand why he had to talk so loudly. It was almost as if he wanted people to know about it. 'Could you not have told him that your spying days are over?' she asked, a tremor in her voice.

'He knows of the connection between my grandmother and his grandfather. I had no choice but to agree to do what he asked of me.'

Jane forced back the angry words that threatened to choke her. 'For what purpose?'

Nicholas hesitated. 'I shouldn't tell you, but he has seen a way that this likeness of mine to his Grace might serve him in getting his heart's desire. I can tell you no more, only think on those matters you know of him and whose residence is in Rome and you might come up with an answer. As it is I must get ready to leave— and you must, too, for you must return to the children.'

'Of course,' said Jane in a dull voice. 'The children.' She thought if it were not for them, then perhaps he would have taken her with him. As it was, it seemed that the future she had envisaged might never materialise. Who was to say that the king and cardinal might not find other missions for Nicholas to go on? That is, if he came back alive from this one. Fear clutched her belly and she felt sick.

Suddenly she heard scuffling behind her and a man's cry. She made to turn round, but Nicholas forced her onwards and said, 'Don't be so sad, Jane. This mission might not take as long as you fear. With fair winds and Our Lady and Saint Christopher on our side, we will soon be together again.'

She thought he sounded more cheerful than he had any right to be and at the back of her mind was the thought that he might be glad to be off on his travels again, having missed the excitement of new faces and new places more than he was prepared to admit.

Once back at the house, Nicholas wasted no time taking his farewell of Jane, having told her that he had arranged for a boat to ferry her to the centre of London where she was to stay at the Raventons' house next to the print works on Paternoster Row before taking ship to Oxford.

Jane felt bewildered, thinking they had still not had that talk he had promised her. It seemed that he had forgotten and she did not want to be the one to remind him. 'What of Pip?' she asked. 'I thought he would be returning to Oxford to be with Rebecca?'

'He will leave on the morrow and has de-cided to travel on horseback.'

She wondered why they could not have gone together. It would have made sense, but she felt that she could not question her husband's orders. Then he kissed her with a passion that she had not expected and was gone before she could say the words that were in her heart.

'So do you think the plan will work, Nick?' asked Philip, who had been busy during his brother's absence from the palace.

Nicholas gave a twisted smile at his younger brother's disguised reflection alongside that of his own. 'As long as Vives doesn't escape be-fore Constable Treadwell returns and no one who knows him gets a close look at you. You certainly look like a Spaniard, swarthy and raven-haired. Don't attempt to practise singing like Vives, though,' he warned, 'or you might break this mirror and I can tell you that it came from Venice and cost almost the same as the ship I hired from our brother to take Jane to London.' He had wanted her out of the way in case anything went wrong. He began to don the garments Philip suggested he wear before telling his brother to take care.

'The same with you,' said Philip seriously. 'Don't forget I'll not be far behind you if any of Vives's other kin were to attempt a surprise attack. It shouldn't take you long to reach the disguising hall and we should have plenty of witnesses to the confrontation before your audience with the king.'

Nicholas nodded and left, praying that all would go smoothly.

The interior of the disguising hall looked more or less as it had done earlier when Jane was there. Perhaps a few more people were gathered, inspecting the decorations and watching and listening to the rehearsals for the entertainment that would take place in the not-too-distant future. Nicholas recognised scarcely any of the faces, but they looked at him as if uncertain whether he was who he appeared to be. A couple even bowed, although it was well known by those closest to the king that there were occasions when Henry enjoyed pretending to be an ordinary man to test them. Just like some of them, Nicholas inspected Master Holbein's work and was aware of the exact moment when his brother entered the hall.

He did not have to wait long before becoming aware that Philip was storming towards him. His brother halted a few feet away from him and let out a flood of Spanish. Nicholas looked down his nose at him and responded haughtily in the same tongue. The next moment

Philip had drawn a sword. There was a con-
certed gasp from those who had turned in their
direction as Nicholas drew his sword. The next
moment the brothers were involved in some
rather nifty swordplay. They had arranged for
Philip to bring the fight to a swift conclusion by
making it appear that he had stabbed his oppo-
nent in the side and then he would flee before
any of those watching could call the guards.

Nicholas was surprised at how well the plan
worked. As he clutched his side and squeezed
the rag he held that had been soaked in red
paint, so that it appeared that he was bleeding,
he waved away those who would have helped
him. He roared at them to go after his assailant. Hopefully Philip would have no trouble
making his escape.

Two of his actors, disguised as guards, now
came to Nicholas's aid and helped him from
the hall. Speedily they made their way to the
players' lodgings where they bound up Nicholas's so-called wounds. As they were doing so,
Philip entered, minus his disguise.

'Well, that part worked,' he said, grinning.
'Now let's see if you can fool the king.'

Nicholas sat down and submitted himself to
his brother's skilful hand. Hopefully he would
have no trouble making him appear pale and
gaunt. His aim was to convince the king that

he had been mistaken for his Grace and an attempt had been made on his life. What with the break-in at the shipyard and the deliberate vandalism of the king's ship, Henry's advisors should be able to convince him that he had serious enemies who had almost taken Nicholas's life. Hopefully the king would then give him leave to return home to his wife and children.

As for his attacker, he had vanished—and Tomas Vives would never be seen again in England.

The following day Jane was waiting at Blackfriars quay for the boat to arrive that would take her to Oxford. She was in company with a large man with a dog, who was in the employment of Sir Gawain. Apparently they were to guard her with their lives. This should have made her feel not only safe, but pleased that her husband and friends were being so protective of her. Instead, she was feeling low-spirited despite the fine weather and that she had now done with the curse until next month. For the past twenty-four hours or more she had puzzled over Nicholas's behaviour and had eventually come to the conclusion that he had intended Tomas Vives to know that the king wished Nicholas to go to Rome, although that did not make sense to her. The Spaniard wanted him dead so why let him know of his movements? Could it be to set a trap?

Her bodyguard tapped her on the shoulder and she saw a ship approaching, its sail billowing in the breeze. Could this be the one she had been told to watch out for? As it drew nearer she saw that it bore the name *Saint Mary*. There appeared to be only one other passenger going aboard and he was clad in a black friar's habit.

The master mariner greeted her and a member of the crew took her baggage and helped her aboard. They were followed by the clergyman. The master offered to show her to her quarters and one of the crew wasted no time casting off. She thought it strange that she and the friar were the only two passengers sailing for Oxford. Once inside the cabin she was astounded by its size. The master left her alone and closed the door after him.

The ridiculous thought came into her mind that she was being abducted and she felt impelled to try the door. It opened without difficulty and now she felt foolish. She closed it again and, tired out by the trauma of the last few days, decided to rest. The bunk was of a fair size and she sat down and eased off her shoes and lay down. She closed her eyes and listened to the swish of the water as the ship forged through the waves. Where was Nicholas now? Would he cross the channel to France, then go overland on horseback, or would he go by ship down the coast, past Portugal and Spain and through the Straits of Gibraltar into the Mediterranean and sail east towards Italy?

There came a knock on the door.

'Who is it?' she asked.

The door opened and a familiar voice said, 'May I come in?'

Jane shot up on the bunk. 'Nicholas!' she cried, scarcely able to believe it was him.

'The very same,' said the figure in the black habit, smiling as he locked the door behind him and approached the bunk.

'What are you doing here?' she asked, bewildered.

'I made you a promise which I had every intention of keeping,' he said.

'Oh!' She did not know what to say, for she was deeply touched and tears clogged her throat.

'Is that all you have to say?' he teased.

She cleared her throat. 'Why are you in disguise?'

Nicholas dragged off the habit and flung it on the floor. 'It saved me pretending to be wounded when making my way to London.' He sat alongside her on the bunk.

'Why should you pretend to be wounded?'

Nicholas explained and she listened without interruption and admiration. Only when he had finished did she say, 'You took a terrible risk, both of you. I do not doubt the king would have had your heads if he knew you played such a jape on him.'

Nicholas nodded. 'Fortunately he accepted that I couldn't travel wounded after apparently being mistaken for him. Also there was also the fact that Tomas Vives appears to have disappeared and could have gone to join his Emperor with the Almighty only knows what information about Henry's plans.'

Jane thought about that and said, 'I am not going to ask where Tomas Vives really disappeared to.'

'No, best you don't,' he said, placing his arm around her waist. 'Instead, I shall tell you where this ship is heading.'

Jane stared at him. 'It's not going to Oxford?'

He shook his head. 'No, we are sailing to Bristol by the route you suggested.'

'But you said it could be dangerous?'

'You once told me that life is dangerous and one has to take risks but the weather is set fair and the master of this ship is very experienced.'

'But what about the children?'

'By the time we reach Bristol, they will have

arrived there. Pip and Rebecca will arrange everything with Tabitha and Ned's help.'

'And Dorothea, you must not forget Matilda's wet nurse,' reminded Jane.

'As if I would, but I also remind myself that my daughter is too young to enjoy all the sights to be seen when we reach Bristol,' he said. 'Still, I cannot wait to show James and the girls the bore wave and then there are the sledges.'

'Sledges?'

'Aye, due to Bristol being a centre for the wine trade there are many cellars there. The weight of wagons would prove too heavy and so the wine is transported by sledge. In winter the children will have fun riding on them.' He smiled. 'So just relax and enjoy the journey, and if there is aught else you feel you need to ask me do not hesitate.'

'There is a matter I am troubled about,' she said, a tremor in her voice as she gazed at him. 'Is this really what you want? To build ships and never go travelling again?'

He looked thoughtful. 'I never wanted to be a shipbuilder, but now I know I can find satisfaction in using the skills my father insisted on my learning. He was disappointed when I received my inheritance and took to travelling.

I think he would be pleased that I'm now following in his footsteps, like Christopher.'

'James's father wanted him to be a stone-mason,' murmured Jane, 'but if you'd rather he worked in the shipyard when he's older, I'm sure he'll settle for that.' She felt Nicholas stiffen. 'What is it?' she asked. 'Have I said something that displeases you?'

He shook his head and smiled. 'Not so long ago I thought Godar was James's father and I cannot tell you how much that pained me, for I am extremely fond of the lad.'

She turned in his arm and stared at him. 'But he's far too young to be so!'

'I realised that only after I left you in Witney. I wasn't thinking sensibly at the time.' He lifted her hand to his lips and kissed it.

She said ruefully, 'I should have told you that I miscarried shortly after I wed Simon, but I was too overwrought that evening.'

'So there was no need for you to have married Caldwell after all.'

She sighed. 'At the time it seemed the only way to save me from disgrace. It was my brother's idea. I did not like deceiving Simon and afterward I did tell him the truth. He forgave me—perhaps because it proved I was not barren. He was desperate for a son and I have to say that I would not be without my dear James and Simon. Besides, we might not be here if it were not for my asking you to be Simon's godfather.'

'I accept there could be some truth in that,' said Nicholas, smiling down at her. 'The same goes for my Matilda.'

Jane sighed. 'I wish she were my daughter.'

'I can't say how much I appreciate your saying that, Jane.' He kissed her.

A delicious shiver went through her and she was overwhelmingly aware of the strength in his arm. 'You are no longer in pain?' she asked when he lifted his mouth from hers.

'No, my shoulder has almost healed. What about you? What of the curse?'

'It is over for this month, I am pleased to say.'

'Really?' he teased, drawing her gown off her shoulders and down to her waist and lifting her to her feet.

'Really,' she echoed.

He pressed his lips against the hollow at the base of her throat before covering her mouth in a passionate kiss.

Her gown slithered to the floor and she kicked it away and began to undress him, dragging out his shirt and unfastening the ties that held up his hose, then that went the way of her gown and then her chemise. Now they were chest to breast and she twined her arms around his neck. She gasped as he placed his hands beneath her bottom and lifted her up. Instinctively her legs fastened about his waist and he carried her over to the bunk. They fell on it, but remained in a tangle of limbs. Their rising passion carried them away on a tide of hot, delicious excitement that seemed to have a life of its own.

Then unexpectedly he felt her pull away. 'What is it?' he asked gently, seeing tears in her eyes. 'Why do you cry?' He licked the tears from her eyelashes.

'Because on our wedding night you withdrew from me. Tell me why?'

'I did not wish to see you suffer the pain of childbirth or to lose you giving birth,' he said simply. 'How would the children and I cope without you?'

'But I want to give you a son,' said Jane, clinging to him. 'I can see him—building ships to your design. He will make the name of Hurst shipbuilders even more famous than they are now. It is wrong in me, I know, but part of me rejoices that Louise did not give you a son, but a beautiful daughter. I might not be lovely like Louise, but I have given birth to two healthy sons and survived. I do not see why I should not do so again.'

'If that is your desire, Jane, then I pray God that it will be so. As for not being lovely, you will always be so in my eyes, my love.'

His love! thought Jane, her spirits soaring, scattering any doubts that might have still lingered about his feelings towards her. 'Then so be it, my dearest husband, whom I love more than the whole world,' she said huskily, surrendering herself to the pleasure that was to come.

* * * * *

Author's Note

On 6th May 1527, the Sack of Rome took place, which resulted in a massacre of a large number of its citizens and the papal guards by the unpaid and out-of-control army of Charles V, Holy Roman Emperor. The pope, Clement VII, managed to escape, but was later captured and had to pay a large ransom for his life. Ever afterwards he had to steer clear of conflict with Charles V and not do anything that displeased him. This meant that he would certainly not allow Henry VIII the annulment of his marriage to Catherine of Aragon. The rest is history.

A sneaky peek at next month...

HISTORICAL

IGNITE YOUR IMAGINATION, STEP INTO THE PAST...

My wish list for next month's titles...

In stores from 1st November 2013:

- ❑ Rumours that Ruined a Lady — Marguerite Kaye
- ❑ The Major's Guarded Heart — Isabelle Goddard
- ❑ Highland Heiress — Margaret Moore
- ❑ Paying the Viking's Price — Michelle Styles
- ❑ The Highlander's Dangerous Temptation — Terri Bris
- ❑ Rebel with a Heart — Carol Arens

Available at WHSmith, Tesco, Asda, Eason, Amazon and Apple

Just can't wait?

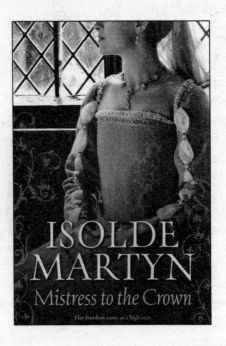